A Thousand and One Coffee Mornings

Miranda Miller

A Thousand and One Coffee Mornings

SCENES FROM SAUDI ARABIA

PETER OWEN · LONDON

ISBN 0 7206 0761 2

PETER OWN PUBLISHERS
73 Kenway Road London SW5 0RE

First published in Great Britain 1989
© Miranda Miller 1989

Printed in Great Britain by Billings of Worcester

For Michael

Contents

Glossary

Arabic words as used by Westerners. (The spelling of these words. varies.)

Abaya   a loose black gown worn by Saudi Arabian women, and also by Western women, over their own clothes.

Bukhrah   tomorrow.

Djibli   a warm wind that blows across the desert.

Ghutra   part of the traditional head-dress worn by Saudi Arabian men.

Haram   forbidden or taboo.

Inshallah   God willing.

Majli   meeting of elders.

Mettahwah   Religious policeman.

Sallah   prayer-time. This occurs four times a day, when the muezzin is called and shops must shut.

Sediki   illegally distilled pure alcohol.

Shariah   Koranic law.

Souk   a traditional market, which occupies a large area of the city.

Thobe   a long white gown worn by Saudi Arabian men.

Kiddieworld

1

Stacie fell asleep at last on the floor of her room, kicking and sobbing convulsively for a few minutes even after her eyes had closed. Lena was afraid the child would wake up if she moved her on to the bed, which in any case was invisible beneath a jumble of toys, dirty clothes, sweet wrappers and puzzles. Asleep, her daughter looked so calm and gentle that Lena stroked her head, the only gesture of affection she had managed all day. The battle between the two of them had begun, as usual, when Stacie woke up at six. Now, at three, Lena could count on forty minutes of peace and solitude, if the baby stayed asleep as well. She thought of phoning some more schools to see if she could find one for Stacie. The child was so bored at home all day and Lena was scared that one day she would really hurt her. But she didn't trust schools any more, though they all seemed great when you first went round there, warm and loving like Mamie's. A lot of them had already said they couldn't take Stacie until she was trained, and although Lena had tried everything – had told Stacie she was a dirty, horrible, disgusting little girl and had smacked her butt until it was red and blue – the kid just loved to make her mad. The whole apartment stank of shit and disinfectant.

Lena closed the door on the children. She wished now she had remembered to give Stacie some more of that medicine, then she could be sure of her sleeping for at least an hour and a half. Josette wasn't so bad. At least you could ignore her crying and she couldn't come chasing and whining the way Stacie did. When she grabbed Lena's knees, Lena had to restrain herself from kicking her. Kids were too damned small, they got in the way too much, it was too easy to hurt them.

11

In the sitting-room Lena sprawled on the couch with a cup of coffee, a cigarette and six of the cookies she had baked that morning. It was almost impossible to cook with Stacie clinging to her legs like a squawking red spider, but Lena loved to cook, loved to eat. Even George said she was a great cook. When the kids were grown and she was living in a civilized country again, with or without George, she would open a restaurant, make fabulous food and be loved. Nobody cared what shape you were if you fed them good. In the kitchen the dishes from breakfast and lunch swayed in dirty pyramids, and on the floor there were the mounds of flour. and sugar she had let Stacie build to keep her quiet while Lena cooked. They had trickled grubbily all over the room and were surging towards the door, where they would be trodden into the carpets to protract George's martyrdom. The sitting-room was submerged beneath an ocean of toys, newspapers, cups, dishes and baby bottles. As Lena explained to George every evening, it wasn't worth clearing up because the kids just made a mess again. He had offered to pay for a maid, but Lena didn't like the idea of having another woman in the house, wouldn't trust George with her.

After her snack Lena put her legs up and sank back heavily on to the couch. She was enormous, getting bigger, she knew. She wouldn't have scales or a full-length mirror in the house. 'I'm on the doughnut and pizza diet,' she would say when she wanted to project herself as a fat, cheerful person. Her fat was a wall of blubber between herself and other people. She knew it desexed her in George's eyes and she didn't like even Stacie to see her in the bath. But it was her power, too: she didn't have to pussyfoot and pretend to be weak and gentle like most women. She trusted her fatness. Women like Helen, skinny as a cockroach after two kids, she hated on sight.

Lena's face was red and raw where she had peeled after sunbathing beside her parents' pool in Ohio. Her unwashed brown hair, dragged back with an elastic band, reached half-way down her back. At college it had been even longer, and George used to draw it like a curtain over her breasts. Now that she was lying down at last Lena still couldn't relax, sleep or even read. She was always like this in Riyadh, every fall she wondered why she hadn't stayed on in the States. Two kids born here, she was like a fucking immigrant. But George still hadn't bought that house in Ohio – when he did, it was Lena's silent intention to get the first plane out to it, take the kids, change the locks, sell it behind his back – and living with her parents would not be easy. They had always preferred her sister Beulah, her husband, children, looks. But America was at least a woman's country, where foreign husbands like George were dependants and hangers-on, the terms on which Lena had married him. In Ohio George kept a pretty low profile, listened admiringly to her father's stories of how he had built up his garment factory, apologized for the violence in his native Beirut and pretended to dote on his two daughters. In Ohio Lena felt she still was, under the flesh and bad temper that had snuck up on her, the bright, vivacious, ripe daughter of the house.

Stacie had been much happier in her grandparents' house. There was always somebody around to make a fuss of her, read to her, take her swimming or to the playground. She even stayed dry for a few weeks. While they were there Lena had hardly seen her daughter, had had no fights with her and accepted with gracious smiles compliments on the child's behaviour. And Stacie had stopped asking for Mamie every few minutes.

Coming back to Riyadh was like returning to a cage, a dirty, airless, stinking cage. Lena thought, I don't even have many friends here since that nasty business at Mamie's. Beulah and Dee have been very supportive, but a lot of the other women have turned real mean. I ought to get started again now, talk to the women who've just come out, go round the coffee mornings and the mother and toddler groups, warn them about Mamie's. But I'm so tired.

Yawning, still unable to sleep, Lena reached out for the new copy of *Epoch Magazine.* There was another story: this time a pre-school in New York City – well, you'd expect it there. And another little old lady, just like Mamie, a sweet old granny type. Lena leaned forward and stubbed out her cigarette in the brown puddle at the bottom of her coffee-cup. She was breathing hard, almost swept off the couch by a wave of nausea, indignation and fear. These people just have to be stopped, I can't bear to think of there being so much evil in the world. Little kids of two and three used in a prostitution racket, raped upstairs while their parents thought they were learning their letters. Senators and showbiz people involved. Lena was weeping, sweating, rocking with pain at the corruption she had to protect her babies from. Mamie comes from New York City, and they're capable of anything there. Sodom and Gomorrah and Aids and kids of nine on heroin and cocaine. All those people who sit around in Mamie's kitchen, men as well as women, even Saudi men – why, everyone knows they all sleep with their daughters and nieces. Who knows why they're really in the house? I don't really think Mamie would do that herself but she's so naïve, maybe she still doesn't realize what's going on. It's Helen. She's the one who takes the kids upstairs for lessons and she's the perverted type, cold and mean looking, with that sniffy English accent. Europeans are decadent too, just like New Yorkers.

This old lady in Manhattan – it all happened in a brownstone, for heaven's sake, the school had a waiting-list three years ahead – she made a fortune out of it. Well, Mamie does like money, what with the school and the video club she must be earning more than George. New clothes and jewellery all the time, trips back to the States every few months. For years the kids couldn't talk. They were too scared. That figured. Sadie had never said anything definite and neither had the other kids. They're just babies – how could they understand? Maybe Helen had made threats, like that old lady's son in New York who killed pets in front of them and told them he'd do the same. Next summer, if Sadie's still acting disturbed, we'll take her to a child psychiatrist, back home, not here. I wouldn't trust an Arab shrink. That was how they finally got those other kids to talk. They played games with puppets, made them act out what had happened with puppets.

Lena's stomach rocked and churned. She went into the bathroom and vomited. But the poison was still inside her. All those important people have good lawyers, maybe they won't even be convicted. They don't have the death penalty in New York State, not like here where they execute such people in public and I'd have a ringside ticket. Then not all the New York parents agreed to prosecute. That's another problem. When it came to the point only Dee supported me, and she probably went and talked to Mamie behind my back. George let me down the most. Saying those things about his own daughter in front of everybody, treating us both like crazies. How can I protect my babies when their father just doesn't want to know? Every night he comes home, complains about the mess, shouts at the kids. When I tell him about all the trouble I've had with them, he shrugs. 'They're girls. What do you expect?' Generations of Christianity, an American wife and he still thinks like some barbarian in the *Koran*. I can't talk to him no more. But I have to talk to somebody.

Lena washed, avoided looking at her reflection in the mirror and went into the bedroom, where she dug out the telephone from under a pile of George's dirty underwear.

'Beulah?' Lena's voice was surly and induced ancient fear and guilt in her sister.

'Hi, honey. You didn't come to Christine's baby shower. I thought you'd be there.'

'I'm still so tired from the trip.'

'But you've been back three weeks!'

'I know. But it's this place, it exhausts me. I just can't stop thinking about Mamie, what she and Helen did to Sadie. I can't rest until I get that school closed down.'

'Oh, Lena! I thought you'd gotten over that.'

Lena wished Beulah was in the room with her. She could hear the boredom in her voice, that disloyal tone George had too. Furiously, she drew flowers on the telephone pad. 'I won't get over it as long as I live. Your niece was molested, for Christ's sake. Don't you care about that?'

'You know I care.'

'Has Kiddieworld opened up again?'

'The girls were talking about it this morning. They stayed open all summer. They've got a lot of new kids.'

'Oh my God! In a civilized country I'd go to the police.'

'You can't do that, Lena. Anyway we don't really know ...'

'Of course we know. That doctor said....'

Beulah felt her strength drain away, crushed by her sister's bulldozer will. Lena always wanted things so much, it was easier to just give in, like their parents had always said. 'OK. So what do you want me to do?'

'You have to keep calling them up. Have you called Mamie since we got back?'

'No. I've been too busy.'

'You promised, Beulah. And Dee promised too, but I don't think she's done a thing either since she got back from vacation. We don't want them to think they're getting away with it. I'm really disappointed, Beulah. You know how upset I get when my friends let me down.'

'OK.'

'And if you don't call her, I'll know. You realize that, don't you?'

'Oh, for heaven's sake, we're grown women. You don't have to give me all that telepathy crap. Now I have to go. Goodbye.'

Although Beulah sounded vexed, her sister knew she would do it. Doodling butterflies among the flowers, Lena wondered if Stacie would be like that with Josette, able to make her do things. But Stacie's not like I was, she's weak. She just wants to be liked all the time. Then she heard her whimper, always her first response on waking up, as if consciousness was unbearable. Heavily, Lena dragged herself into the air-conditioned room.

'Shut up. You'll wake Josette.'

Stacie lay on her back, wearing only a T-shirt and pants, staring. up at her mother and crying drearily, without energy or purpose. Tears poured from her eyes more naturally than words from her mouth, although she was nearly three now and ought to be talking more. Lena was afraid there was something wrong with her, that she had been traumatized by whatever had happened at Mamie's.

'What's that stink, Stacie?'

'No. Not dirty. Josie dirty.'

'Oh my God, you're wet again. Do you want me to put you in diapers again like a baby? Like a stupid, dirty, disgusting little baby?'

'No, Mama.'

Lena smacked her sharply on the buttocks, dragged the sheet from under her and went into the bathroom, where she stuffed the sheet in the washing-machine. Stacie followed, her sobs building up to a crescendo of screams. Her fair skin turned scarlet, her teeth stuck out and her nose had been stuck on to her face at the wrong angle, giving her an impish, malevolent look. Around her crooked face her thin, white-blonde hair straggled.

'You're so ugly when you cry. Bad, ugly girl.'

Stacie's screams turned into long-drawn-out hiccupy sobs. 'Mamie,' she gasped. 'Not Mama – Mamie.'

'What did you say?'

'Want Mamie.'

'No. Mamie is very bad. Do you understand? She hurts children, she hurt you. Mamie's school is bad, mean. Mama will find a new school, a nice school.'

'No!' Stacie screamed between sobs. Lena could feel her hot, salty breath burning her knees. Her tears dripped on to the tiled floor. 'Not new school, Mamie school.'

Josette had woken up, and her less developed lungs could be heard just behind Stacie's. Lena felt her panic rise as she rushed to

turn on the washing-machine, get the disinfectant, prepare
Josette's bottle and drag the nappy-bin into the bedroom. The
telephone was ringing, but she couldn't stop to answer it. The
noise is insane. Now they're both awake, the noise and the smell
will get out of hand again, I'll lose control, George will come home
and be furious. What do you do all day? He'll shout with that
temperamental Mediterranean act I used to find so exciting. I live
in a cage, with two stinking, screaming kids and a stupid man who
thinks he's Rambo.... Rehearsing her next row with George,
Lena marched into the bedroom with Josette's bottle and nappy..
Stacie still clung, sobbing, to her legs.

2

'Hello? Kiddieworld?'
'That's right.'
'Is that Mamie?'
'Who is that?'
'Oh, you don't know me. I've heard so much about your school.
I hear the kids just love it and you even do work with handicapped
kids. Is that right?'
'That's right,' Mamie said cautiously, not recognizing the
woman's voice. Perhaps she was genuine.
'Everyone tells me your pre-school's the best in Riyadh. I'd just
love to send my daughter there. But I can't. You know why?
Because you molest the children. Or let Helen molest them. How
can you do that, Mamie? You have to get rid of Helen. She's
warped, she's twisted, you have to....'
Mamie slammed down the receiver. She took out her pink
chiffon handkerchief and sobbed into it, crouched in the corner of
the hall. She turned away from the front door, from the sitting-
room where the children were singing and from the kitchen where
Helen was getting their orange juice and cookies, and faced the
wall as if she was being punished. She couldn't cry in front of any
of them. But it was such a shock, the first of those calls since before
her vacation. Don had told her not to answer the phone, to let him
or Helen do it, but Mamie said, 'I'm a grandmother, aren't I?
This is my house, my pre-school. I'll answer my own phone.'
But it hurt so much. There had been at least five different voices
altogether, American and English. There must be dozens of

women saying those things about her. She crouched in the corner
again and cried, less like a grandmother than one of her pupils.
Mamie was only five feet tall, with obstinately yellow hair, bangs,
large blue eyes and cherry-red lips and nails. She had retained
throughout her life the look of a pretty little girl and still wore a rich
variety of brightly coloured frills, sashes, bows and puff sleeves. A
child model, always carefully made up and neatly dressed. She
often said, the kids love me so much because I'm a lot like them.
They do love me, she remembered, and went back into the sitting-
room to check.

They were standing in a circle singing, conducted by Leyla, the
third teacher, a young Egyptian woman who had been educated in
America. There were about twenty children and almost as many
nationalities. In age they ranged from Lakshmi, an Indian two-
year-old with vast liquid-black eyes, and Jack, an American seven-
year-old with a mental age of two. Jack's brain had developed in
the year since he had arrived at Mamie's. Mamie knew it and it
had also been measured, proved and confirmed scientifically. He
was a blond, handsome, ironically intelligent-looking boy who
could now go to the toilet on his own and join in the daily
repertoire of songs and rhymes. If anyone smiled at him he would
run over to hug them, even more spontaneous in his affections
than the younger children. When Mamie came into the room he
ran up to her and stood beside her to show off how perfectly he
could count his fingers: Tommy thumb, Tommy thumb, where
are you? Here I am. Here I am. How do you do?

The circle of children almost filled the room. Mamie's school
was also her house, on the compound owned by the International
hotel chain Don worked for. Officially they were not supposed to
open a school there, but it had survived for five years. The house
was small and spotlessly clean. There was a brass souvenir hookah
with a pink and green lurex pipe and numerous brass and copper
nicknacks from the *souk*: miniature coffee-pots, pestles and
mortars, tea-trays and clocks that chimed four times a day at
prayer-time. A row of little china animals played musical
instruments, jostling framed homilies, Venetian glass ashtrays
and a shelf of dolls wearing national costumes. They were all
presents from Mamie's wide circle of friends, most of them parents
of children who, over the last five years, had been kept happy at
her school. The walls were dominated by large, anodyne, pastel
portraits of her four adult children, done from photographs by a

Korean artist of great talent but no originality who worked from a booth in a Riyadh supermarket. The small, neat three-bedroom villa with its brown stucco façade and garden full of swings and paddling-pools could have been transposed, without incongruity, to any British or American suburb.

Mamie hugged Jack and smiled at the other children. Helen saw, as soon as she came in to announce that drinks and cookies were ready, that her friend's smile was brimming and trembly. She let Leyla take the children through to the kitchen and squatted beside Mamie's chair. Helen was tall and very slim, with straight red hair and a white, pretty, nervous face. Her long neck and fingers and large green eyes gave her a fragile look which was contradicted by her ex-nurse's air of common sense and toughness.

'What's the matter, Mamie? Have you had another call?'

'I wasn't going to say anything.' Mamie huddled over her lace-edged handkerchief. Even in her grief she was dainty and never cried into the same handkerchief twice.

'Why not? Was it Fat Lena?'

'No. An American voice, but not her.'

'What did she say?'

'Oh, the usual. She started out all nicey nice to disarm me. Said she'd heard we run a great school but she couldn't send her daughter here because we molest the kids.'

'What a load of rubbish. Did she mention me?'

'Yes. But don't . . .'

'I don't care what they say. I just want to know.'

'They want me to get rid of you, Helen. They hate you. I really don't know why.'

'Well, I'm not going. If I did, it would be like admitting I'd done something wrong.'

Helen stood with her thin arms folded, tall and very straight, shivering because the acts that she had been accused of six months before still made her feel cold and sick. She had been educated at the convent near London, where her daughter now boarded, and had never rejected Catholicism or gone through the wild phase expected of ex-convent girls. After a brief career as a nurse she had married Peter, her first boy-friend, had had two children and lived near Epping, where Peter managed a hotel. Although, in her cotton shirt and striped jeans, Helen looked like an ordinary woman in her mid-thirties, she was almost eccentrically conventional.

Until she followed Peter to Riyadh she had always felt secure
inside her family. She hadn't wanted to leave her children in
England but wished them to have a 'good' (private) education and
felt that, at twelve and fourteen, they would be all right without
her.

But Helen's arrival in Riyadh had provoked the first real crisis
in her life. She had suddenly found herself childless, alone for most
of the day and for many evenings while Peter worked. Although
Helen was a puritan herself she was out of tune with the Islamic
fundamentalist intolerance that scourged Riyadh. She hated the.
concrete and stucco compound where employees of the hotel group
lived in isolation, the deserted streets around it, the impossibility
of legally attending mass or even going out to the shops without
making elaborate arrangements for transport and chaperones.
One day, by chance, she discovered an underground Filipino
priest with a chapel hidden in his villa. He was one of many such
secret Christians, employed as a 'consultant' by a multinational
company, and at weekends he saved the souls of his colleagues.
Many foreigners in Riyadh, agnostics at home, found that the
illegal services had a kind of bootleg charm. For passionate
believers it was of course inconceivable that their children should
go unbaptized or unchristened, and many of these underground
priests and vicars found Riyadh a more exciting place to worship
in than their own parishes.

This particular priest alternated between services in Spanish
and English, and Helen happened to pick a Spanish Friday to go
to Communion. She thought the service was overloaded with
flowers and incense and gaudy pictures. Inside the hall a vast
Filipino family huddled around a new-born baby waiting to be
christened. It was all very exotic, sickly and touching. Helen left
feeling relieved and walked home in her long black dress. She had
some satisfaction in practising her religion as a gesture of
rebellion. At home her children and most of her friends sneered at
her for being so unfashionably devout. Helen passed Saudi
women, also in black, with long veils, women reduced to shadowy
death wishes, as the medieval Catholic Church had wanted to
reduce its female subjects. For the first time Helen felt nostalgia for
a freedom she had never even noticed; freedom to move, drive,
work, dress and worship as she liked. She went home to a childless,
manless house, for Peter was working yet more overtime to pay for
the children's school fees and the bigger house they wanted to

buy. In the void of the dull company house there stirred in Helen a strength she had never called on. She learned how to be alone, and although she didn't like it she regained a calm integrity, a subtle pleasure in endurance, which had characterized her as an adolescent. Her neighbours found her aloof and Peter was puzzled when he came home to find her reading *The Life of Saint Theresa*. The house smelled of candles, incense and scones. Peter, a cheerful agnostic, humoured his wife's religious tendencies and was still passionately in love with a kind of purity, a clean, straight quality he saw in her. It didn't occur to him there was any. connection between the two. Secretly he was pleased to see her reduced by Islam to the faunlike shyness she had had when he first met her.

'I'm going back to work,' she announced one Friday night as they ate roast lamb and listened to the World Service.

'You're not allowed to work here, are you?' He loved to think of her waiting for him, cooking and praying.

'There are plenty of jobs for nurses. I might have to leave the country for a while to get my visa changed.'

'I thought you were enjoying your rest,' he said reproachfully, as if waiting for him to come home was an occupation most women would jump at.

'No,' she said quietly. 'Women get neurotic here doing nothing. I'd rather work.'

Helen didn't analyse it more than that. She wasn't a Freudian or a feminist. She had only an instinct for sanity.

A few weeks later Mamie rang her bell and sucked her in to the perpetual warmth of her kitchen. After the children left each day at two, a big, noisy circle of adult friends came to visit Mamie. At first Helen stood outside in the garden, where Lego, sand, buckets, paddling-pools, cars, lorries and Fisher-Price people sprawled in the dust. Mechanically, Helen began to tidy them, surprised to find the garden so similar to her own, ten years before, when her children used to play there. Mamie rushed out to hose the garden, paused in the hall to listen to the history of a friend's breakdown and ran into the kitchen to see if her strudel was burning. She made Helen smile, raised her temperature, which had dropped to such a low point in her own silent, air-conditioned house. Helen returned to the sitting-room, where she vacuumed and stared at Mamie's friends. There were two American women, an Indian woman in a sari who had brought a plate of fresh

chapatis, a Japanese business man who wanted to send his son to
the school and a young Saudi in a *ghutra* and *thobe,* Abdul Aziz,
who spoke with a pronounced American accent and great affection
of his student days in Colorado. Helen kept looking nervously at
the open front door, waiting for the morality police to come and
break up this scandalous party. She had never spoken to a Saudi,
male or female, before. Peter referred to his Saudi bosses as if they
were extraterrestrials with pretensions as human beings.
Throughout the city, she had been told, an inverted apartheid
ruled, with foreigners and Saudis hardly mixing except on formal
occasions, when segregation of the sexes was rigidly observed. The
presence of this smiling boy, who guzzled strudel and confided in
Mamie, amazed her.

Helen kept going back to the house. It was always warm, noisy
and crowded. Mamie came to seem less brash, rapacious and
superficial than Helen had at first thought she was. Certainly she
had a loud voice and made a lot of money, but Helen's judgement
was suspended by Mamie's generosity: she was always listening,
advising, feeding, helping. She can't help being brassy and
American, Helen thought, any more than I can help being
repressed and English.

Mamie had lived all her life in an extended family, and when
one was not available she formed another instinctively. Children
were her chosen material, but she could attract adults too. Far
more observant than she seemed to be, Mamie soon perceived
Helen's loneliness and integrity, and drew her into her circle.
Mamie could toss people like pancakes, deftly knead and mould
them. She made Helen feel they were soul sisters, united by their
homesickness, their love of children and appreciation of the
problems of living in Riyadh. Differences of personality,
nationality, age and background diminished, and soon Mamie
presented Helen with a job at the school and a badly needed new
identity to go with it. To Mamie's soft, loving, vulnerable mommy
Helen played the prim, strict aunt. The children liked her, the
school thrived and she was happy.

Mamie was still crying. Helen knelt in front of her and took both
her hands, pouring strength into her as Mamie had once poured
confidence into Helen.

'Listen. You've got to stop letting them hurt you. That's why
they phone you and not me. They know you can't take it.'

'I just can't go through all that again. Waiting all night for the phone to ring. Even when my kids call me from the States I'm shaking, I'm so scared they're going to say terrible things to me. Don't touch me, for God's sake.'

'Why not?'

'Someone'll see, then they'll start on us, say we're perverted. This place is a glasshouse. My God, and I've never even looked at a man except Don. But if they said I was having an affair with another guy, I don't think I'd mind, I'd even be kind of flattered. You know what really scares me?'

'What?'

'How do we prove it? Suppose they get real nasty and denounce us to the police. These things do happen. It's only our word against theirs. Last time when we had that parents' meeting they believed us. But if it happens again, if the police come round? Why should they believe we're innocent?'

'But we are,' Helen said blankly. 'Those things they said we'd done, I'd done, they'd never even occurred to me.'

Then she was silent and gazed out of the back window, where the children in the hot garden jumped in and out of the paddling-pool. Because now of course they had occurred to her. Every time she took a child to the lavatory or changed Lakshmi's nappy, Fat Lena's fantasies were in the room with her. Innocence was only not knowing; she hadn't known that anyone could suspect her of sexually abusing small children. Now the suspicion poisoned all her relations with the children and even her memories of playing with her own children. Furious, Helen slapped away a tear.

'Don't you start,' Mamie said, wiping her eyes and relieved to see she was upset. Helen's coolness and toughness sometimes appalled her. 'Oh my God, will you look at what they're doing out there! They've all taken their panties off!'

'They're only little kids,' Helen said fiercely.

'But Abdul Aziz'll be here soon, if he finds his kid naked with a crowd of little girls. You know, we've got to get more Saudi kids in the school, otherwise they'll close us down.'

'But Abdul Aziz seems so Westernized.'

'It doesn't matter. They're all the same. You meet them in New York and it's all Scotch and blue jeans. But when you see them back here you'd think they'd just ridden out of the desert on a camel.'

Mamie rushed out and yelled at the children to get dressed. Helen, who followed slowly, smiled on hearing again the Brooklyn percussion in her voice.

That afternoon Helen went home with one of the children, Katie, and her mother, Sally, an English teacher from Brighton. The compound where Mamie and Helen lived was an underprivileged one. It had no swimming-pool and no transport laid on for the women. We're poor relations, Mamie used to complain as mothers brought their children to the school in chauffeur-driven limousines and panicked because their houseboy had left. But both she and Helen had open invitations to borrow cars and pools. After six months in Riyadh Sally was still completely disorientated, hunting for sympathetic women. All her life she had been surrounded by women she could talk to, who shared most of her attitudes and cultural references. It wasn't the Saudis (with whom she had no social contact) whom she found alien, but the English-speaking women. She was beginning to like Mamie, although at first she had found her Bette Davis looks and raucous manner off-putting. Sally kept trying to make contact with Helen, the sanest woman she had met since her arrival, but she was puzzled by her melancholy air.

'This is a lovely compound. What does your husband do?' Helen asked politely as they lay beside the pool in the blazing October sunshine, watching Katie dive and leap like a shiny, brown otter.

Sally didn't bother to reply. She was sick of the endless one-upmanship over accommodation and husband's salaries that plagued the women of Riyadh and thought Helen should know better.

'I am glad Katie's so happy at your school. I thought I'd go nuts the first few months here, incarcerated alone with her. There aren't any kids her age on this compound. I used to try to take her out for walks in her pushchair – in Brighton we used to go on to the Downs every day. But this city's impossible to walk in. There's no shade, they plant the trees in the middle of the pavement and then, just to make sure you can't get past, dump some rubble and leave a few uncovered manholes.'

'I know. I nearly broke my neck the other day, walking to the supermarket. Katie's a very nice little girl.'

'She is now. A few months ago she was having tantrums five times a day. So was I. We just got so bored with each other. But now she's at school I'm thinking of going back to work.'

'As a teacher?'

'I thought I might give private English lessons to Saudi women. I'd love to meet some of them.'

'Be careful.'

'Everyone says that. All the foreign women here seem to be terrified of doing anything, at the coffee mornings and mum-and-toddler group all they talk about is how dangerous everything is.'

'It really is a dangerous place, you know.'

'Why was Mamie crying?'

Helen sat up, very formal in her black, one-piece swimming-costume, and white skinned because she had hardly sunbathed. She smothered herself in coconut oil. 'If I have any more sun I'll peel until I look like a boiled shrimp. Can we put the umbrella up, please?'

Sally, who was dark skinned and scorned precautions against the sun, which she still regarded as the one delight of Riyadh, stayed outside the circle of shade. She screwed up her eyes and frowned at Helen, who carried on anointing herself, evading Sally behind her sunglasses.

'Mamie said something about phone calls?'

'Did she really?' Helen looked up. As she was capable of discretion in any circumstances, Mamie's big mouth exasperated her. 'Well, since Katie's at the school, I suppose you ought to know. Most of the parents do.' Cautiously, she took off her sunglasses and blinked at Sally, dazzling with the sun behind her, whose brown eyes were very shrewd. Helen whipped on the glasses again.

'I know what the gossip's like here. It's vicious. That's why I stopped going to the mum-and-toddler group. I heard so many nasty stories I became quite paranoid.'

'Stories about Kiddieworld?'

'No.'

'Well, I'd better tell you in case you do. Last winter there was a woman called Lena who had a child at the school. She's American, married to an Arab, Lebanese or something. He treats her badly, according to Mamie. Her little girl, Stacie, was like an animal when she first started at the school, always biting and kicking and screaming. She was about two then, a real brat. And she stank. I don't think Lena ever gave her a proper wash, and Lena was none too clean herself. But Mamie managed to get on with her. She likes everyone who doesn't actually beat or rob her.

She talked to Lena a lot and they used to cook together in the afternoons. Lena's a compulsive eater, as big as a heffalump. She never stopped going on about how wonderful the school was, how Mamie was her best friend. She never liked me much. Stacie was happy at the school – she started to behave more or less like a human being although she was still disturbed. And Lena began to act as if she owned the school, and Mamie too. She was always there, whenever new parents came, she'd rush up to them and tell them how lucky they were.'

'You hated Lena?'

'There's something repulsive about her. Even before all this, I thought so. She's so fat and greedy and slovenly and loud.' In her fastidious slenderness, Helen writhed with antagonism.

'But Mamie liked that?'

'Mamie's so open. She really wants everyone to be her friend. She manages it with small children, but she can never get used to the idea that adults are more complicated. Then she likes flattery – don't we all? – and Lena admired her house, her clothes, her cooking, her gift with kids. But it was unbalanced, as if Lena was stuffing herself with Mamie's life, gobbling it up so fast that she'd soon feel gorged, sick. She kept introducing friends to Mamie, insisting they sent their kids to the school. As soon as her sister's baby was born, Lena made her put this child down for Kiddieworld. As if it was Eton or something. Then one day Stacie got a rash on her bum.'

'Katie got that last week. I think it's this dry heat.'

'What did you do about it?'

'Took her to the doctor, kept her out of the pool and put some ointment on it.'

'Well, Lena went to an Egyptian doctor who said it was either a nappy-rash or the child had been sexually interfered with. Stacie was still in nappies and the only time she got a good wash was at school. Anyway Lena came rushing round to the school. She had this friend with her, Dee, who'd just started sending her kid, a baby called Cindy, about eighteen months old. Lena started to scream at Mamie as soon as they got inside the gate, in the front garden, in front of all the children: "That doctor says my baby's been interfered with. If she's been abused it must have happened here. She goes straight from home to your school every morning."

'Mamie didn't even deny it. She took them into the sitting-room and got Lena to repeat what she'd said, then burst into tears.

When I came into the room a few minutes later Lena and Dee were standing over her, threatening to take their kids away, get the school closed down, go to the police, and Mamie just looked terrified. She has no defence against nastiness. She once said to me, "The thing I can't understand about the Catholic Church is all that stuff about sin and wickedness. Nobody's wicked." Dee became hysterical, started saying her child had had a rash on her bum as well.'

Katie climbed out of the pool and ran to her mother, who absent-mindedly wrapped her in a sun-warmed towel. The child giggled because the mummies were talking about bums. The two women were so absorbed in their conversation that they couldn't change the subject. It was the first time Helen had tried to talk about it like this, dispassionately, to someone she didn't know very well. Her voice had its usual reticent note, her face was grave and still, but she relived the scene as she tried to describe it and her shame still grabbed her by the throat, made it swell and burn. Katie rolled over on to her back, kicked her legs in the air and waited to bask in the attention of her mother and her favourite teacher.

'Katie, why don't you go and get yourself an ice-cream and a milkshake out of the fridge?'

'I wanna cookie.' All the children at Mamie's picked up strong Brooklyn accents.

'Ask for it properly.'

'Please.'

'Help yourself to whatever you want from the kitchen.'

The dangers of white sugar and tooth decay seemed negligible now. As the child ran off Sally leaned towards Helen, galvanized by her story. And for the first time Helen realized that it was a story which had to be aired and given shape, simplified, to become bearable.

'Go on, quick. She'll be back soon.'

'I was furious with them both, and with Mamie for looking so guilty – yet I felt guilty too. Isn't that strange? But I was determined to fight them. I said to Lena. "Are you accusing us of some kind of perversion? Because if so you'd better get the police." Then they started to prevaricate. Lena said, "I don't know if it was you. Maybe you've had men in here." Then Mamie stopped crying and she and I just screamed with laughter. I said, "What do you mean, men? The gate is locked from the minute the

kids arrive. Nobody comes here except for the teachers, the kids
and their parents. Do you think men come climbing over the wall
or something?"'

'Then Mamie looked at Lena, who she still thought of as her
friend. "Honey, do you honestly think I'd do anything like that?
You know how I love these kids." "Maybe you love them too
much," Lena said, and after that Mamie couldn't look at her.
Then Dee started: "I have seen men in here, sitting round the
kitchen table for hours. Ay-rabs too." That just made me so
angry, I practically spat at her. "Aren't we allowed to invite our
friends round in the afternoon? Do you expect Mamie to live in
purdah?" Lena stood up. I know she can't help being so fat and
unhealthy looking but at that moment she was like a greasy,
sweaty jelly poisoned by her own malevolence. I've never seen
anybody look so ugly. I really hated her. I still do, God forgive me.
"Take Stacie away, then. You're sick. If anything's the matter
with that child it's because you don't love her or look after her
properly." I know I shouldn't have said that. Afterwards I felt
bad, specially when I remembered she was pregnant. Then Lena
said again that she was going to get the school closed down, Dee
muttered something about taking Cindy away, and they left.

'Mamie and I decided we had to talk to the other parents before
they did. So we arranged a meeting a few days later. I told Lena
this was her chance to get the school closed down. The meeting was
on a Friday, so most of the mothers and even the fathers came.
Lena turned up with her husband, who's a real smoothie, terribly
handsome and elegant, gold rings and tiepins, looks like a
croupier. Most people brought their kids, so we sent them off to
play in the garden. It was rather horrible, hearing them all
through the meeting, catching glimpses of them out of the
window. They kept looking in, specially Stacie. She seemed to
know it was to do with her.'

Katie trailed back. Her pot belly stuck out over her red
swimming-trunks and her orange, plastic water-wings made her
look like a clumsy insect. She was annoyed that her mother had
hijacked Helen. Sally looked around desperately for toys, other
children, anything to prolong the illusion of her child's childhood.
She had always vowed to be open and frank with her daughter, but
surely it was too soon to expose her to the most brutal adult
realities? Sally found paper and felt-tip pens.

'Why don't you do a lovely drawing for Mamie?'

'No. For Helen.'

'All right, darling. Go over there, there's more shade.'

'No. Here.'

Katie lay face down on Helen's towel, her legs glued to her teacher's oily thighs. Helen flinched and moved away.

'What shall I draw?'

'A big, big city with lots of houses and cars and people and trees and flowers.'

The two women drew closer and lowered their voices, trying to speak in code like conspirators.

'Tell me about the meeting. I wish I'd been there.'

'The parents were marvellous. I stood up at the beginning and told them why we'd asked them to come. Three of them just laughed, said it was ridiculous and went home. One man, a lawyer, stood up and said that if this wasn't such a crazy country we'd be able to sue for defamation of character. Then I introduced Lena. She stood up and it was like a pantomime. People didn't actually hiss but you could sense the hostility. Dee was very quiet, she looked really nervous, and Lena's husband . . .'

'Finished.'

'That's lovely, darling. Now do a birthday card for Granny.'

'Do you like it, Helen?'

'Very much.'

'You can keep it for ever and ever. Put it on your wall.'

'Thanks.'

'Katie, let us talk now, darling.'

Katie hurled herself on to her mother's lap and pressed her hand over her mouth.

'Katie, don't be silly, I want to talk, I . . .'

'Mummy! Never talk!'

The child clung to her like a baby monkey, ravenous for adult attention. Sally cuddled her and spoke literally over her head. 'Go on. She won't understand.'

'Really? Well, Lena's husband was amazing. He didn't even sit next to her and he kept eyeing all the other women in the room, lighting cigarettes for them and smarming all over them. All the time I was talking, and even after Lena started, he was chatting up this very pretty Japanese mum who'd come along on her own. I felt sorry for Lena, I really did, despite everything. His manner was so deliberately insulting, not just as if he didn't support her, but as if he'd only come along to sabotage her. She kept looking at him rather pathetically, and he didn't even look back. She was quite nervous, and although she always has a hard, thick-skinned manner, I could tell she was hating it. She knew nobody believed her. Every few minutes she'd be interrupted. How do you know? How can you prove it? Why couldn't it have been a rash? The whole room was against her and she was getting more and more rattled and incoherent. Then her husband stood up and said, "I don't think we should take this any further. Lena knows Stacie's a funny kid. One day last week I went into her room and found her sticking pencils up herself. If she had a rash, who knows where it. came from?"

'A few people laughed. Lena couldn't speak after that. She went out into the garden to grab Stacie – who didn't want to leave – and dragged her out to the car. Of course anywhere else in the world she could have salvaged a bit of dignity by getting in and driving off, but, this being Saudi, she had to wait for her husband to come and drive her home. He left like royalty, smiling at everyone, pressing Mamie's hand and telling her how wonderful she'd been, apologizing to me. He was charming and at the same time terribly cruel. All that charm was aimed at humiliating Lena. Then Dee ran up to Mamie, sobbing, told her she was sorry and said Lena had made her say all those things. She said she trusted Mamie more than her own mother and she really wanted to keep Cindy at the school. Dee's about twenty, just a little Midwestern kid who does whatever grown-ups tell her. Mamie was tough for once. She said she couldn't have Cindy at the school any more.

'Then the parents kept coming up to me and Mamie, telling us how much they liked us and the school. A lot of people were in tears and we were all hugging each other. Someone had brought along a couple of bottles of black-market whisky – about fifty quid a bottle – and we were toasting the school, Mamie, me, we were all so relieved. We really thought it was all over. My kids were coming out a few weeks later for the Easter holidays and I'd dreaded having to tell them. My daughter's ever so sharp, she always knows if I'm upset. We're very close.'

'Have you got a little girl, Helen?'

Uneasily, they realized that Katie had been listening to every word.

'Big girl. She's fourteen.'

'How many is that?'

Helen held up all her fingers and four toes.

'Where is she?'

'In England. She's coming out here at Christmas.'

'Can I play with her?'

'Oh, she'll be at the school all the time. There's nowhere else for her to go,' Helen added sadly.

'So when did the phone calls start?' Sally asked.

'Almost immediately. Always different voices, British and American. Mamie couldn't recognize Lena's voice, but of course she's quite capable of disguising it. They usually phone at night. Mamie's been on sleeping-pills for months. She's become an insomniac. But it's me they're really after. They want to force me to leave the school. But I won't.'

4

George's first precaution when he got home each evening was to lock himself in the bathroom, take a shower, wash his hair and clean his teeth. For a few minutes the roar of the water drowned the background noises of his household; Stacie banging on the door, Lena yelling at her, Josette screaming. He washed away the dust of his exhausting drive from the shop and then with Badedas and Head and Shoulders exorcized much of the stink of family life. But as George dried himself his resentment and indignation mounted: soon the door would open on squalor and pandemonium, a spiteful parody of the domestic harmony he had grown up with. This image of a family as an art form, a gilded triptych of a dignified patriarch supported by a modest female saint and smiling cherubs, was always in George's mind and accounted for much of his unhappiness. Both his parents had been bombed to death in their beautiful frame, and the other cherubim were like him dispersed to marriages of convenience around the world. All he had salvaged was an American passport and a gold signet-ring. George put on his olive-green bathrobe – he had all his clothes laundered, never let Lena near them – and reluctantly stepped out of the fragrant steam on to the fetid carpet.

Stacie, who had been waiting for him all day, climbed up his legs and clutched at his neck.

'Hi, sweetheart. You're strangling me.'

'Daddy! Daddy!' She buried her face in his neck and planted dry, fierce little kisses on it.

George let her adore him. It wasn't her fault she was so ugly and unkempt looking. His sisters had been beautiful, with rich dark hair and eyes, tiny gold earrings and white broderie anglaise dresses with matching panties. 'You OK? You wearing a diaper or something? Been a good girl today?'

But Lena had also been waiting for him. She swayed out of the kitchen like an oil drum on legs. It seemed to George that every day she expanded, became greasier and more rancid. It was weeks since they had touched. In the vast bed they could roll far away from each other and dream their separate revenges. They hadn't fought physically since Stacie had come into the sitting-room late one night, woken by their yells, and found her father dragging her mother by her hair, red scratches all over his cheeks. For the time being their violence was formalized, verbal.

'No, she hasn't. Accidents all day long. Is there something the matter with your nostrils?'

Nervously, George loosened the child's grip and lifted her down to the floor, where she clung to his legs.

'Stacie! Leave your father alone. He's tired. Go play with Josette.'

Stacie dragged herself into the bedroom. The baby was screaming, stinking. Her sister watched her through the bars of her prison cot. You couldn't play with her, she wasn't a proper child. It would have been better if they'd bought a kitten or a puppy. Babies were stupid, ugly and dirty, although Josette didn't understand that yet. Stacie wondered why grown-ups went out and bought children in hospitals when they didn't want them. Mommy left Josette screaming like that for hours. Her face was like a red, squidgy rubber football. Tears and slobber and pee made her shiny all over. 'They won't come. They won't like you if you do that,' Stacie said quite gently. She pushed her hand through the bars and let her sister's slimy hand grasp one of her fingers, then suck it ferociously. Josette no longer screamed and Stacie felt some of the loneliness sucked out of her.

George made a great play of finding a clean spot on the sofa to sit down on. Combative, huge, her arms dangling like a Japanese wrestler, Lena watched him from the doorway. They drank fruit juice together because they were afraid of the effects of home-brewed alcohol.

'I may have to go out to dinner with some clients.'

'Tonight? Why didn't you tell me? I already fixed dinner.'

'I didn't know. They run a department store in Dubai. It could be a big contract.'

'So? Invite them back here.'

'I wouldn't invite a pig's asshole back here.'

'I'm sure you could find some use for a pig's asshole.'

'Lena, why are you so ugly?'

She felt the pain and hatred rise to the pitch where she would attack him. It was some satisfaction to her to know that she was stronger than him, certainly heavier and quicker on her feet. I could throw him off the couch and crack his head against the coffee-table quite a few times before he had time to retaliate. Last time we had a fight in here we smashed the table and that louse of a Saudi landlord made us pay a fortune to replace the glass top. And Stacie came in. She will now any minute. I know I'm a bad mother but I don't really want to murder him. Not in front of her.

Lena turned away, didn't look at him so that he couldn't look at her. 'Get out, then.'

'I'm just finishing my drink.'

He sat back on the sofa, sipped his drink, smiled and crossed his legs as if he was having a party all by himself. Lena used to admire his elegance and style, the way he always looked clean. She had thought that, living with all his attractiveness, some of it would rub off on her. But love of his grace had not made her more graceful. It seemed to her now that every time she had admired his charm she had put on another pound, stumbled or lost her temper. She had perceived the treachery implicit in that cheap salesman glamour, and now she felt as much distaste for his smiling dandyism as he did for her sluttishness. Lena was the more bitter of the two, she wallowed in her ugliness and permitted herself no comfort there. Even food, her one pleasure, was a confirmation of her unlovableness.

Stacie came in and sat on her father's knee because he smelled better. She was used to squeezing between these silences of theirs, which sometimes continued for hours, although she wasn't allowed to interrupt them.

'You gonna eat supper with Stacie?'

'No, honey. I have to go out.'

'Stacie come?'

'No. I have to work.'

'And then Daddy will have to stay out all night, working, and maybe all weekend. Working.'

Stacie was frightened when her mother used that voice. It was like a joke but not funny. In the bath and at bedtime her hands would be rough, she would push and slap, and when Stacie cried she would just smile, as if crying was right. Her father was happy, he was the only one of them all who never cried or screamed, and Stacie thought the secret of his happiness lay in his ability to get out of the house.

'Stacie come with you. Please.'

'I'd love to take you, sweetheart, but I can't.' George stroked his daughter's strawlike hair to make sure she was on his side, kissed her, and amiably left.

Stacie stared after him. Her voice froze as the door sliced him in two and wiped him out. She knew that if she tried to talk to her mother the words would come out all wrong, baby words. Then she would be stupider than Josette. Her mother would tell her so and probably hit her.

Lena was furious with George because he hadn't even said goodbye to her, had kissed Stacie but not her, had made Stacie look at the door after he left in that dumb way. I get all the shit, mess, noise and resentment. George just walks in, charms Stacie and walks out again.

'I better feed Josette and fix your supper.'

Stacie took her mother's hand because she had been crying. She liked it when her mother was sad. It was her anger that frightened her. The hand was enormous, red like a piece of meat. Her mother staggered down the corridor, sighed as she reached into the fridge for the baby's bottle and grunted. It must be so heavy to drag that body around. No wonder she was always tired, never sang or whistled like Daddy. While the fridge door was open, Stacie snatched the pizza she was supposed to eat for her supper. She wanted to make her own food, then her mother wouldn't be so tired, so angry, so sad.

'Stacie! I told you! Don't grab food like that. I'll fix your supper in a minute.'

'Stacie big girl. Not bad.'

'Don't use that stupid baby talk. Say "I". "I'm a big girl."'

'I'm a big girl. Not bad.' She reached up on to the dresser for a plate to put her pizza on and knocked over a stack of cups and saucers, which fell with a clatter and broke on the hard, tiled floor. Stacie wailed, terrified, while Lena swore at her and swept up the jagged pieces.

'OK. Now stop crying. I'm the one who should cry. I'll stick this in the oven. Now let's go feed Josette.'

But Stacie couldn't stop crying. She couldn't bear her failure to be good, clever, loved. Her father and Mamie disappeared, however hard she tried to make them love her, and her mother was always mad at her.

When Lena came back into the kitchen, the child was still crouched in a corner, crying.

'Oh for Christ's sake shut up. Eat your pizza and go to bed.'

But Stacie couldn't eat, her throat was too swollen, she couldn't get words up or food down. Lena coaxed her, smacked her and said she would buy her a toy in the morning if she ate up her supper.

'Open your mouth, then.' Lena rammed in a spoonful of the red syrup which would save her from losing control altogether.

Stacie sucked the spoon greedily. She knew she would stop crying soon and go to sleep. The bedroom was dark and cool from the air conditioning, which had been turned on all day. Above its faint roar Josette snored. Stacie got into bed. The diaper scratched between her legs and she felt her mother's hand, heavy and tight, waiting to get away from her.

'Don't go. Stacie wanna story.'

'What about?'

'Bout Mamie's'

'Now don't start that again. I'm too tired to tell you stories. Think about Grandma's house. Think about Santa Claus. You want Snoopy? Goodnight, honey, see you in the morning.'

Stacie thought about Stacie, who made people want to go away. She shut her eyes and listened to Josette's breathing rise and fall like the sweet red waves coming to wash her away until morning.

Lena sprawled on the sofa and had a glass of home-brewed wine with soda to celebrate getting Stacie to bed without any serious violence. Although she was furious with George for having gone out, Lena was least unhappy when she was alone like this. She never believed his stories now, assumed he ran off with a string of women. How he managed it in such a repressive city she didn't ask. That was his problem. Although Lena hadn't had a religious upbringing, there were only angels and devils in her life, and the angels fell thick and fast. For years she had adored George, hadn't even noticed that there was anything to put up with. She had been genuinely, touchingly, grateful that he stayed with her. Now she often wished that he would leave. At night she lay awake hoping he had died in one of the car accidents so common in Riyadh, gone off to Timbuctoo with his latest girl-friend, disappeared any which way. She wanted him out of her life, but for some reason hadn't the strength to push him. She ate the stuffed peppers, rice and chocolate mousse she had cooked for the two of them. She often did this, then blamed George for her weight problem. She was eating for two, three, four, trying to fill the awful hole inside her.

She gave Beulah time to finish her supper, then went into the bedroom and dialled her number. Charles, her brother-in-law, answered.

'Hi. You're not going out with these clients?'

'What clients, Lena?'

Charles was always formal with her. It had been a kind of double marriage, the two American sisters and the two Lebanese partners. But Charles had never felt any doubt as to which couple was the more attractive and successful.

'George said they were staying at the Intercontinental. Opening a department store in Dubai or something?'

'I really don't know, Lena. George makes his own arrangements.'

'That's what I figured.'

'You want to speak to Beulah?'

Beulah sounded tougher because Charles was there. He protected her, she told him everything and never complained about him. It made Lena sick.

'Hi, honey. I was just wondering if you went to that coffee morning?'

'Yes, Lena.'

'How was it?'

'Oh, just fine.'

'Did you mention . . . any more news about Kiddieworld?'

'I made that call last week, if that's what you want to know.'

'And Dee? Did you see her?'

'She said she'd be calling soon. And there was some talk about Mamie's, as a matter of fact. Some of the girls who just arrived were asking abour pre-schools. So we warned them.'

'Yeah? That's great. I really appreciate that, Beulah. Shit, Stacie's just woken up again. You know, she always has bad dreams now. Oh, and did you see the new *Epoch?* That little old lady in New York City got life.'

'That's a stiff sentence.'

'You think so? It's a pity it didn't happen some place where they have the death penalty. She'll be dead in a few years anyways. I have to go – my baby needs me.'

5

In the middle of the night Mamie reached out for the telephone. Out of the foggy clouds of the sleeping-pills that no longer gave her sleep, past the sour blasts of Don's nocturnal breath, she threw her voice. 'Hello?' It might be one of the children calling from the States. They always forget the time gap.

'Hello? Is that Mamie?' An English woman. A new one.

'Oh my God. Can't you let me sleep?'

'You don't know who I am.'

'I'm going to put the phone down. I'm going to hang up on you,' Mamie said shakily. Don had woken up and was leaning towards her, mouthing 'Hang up.' But Mamie couldn't, she was mesmerized, she had to hear.

'I just want to talk to you about your school.'

'At this time of the night? It's three o'clock in the morning.'

'I can't sleep, thinking about what you did to those children. Is it still going on? It's so terrible, how can you let it happen? How can you sleep?'

'I can't with nuts like you calling me up all night.'

Beside her Don silently cheered her on. Mamie thought of Helen, who had told her to be tougher, told her not to let them hurt her. But Mamie's voice shook.

'Have you got rid of that woman? That Helen?'

'Helen's a fantastic teacher. She's my best friend.'

'You're a pair of dikes. You molest the children, those poor little children. You're disgusting. And I hear you're making money out of it now, running a vice racket for one of those Saudi princes.'

'You're insane.' Mamie was trembling so much she nearly dropped the receiver.

Don grabbed it from her. 'Who is this?'

'I'm just an ordinary mum. We've decided to get together to do something about what's going on at Kiddieworld. We're going to get it closed down.'

'Bullshit. Ordinary, crazy, interfering bitches. Get off of my wife's back. Next time you call you'll be recorded and we'll get the police to trace you. Right? You still there?... She hung up.'

Carefully, Don replaced the receiver and put his arms around Mamie, who was sobbing and shivering. Despite his deep, growly, Brooklyn voice he was only an inch taller than her. Behind his ears were clumps of gingery clownish hair, massaged by him every evening to encourage growth. The rest of Don's shiny bald head sloped towards his prominent squashed cauliflower of a nose, which he had inherited from his father, an Irish boxer. Even when Don was young it was his most noticeable feature, and now he was in his fifties the rest of his face strained towards it. 'Oh boy, what a schnozzle!' Mamie used to say affectionately, before she came to live in Saudi Arabia and repressed her Yiddish vocabulary. Still, she was relieved that none of their children had inherited that nose. Don held her for a long time.

'How can they hate me like that?'

'They got nothing else to do.'

'But why me? And why Helen? She's so good. I'd trust Helen with anything, anybody.'

'I'm going to see the Chief of Police. We had him in the hotel over that rape case. He's OK.'

'Don, no. Don't go to the police. The things they do to people here – they could have us executed in Chops Square.'

'For Christ's sake, you ain't done nothing wrong. It's those women who call you up, those ordinary fucking psychopaths. They're committing a crime.'

'But who would believe us? These things do happen, I know they do, I've read about cases like that. Even in the States, in New York City, it happened recently. And there was another case last year, in a pre-school in California.'

'That doesn't make you guilty. For God's sake don't start to feel guilty. Now you're reasoning like them – it happened at home so it's gotta be happening at Mamie's.'

Neither of them could sleep. At five o'clock Mamie said, 'I was thinking of going back this summer anyways. What's it matter if I go now instead?'

'If the school closes, they win.'

'I can't stand this. I feel so dirty. I'm scared to pick up the phone. I can't live like this.'

'You'll be letting Helen down if you go home now.'

'I'll have to talk to her. But I been thinking, by next August we'll have enough to help all the kids buy houses near us in Seattle.

We'll all be together again, near the grandchildren. I often think it's crazy, pouring all this love into other people's kids. They go away, they forget you. Then when something like this happens. . . .'

'You just happen to be a genius with other people's kids. Everybody says so. Twenty years now you been running pre-schools, thousands of kids, and they all loved you.'

Mamie gave a long, shuddering sigh, because it was true, because feeling loved was the basis of her personality. Being hated destroyed her.

Don, who worked shifts at the hotel, spent as much time as he could at home. Whenever he came back, the house was full of people, as all their houses had always been. He could smell pancakes or strudel or pizza, and as soon as he saw Mamie's face he could smell whether or not there had been another phone call. He did connect a tape recorder to the phone but didn't go to the police because Mamie panicked and sobbed every time he suggested it. Over a month, they filled a tape with hysterical, vindictive monologues. There were six women, each of whom phoned at least three times. Mamie thought she recognized Lena's voice, but she couldn't be sure. Often she thought she recognized friends' voices. On the rare occasions when she was alone in the house Mamie locked herself in the bedroom and played the tape back, again and again.

' . . . they were all talking about you at the last mum-and-toddler group, Mamie. About those films you've been making, using the kids. Doing things with dogs and Arabs and black men – oh my God, Mamie, how can you be so obscene? And who watches them, that's what I want to know. I suppose you hire them out with your other videos? Well, we're going to get hold of a copy and take it to the police. We're really going to get your school closed down, Mamie. We're going to start phoning the parents of those poor little children, too, tell them what's going on. . . . '

For a moment Mamie thought the low, husky, English voice sounded like Helen's. Disguised, of course. They all disguised their voices. If it was Helen, if this was all her fabrication like people who faked their own kidnappings? Mamie buried her face in her pale-pink bedspread, which her elder daughter had embroidered with hearts and rosebuds. The thought that she might not be able to trust Helen upset her even more than the accusations.

She heard Don open the front door and stumble through the house looking for her. He was exhausted after ten hours at work, drained of everything except the desire for food, sleep and Mamie's presence. She had always been there, had insisted on being at home when the kids came home from school as well. Of course she led her own life, had her own friends, more than he had in fact. She was a lively woman, sociable, loved to talk. Don often moaned about the way he never got her to himself and, when he did, she never stopped yapping.

'You sleeping in there? Why d'ya lock the door?'

Mamie unlocked it and ran back to hide her face in the covers again. Don was amazed that she wept so childishly. Surrounded by photographs of her children and grandchildren, a matriarch and a business woman, she snivelled and bawled. He fetched a box of tissues, knelt beside her, put his arms around her and gently mopped her face. Smears of mascara, foundation, blusher and lipstick rubbed off on to the tissue.

'See, look at this stuff, looks like one of those kids' drawings. You want me to put it up on the wall? I always said you use too much junk on ya face. Why can'tcha be like me? I'm natural – look how pretty I am.'

She raised her face, smiled feebly and caught sight of herself in the dressing-table mirror. Three of her, three streaky-faced hags with yellow hair. 'Sorry, I ought to act my age. I look like a hundred and one.'

'You been listening to that tape? You're crazy. Like Helen says, you gotta rise above it.'

'What are you doing with that thing?'

'Erasing it. I went to the telephone exchange today, changed the number.'

'That won't stop them for long. How about the parents? How'll they know? It'll look like we closed the school down.'

'So send the parents a letter.'

She was quite helpless. He made a salad and some tuna sandwiches, which he brought up on a tray. They ate together in the bedroom, then he ran her a bath and sat on the edge of it while she disappeared under the bubbles. She had a whole shelf of bath foam and talcum powder, presents from kids and parents. Mamie's head bobbed above the white foam, rising above it. Her eyes were blue again and her skin pink. She smiled at Don, who grabbed her hand and pulled it out of the water.

'And what would Jack do without you? He'd be back in some
institution, some kinda cage.'

'I know that. But you gotta take the signals, it's no use staying
on for ever. Like New York City, we loved it, it was our home. But
things just got too tough there. It was too dangerous with the kids.
I didn't feel I could go out no more. So we moved.'

'Soon it'll be Christmas. Did you ask Chuck if he'll do Santa
Claus?'

'Not yet. What is it – you don't want me to leave you on your
own here?'

'If you leave, I leave. Those guys stuck out here on their own,
I seen them fall apart one after the other. They have asinine affairs
with nurses or drink themselves crazy or go gay – did ya hear
about that Aids emergency? They're testing all the new applicants
for visas to come here for Aids now. Even encouraging wives to
come out with guys, wouldya believe.'

She smiled, but it wasn't as funny as it would have been a few
months before. 'The way those phone calls make me feel, I'm
suffering from Aids and herpes and leprosy and the clap. I have to
go, Don.'

'OK, I can't stop you. Only if we go now, we'll have to forget
about buying that third apartment.'

6

Sally kept hearing rumours that the school was going to close. She
looked at several other nursery schools, British and American, but
the former were too bossy and chilly and the latter seemed to her
to be brat factories. She realized that Mamie's school was special,
the only place in Riyadh where she could cheerfully leave Katie
each morning. She became obsessed by the phone calls: every time
she answered her telephone, Sally listened for the spiteful voices
and, when they didn't come, she felt relieved, even surprised.
They might just as well have picked on her as on Helen. It was so
easy to make such accusations and so impossible to disprove them.
She was scared to phone Mamie, even to tell her when Katie was
ill, in case she inadvertently made her suffer. So she telephoned
Helen instead, several times a week, to ask how Katie was getting
on and to reassure herself that the school was still there. She was
aware that she was becoming a nuisance, the kind of mother

teachers curse. But Mamie's was her linchpin, the only fixed point in the lonely and bewildering life she was forced to lead in Riyadh. Although she longed to go back to work, Sally put off job-hunting until she was certain she could count on the school.

In the mornings, while Katie was at school, Sally read voraciously and wrote long letters in which the story of Mamie's phone calls kept cropping up. She imagined the bizarre story being disbelieved by her friends: things like that didn't happen in Brighton. She mentioned the phone calls to those of her neighbours who also had small children, asking them to defend Mamie and Helen if they ever heard them being slandered at one of the mum-and-toddler groups. All the women she told looked embarrassed and evasive, as if it was a lapse of taste for such things to have happened and even more tasteless of Sally to try to involve them. One day she asked the driver to come half an hour early at picking-up time, the next day forty-five minutes. She felt more at home at the school than anywhere else in the city.

Mamie accepted her as a new member of her kitchen circle, one of the mothers who stayed on for coffee and cakes and gossip. Sally had never known anybody who absorbed other people's lives and emanated warmth as naturally as Mamie did. Often when school was finished Sally hovered on, holding Katie's hand, reluctant to go home.

'You still looking for a job?' Mamie asked briskly one afternoon when Sally was in the garden helping to put toys away.

'Yes.'

'Leyla's leaving beginning of December. You want her job?'

'So you're not going to close down! I knew you wouldn't.'

'I just don't know. I keep on getting those calls.' Suddenly Mamie's make-up mask cracked as she sobbed.

Sally put an arm around her shoulder. 'They're mad, those women. They're the ones with problems, not you. But please don't close the school. I just don't know what I'd do without it. It must be terrible to get calls like that, to know people hate you, but you mustn't let it destroy you.'

'Don't cry, Mamie,' Katie said.

And it occurred to Sally there was something wrong, it wasn't normal for a three-year-old to have to tell her teacher not to cry. The she felt ashamed because it seemed petty and mean to be embarrassed, like her neighbours, by suffering.

Soon after she started work at the school Sally joined Helen in a conspiracy to protect Mamie. Whenever the phone rang, one of them would answer it, sometimes even snatching the receiver away from Mamie. When Mamie's mascara smudged and her voice wobbled in the middle of a rehearsal for the Christmas show, Helen rushed her upstairs to lie down. In the afternoons one of them always stayed with Mamie until Don came home.

But it was still Mamie's school, and she was proud of it. 'they're still lining up to come to Kiddieworld. You know, we have a waiting-list six months ahead. They just feel at home here – well, none of the other schools makes pancakes. Jack's dad just signed a contract for another year because of my school. His mom says they're afraid if they go back to Kentucky now he'll never learn nothing. I guess it's true. I really can do anything with those kids.' She was depressed only between boasts. For twenty or so lonely women her kitchen was the only place in Riyadh where they could relax and complain in peace about husbands and neighbours. All the children went to Mamie's willingly each morning, as they would have done to the house of a particularly devoted grand-mother. She hugged them hello and goodbye, mopped up their tears and made pancakes on their birthdays. In Brighton terms, Mamie was outrageously sexist: Sally watched with irritation as Katie was transformed from a denim-clad tomboy to a rather coy little girl who would wear only dresses, preferably miniature copies of Mamie's wardrobe, pastel coloured with an armoury of sashes, frills and smocking. Little girls at Mamie's didn't play with guns or dress up as Superman, and little boys were encouraged to be noisy and mildly rough.

Working together, Sally and Helen became close. Younger, slimmer and more active than Mamie, they bustled and organized, but they weren't loved as much as Mamie and they were both aware that it was her combination of warmth, softness, generosity and brashness that made the school so special. Without her the school would close and they both desperately wanted to keep it open.

Meeting in the kitchen one morning they whispered reports to each other.

'Where is she?' Sally asked.

'She's lying down. She had another call last night. Don forgot to leave the tape recorder switched on.'

'I'd like to push those bitches over a cliff.'

'I do pray for them.'

But Sally forgave Helen her religious impulses and liked her anyway. The differences between them, which might have seemed enormous in England, were negligible in Riyadh.

The build-up to the Christmas party was intensified by its illegality. In the hot garden the children cut out red crêpe paper hats and stuck cotton wool around the edges. One of the fathers, Abdul Aziz, who owned a toyshop, promised a sack of free toys for the party. 'That guy's fantastic,' Mamie said. 'I just hope they don't catch him and chop some bit off of him.' There were rumours that Christmas was particularly unpopular that year; the Christmas tree at the American school had been confiscated by the religious police, all requests for leave on Christmas Day were being refused and Christmas puddings in the supermarkets had been relabelled 'holiday puddings'. The teachers strained to choose a programme of songs which were seasonal without being offensively religious, so that Saudi friends could come to the party with a clear conscience. They decided on 'Jingle Bells', 'Santa Claus Is Coming Tonite' and 'We Wish You a Merry Christmas'. When the children stood in a wide circle to rehearse each morning, Helen and Sally had to rush around shutting all the windows and doors so that their subversive voices wouldn't carry.

One afternoon Helen and Sally stayed on to help Mamie make Chuck's Santa Claus costume. He was a huge Texan baseball player, so they had to cut out acres of scarlet felt and long streamers of cotton wool. Mamie, who made most of her own clothes, set about it briskly and professionally. 'I couldn't find any red buttons that were big enough, so we'll have to use these black ones.'

'Don't bother with buttonholes,' Helen said. 'He's only going to wear it once. The belt'll hold the jacket together.'

'We could keep it for next year?' Sally looked at them for her daily reassurance.

'I got six cardboard boxes of tree decorations and lights and stuff from last year.' Mamie occasionally became impatient at her own sentimentality. 'I must be stupid to keep all this stuff. Anyone would think we're gonna be here for ever.'

'But it's right to do it properly.' Helen regretted her remark about the buttonholes. 'It's more fun for the children like that. And for us. Peter wants me to do a turkey, and I'm getting my daughter to bring out some chestnuts and brandy butter. I do hope she's not searched at the airport.'

'Well, I guess it's fun anyway. Last year wasn't so good. We had this big fight over whether or not to do a nativity play. I told them, that's just asking for trouble. Oh, and the year before that we found out just in time one of the kids' uncles was a *mettahwah*. We had to call it parents' day. Just pulled some crackers and ate some mince pies. This is going to be the best one yet.'

Mamie sighed, because Riyadh Christmases seemed to stretch behind her in a long tradition, yet really there was no past or future here. Next year in Jerusalem, Dad used to say at Yom Kippur. I could be arrested for saying that here. They'd think I was an Israeli terrorist. Crazy city. 'Next year in Seattle, I guess.'

7

On Christmas morning Mamie woke up very early, choked with anxiety and excitement. She felt as she used to when, as a little girl, she got up in the middle of the night to put on her school clothes. Such a need to be good, to please, to be approved of. Yet it wasn't really Christmas at all; there was no nip in the air and no children in the house. Beside her Don snored even louder than usual. Great rumbles and bellows echoed out of his cavernous nostrils. At the foot of the bed were their presents: a neatly wrapped bottle of Givenchy perfume and another gold bracelet, a bottle of aftershave and *The Car Lover's Guide to 4-Wheel Drive Vehicles*. They'd open them later, when she brought up the tray of eggs and breakfast beef. Mamie took off her pink, lacy nightdress and put on her new Mother Christmas outfit, which she had made herself: a tightly fitted scarlet jacket with a wide black belt, neat scarlet skirt and tiny, black, high-heeled boots. At once she felt better, firmer inside her clothes; nakedness really wasn't a lot of fun past fifty. She did her make-up and hair very carefully, took the phone off the hook and switched off the tape recorder. She might miss the kids, but she would phone them after the party.

Sedately, Mamie and Don opened their presents and ate breakfast. There were no surprises and Mamie preferred it like that. Surprises were things you created to delight children: those that had been sprung on her lately were an aberration, a slap in the face so vicious that she wished to have no face. All morning she bustled, laid out the food she had spent days cooking, wrapped and labelled a present for each child and drank coffee until her heart skipped with ersatz happiness.

By midday the house was so full of life that Mamie feared a raid by the religious police. The children, in party clothes and the Santa Claus hats they had made, were lining up to perform 'Jingle Bells'. This marriage of their two separate worlds, home and Mamie's, made them feverishly self-conscious. Those who knew how to show off, did, and those who didn't, collapsed, like one two-year-old Filipino who refused to wear his hat or go on stage. Wherever there was a child, there was a camera pointing at it. Japanese fathers aimed video cameras, English and American mothers held modest Instamatics and Don sat in a corner with a video camera, recording the entire party for posterity. The lenses distanced the parents from each other, which was a relief to all except the few who had already made contact with each other at picking up time. Total absorption in loading a film or adjusting a flash made it permissible to ignore your neighbour, who was similarly occupied. Abdul Aziz, the token Saudi guest, was regarded with suspicion by everybody except Mamie and Helen, who knew and liked him. In his immaculate white robes he looked very young and formal. The other parents muttered to each other that you couldn't have a drink with one of them in the room, that they would be introducing Koranic instruction for the foreign three-year-olds soon, that the mothers wearing short sleeves and low necklines felt nervous with him around. This hostility created a fleeting bond between English, American, Indian, Japanese, German, Filipino, Egyptian and Korean parents, before they turned back to their own offspring and cameras.

Upstairs in the bathroom Chuck swore as he ripped his scarlet felt breeches, trying to get them on. Mamie seems to think Santa Claus has no goddamm balls. Her school needs stories about Santa Claus exposing himself with little girls on his knees like a hole in the head. He found a giant safety-pin in the nappy changing box (it was part of Helen's puritanism to advocate terry towelling instead of disposable nappies) and incompetently mended the rip in his pants. He would have to keep the sack of gifts anchored there for cover. Chuck straightened his cotton-wool beard, looked at his watch, reminded himself of all those meals Mamie had given him and grinned fiendishly as he opened the bathroom door.

Sally hadn't brought a camera. She tried to enjoy the party but she was annoyed because James hadn't been able to get even Christmas Day off from his teaching job, and she felt uncomfortably aware of being the third teacher, whom most of the parents didn't know. In her jaundiced mood the party struck her as a bizarre exercise in kitsch. She sat and watched Katie, who had been opening presents since six o'clock that morning and was now about to tear open Mamie's gift from Santa Chuck's sack. Out of the silver and gold wrapping-paper Katie pulled a doll, whose legs fell off as she waved her triumphantly at her mother. Sally hugged her daughter and squeezed the pink plastic limbs back into the nasty-looking round gaps in the doll's trunk. The plastic emitted a sweet, cheap smell that overwhelmed Sally with nostalgia for her own childhood. Katie paused abruptly in mid-wail, grinned, snatched the doll and ran back to her friends. The happiness of the children is real, Sally reminded herself. The rest of us are just ghosts. Kids lined up to be photographed: with Santa, together, with their toys, with Mamie. Of all the adults there, Mamie was the only one who looked joyful, focused, like the essence of Christmas released from an expensive atomizer. Sally thought again, it's so rare to love children as Mamie does. I wish I could.

Helen was wearing a black lace dress which accentuated her height and thinness. Against her red hair and white skin, the black was dramatic and tragic. Sally wondered if she had just returned from some underground mass and hadn't had time to change. Helen came over and sat beside her.

'Mamie's so good at all this,' Sally whispered. 'I feel I ought to be helping, but I'm not sure what to do.'

'Don't worry. She's a great organizer. All we have to do is enjoy it.'

'Are you OK? You look a bit sepulchral.'

'I'm just fed up. My son and daughter wouldn't come along. They've gone off to some barbecue in the desert. And my husband's working overtime again.'

'So's mine.' Sally thought bitterly, I never used to refer to him or even think of him as 'my husband'. Sometimes now I even call him 'Daddy' to Kate. I swore I'd never do that. This morning Katie opened her presents, got dressed and went to the party. She hasn't asked for him once. Daddy's absence is a matter of course, he just pays and drives and appears at bedtime. When people ask what he does, Katie says, 'He drives around in the big car.' And I don't know much more about how he spends his days. Doing something in an oil refinery, somewhere in the desert, a long way from me.

Sally looked more closely into Helen's thin, pale face, at the expression of suffering intensified by her black weeds, and turned her attention to her friend. 'Has there – there hasn't been another phone call, has there?'

'Yes.'

'When?'

'Six o'clock this morning. And they phoned me this time. Mamie had left the phone off the hook. Wouldn't you know they'd choose Christmas. I could hear children in the background too, screaming with excitement as they opened their presents. It's funny really. I never thought they would phone me. I thought I looked so severe and tough. In a way I thought Mamie brought it on herself by being sweet and warm, made it too easy for them. And I imagined that, if they did start on me, I'd scare them off, I'd be so ferocious – but I just burst into tears.'

'What did she say? Was she English or American?'

'American. Oh, the same. I'm a monster, I'm perverted and filthy and – oh God I can't. This is so stupid.' Helen turned her face away from the party while she tried to control it.

'Sorry, Helen. Shall I shut up about it?' Sally gripped her arm.

'No. Perhaps it's better to talk. Then Peter and the children came out of their rooms – our phone's in the hall so they could hear my voice. They thought someone had phoned from England. I slammed the phone down and rushed into the bedroom with Peter following me. I told him about Mamie's calls but he kept dismissing it, saying it's best to ignore nutters like that. He was angry that they'd started on me, too, but what could he do? He had to get dressed for work and the kids were hammering on the door asking what the matter was. I couldn't tell them. I'd always meant to talk to them about it, specially to Adrienne, because she's a bit older and we're very close. . . .'

Mamie came over to them, her eyes bulging turquoise with compassion. She gripped Helen's hands and, with a sensitivity that surprised Sally, whispered, 'What is it, honey? Did they get you, too?'

'I had a call this morning. Sorry, I wasn't going to tell you today.'

'Of course you have to tell me. Like you always said, we got to share this thing. Oh Jesus, what're we going to do? Now you'll have to leave your phone off the hook too – nobody'll be able to phone the school, we'll go out of business. Well, maybe that wouldn't be so bad. C'mon, they're looking at us. I'm going to make you girls some cawfee.'

For the rest of the party Sally watched Mamie bustle and wisecrack, feed and wipe and hug. You could see how much effort it cost her. Towards the end she looked drained and could hardly disguise her relief when people started to go home. Yet Mamie looked and felt triumphant, too, as if she was glad it had started to happen to Helen.

8

As soon as the calls stopped, Mamie started to get the dreams instead. The first morning she awoke with only a vague sense of unease, saying that she hadn't slept well.

'You take too much dope.'

'It's not dope, Don, just sleeping-pills. Anyways I didn't take none last night.'

'Must've been the bugs biting.'

They were hungry, those bugs. They gnawed and sucked and drained her. Each morning at about five she woke up feeling like the leftovers from a vampires' banquet. The dreams, which hardly varied, came back to her in fragments during the day. They nudged her consciousness, sneaked out of corners, finished her sentences for her and left her gaping. Did I really dream that? Think that? Some part of me is guilty then. They were right.

The dreams were set in the sunny garden, suffused in that strong, pure, blue-gold light which still washed over Riyadh as if the desert had never been smothered by concrete. That heroic, nomadic, pre-industrial light illuminated her dream garden, where it was just warm enough to sit in a deckchair feeling drowsy, carry ice-creams in and out, fill the paddling-pool for the kids and make the blonde ones wear hats. In her dream chair Mamie sat back, shut her eyes and sighed as she felt the sun on her skin. She was so tired, it was so long since she had slept well, that she almost drifted off into a sleep within a sleep.

She was pulled back by the silence; the comforting burble of splashes, shrieks, giggles, chants and whines had stopped abruptly. Mamie strained to open her eyes and shout to Helen to check that the kids were all right. But her eyes, her muscles, had run out of batteries. She was paralysed alone in the dark without sounds or power or signals, yet she knew there was something very nasty out there. Helpless on her back in the low deckchair, Mamie struggled to kick and shout.

Then she levered herself up, pushing with both hands against the hard wooden bars of the deckchair. Her arms and legs were flying buttresses, her body arched in the position they used to call the crab when she was at school, a crab flailing helplessly on its back. Then she rose, floated up above the garden, the deckchair flat beneath her like a green and yellow striped cloud. Sight and mobility restored, Mamie the corny-haired goddess hovered above her garden of delights.

Now she could see how the children played. They were rolling together on the grass, in the bushes and in the round paddling-pool. In couples and threes and fours they groped, kissed and gambolled. They don't understand, they don't know it's wrong, Mamie thought, and she rocked her deckchair cloud as she lurched down to stop them. The plants came alive and twisted around the little bodies, stroked and caressed them. Three adults came out of the back door and advanced on the writhing mass of small pink bodies, green tentacles and bright flowers surging towards them. Mamie couldn't look at the adults, because she knew they were going to corrupt the children, do all those things she had been accused of. She twisted and rocked, trying to dive down into the garden. But she couldn't, because she was the adults and the adults were her.

Mamie awoke from this dream in such an anguish of guilt and fear that she could only sob. Night after night Don woke up, held her and tried to rubbish her subconscious.

'You had the same dream?'

'I told you, it's always the same. Only some nights the vegetation's different or there are different kids. Sometimes our kids.'

'Maybe it's indigestion. Maybe you're eating something that doesn't agree with you.'

'I feel so dirty,' she sobbed.

'You? You're spotless, the nicest dame I ever met.' Don sat up in bed, holding her, weeping himself because her grief was so crazy.

Every morning Mamie looked more grotesque. Her make-up was cracked and her eyes, staring and full of shadows, saw through the day. Helen also turned up at school looking as if she had spent the night in hell. When Sally asked, Helen said, yes, they called almost every day and there were more of them now.

'Can't you just leave the phone off the hook all the time?'

'What about my children? They're back in England again now. How would I know if they'd had an accident?'

Sally felt apologetic towards them both, as she would with friends who were very ill. Their suffering made them unequal, morbidly sensitive, and disqualified them from normal responsibilities. Sally, who had to run the school now, resented the situation and ran it badly. The children felt rejected by Mamie and missed her spontaneous hugs and pancakes. Most of the day, she sat on the couch in the sitting-room, her face a sad, lopsided mask, her body clenched inside her elaborate clothes, which were now always crooked and seedy looking. She hardly even dared to touch Don any more. Jack regressed and the other children ran wild, behaved badly and stampeded like ponies mounted by new and heavy-handed riders. Mamie had made her surrogate family in Riyadh so successfully that they really felt like her children. And now she didn't want them any more.

Occasionally, after a few cups of coffee, Mamie would perk up. On Khalid's birthday she even started to make pancakes and boast a little. Sally watched as she deftly cracked eggs, mixed and tossed. Children drifted in from the garden to stare up at her. They tried to gauge her mood, grab her hand or bury their faces in her apron. Then, shyly, they ran away again.

All the time she cooked, Mamie kept up a nervous, husky monologue. She accepted the children's caresses as offerings to a shrine she knew was worth worshipping at. 'You know, Kiddieworld still has the best reputation of any pre-school in Riyadh? We got a waiting-list until next Christmas. They're phoning up all the time, just begging me to take their kids. I could have fifty kids here if I wanted, easy, only where'd I put them? If I had a bigger villa – but I figure it's better to stay small. That way I know all the kids, they know me.'

'They really love you, Mamie,' Sally said softly.

'I know it. Kids always do, I guess some of the mothers must be jealous of me. You know what Jack's mom said to me the other day? She said, "Mamie, if you hadn't taken him in, I don't know what we'd have done. He'd still be like an animal in a cage." I just have this gift, you know, specially with handicapped kids. I often thought, maybe I should go back home and open up a special school for them.'

'Don't go. These children really need you. The school couldn't carry on without you.'

'Helen's real good with them, but they don't love her like they love me. And you, too, you're doing great. A lot of it's just experience. I been running pre-schools for twenty years now – I'm a mother and a grandmother for Christ's sake, I ought to know how to handle kids. I seen everything, every kinda kid, nothing surprises me. And they know it. You just got to know how to love them. . . .'

Mamie stopped in mid-sentence, mid-pancake, and that glazed, masked look dropped down over her face again. Because she didn't know how to love them any more and something had surprised her.

February came, with heavy, murky days. The *djibli* blew across five hundred miles of desert and deposited in Riyadh dirty yellow trails of sand. The mystical blue sky clouded over into a khaki sulk. Sally thought it spread depression and bad temper even faster than an English February. Rain was prayed for, and finally came in huge torpid drops squeezed from dusty clouds. The children played less in the garden and, instead, invaded the house, broke things, pushed each other downstairs and made up rude words to substitute for their nursery rhymes. This year Mamie had no patience with them. She shouted at them all the time, put them in the corner and told them off in front of their mothers. 'I don't know what's got into them this year,' she kept saying, 'I never knew kids so mean and spiteful.' Then, after they'd all gone home, she would weep and repeat like an incantation, 'I love them all.' The dreams recurred again and again, with few variations, and now her revulsion was mingled with boredom. It was like watching a film for the hundredth time. The sour aftertaste left by the dream and her sense of failure with the children even got in the way of Mamie's friendship with Helen. Each was locked in her separate unhappiness, powerless to help each other, although they both knew exactly what was the matter. 'I know just how you feel,' Mamie often assured Helen. Yet she didn't really know because Helen's emotions were a self-contained universe, with more plains and shadows than her own. Helen didn't weep at school or talk about her insomnia or scream at the children. She only became quieter, paler and more exhausted. She no longer had the energy to protect Mamie, or do anything except plod through each day and night, dreading the next phone call. Anyway she was tired of Mamie's noise; she perceived her now as she had when they first met, before her heart was warmed and stirred by Mamie's generosity. Secretly Helen thought Mamie should shut up, now that she no longer got those terrible calls, should stop all that noisy suffering. I'm the victim now, Helen thought. I need to be comforted and hugged and there's nobody. But she didn't demand it because the corset of her unselfishness was laced so tight.

There was one last time when the two women came close to each other. Helen was just about to go home one afternoon when she saw Mamie through the half-open door of the sitting-room, where she was on the couch. She sat very erect, with her legs crossed, daintily mopping the tears that ravaged her make-up. Helen remembered the first time she had seen Mamie like that, after Lena and Dee first came round with their accusations nearly a year before, and realized how much both of their personalities had been eroded since then.

'It's not worth it!' Helen burst out, very tall and thin in the doorway.

Mamie glanced up, amazed because it was so uncharacteristic of Helen to burst. 'Have all the kids gone home? And Sally?'

'They all know anyhow. Everyone knows. We go on behaving as if there was this big secret.'

Helen sat down beside Mamie, who blew her nose and shuddered, reversing the tide of her grief. 'I don't think I ever cried so much in my life.'

'We must be stupid to stay here.'

'You really think so? But I thought . . . it was you who always said we had to stay and fight. Won't it mean they've won, if we go now?'

'They already have. Look what they've reduced us to.'

'Sometimes I still think we could bring this thing out into the open. Don said last night, "Why don't you just phone Lena, ask her to come round and talk about it?" I told him he was crazy, but then later I thought, why not?'

'Lena's not here any more.'

'What?'

'She went back to the States a month ago. Left her husband. Sally heard through a friend.'

Mamie was appalled, then relieved. Her pain had always had

Lena's face, the face of betrayed friendship and irrational hatred. If the hatred was diffused and faceless, it was for some reason easier to duck. She turned to Helen with her most childlike smile.

'Then we can go home? You want to go?'

'Yes.'

'I kept thinking, I have to stay because of Helen. Because there was this battle we had to fight together.'

'I did think that, but now I'm too tired to care. And it's not real here any more, even the calls aren't real. Althought they hurt.'

'Pain is for real.'

'Well, Peter says I'm being a martyr, and I'm beginning to think he's right.'

They sat together on the couch, planned in low voices and saw straight ahead to visas, triumphant homecomings in the arms of children who wouldn't go away. Around them expatriate life, even the school they had built up, faded until it was less vivid than Mamie's dreams. She could almost feel her memory filing events, sorting them, retelling the story of her time here: the telephone calls would eclipse all the friendships, the success of the school and the money she and Don had made and spent. Once or twice a year, long after she had lost touch with all her other Riyadh friends, she would write to Helen in memory of painful dreams.

*   *   *

One morning Sally and Katie approached Mamie's school through the shadows and sprinklers on her compound. They were both relaxed after weeks of baring their flesh on Italian beaches. Katie swung her lunch-box as she skipped beside her mother, who was telling her a story about a phoenix that hatched out of an Easter egg. As she improvised, Sally squeezed her daughter's hand, anticipating the pleasure of letting it go again in a few minutes. Mamie and Helen would make a fuss of Katie, cuddle and feed her. Sally would be able to turn and walk away without a twinge of guilt to enjoy five child-free hours of reading and letter writing. She thought, I'd rather leave Katie there than with my own mother.

The child's attention wandered from the story as she looked towards the high wall. Behind it were her friends, toys, songs, cookies, laughter: the party at which Katie was always welcome.

She pulled at her mother's hand and dragged her across the road.

But the metal gate was padlocked. Sally shook it, impatient to reach the haven of the toy-strewn garden.

'Mamie! Helen! It's meee!' Katie yelled in her hide-and-seek voice.

The wall was silent and cold, too high to see over, too solid to see through. For a moment Sally hoped it was the wrong house. They were interchangeable, those grey concrete cubes, but the way to Mamie's school was the only route in the city their four feet knew by instinct. In the dust under the gate sprawled a miniature legless Texan with a big hat and a plastic grin. Sally scooped up the play person and rolled him compulsively between her hands as Katie's coyness turned to anguish. She assaulted the gate with her lunch-box and, when that didn't bring Mamie, flung her whole body against the metal, beating at it with her fists and banging her head. Sally had to drag her away, and in the struggle dropped the plastic oil man, who rolled once more in the dust.

Villa Despair

1

Rosemary sat alone in the office, her skin like underbaked dough where it protruded from her drooping, pink cotton robe. It didn't protrude much because Robbie insisted that she observed the strictest rules of dress and, like most of the foreign women in Riyadh, she wore ageing hippie clothes; sad ankle-length dresses with long sleeves and high necks. She was perpetually dressed for a party that had ended in the early seventies. Rosemary looked rather like an anaemic horse as, with her long upper lip raised over big, honest teeth, she stooped over Robbie's official school accounts. His private figures were locked away in their computer at home under the code-name BINGO. Through the thin walls of her office Rosemary could hear the rhythmic chanting and shuffling sandals of dozens of students. She could just distinguish Beethoven's Ninth, coming from Bertram's room, and 'Amazing Grace' emanating from Chris's class. It does cheer things up to have music in a school and attracts such a nice type of teacher, although Robbie doesn't agree. The ICBM, or Intercontinental Choral Balletic Method, had been the brain-child of a failed opera singer who had made a fortune out of his chain of schools.

Mansour, the one-eyed Kuwaiti fixer and odd-job man, knocked and came in with a glass of mint tea. The teachers pronounced his name, with relish, as ManSewer. Rosemary drank the hot, sickly, fragrant tea and tried to avoid his disconcerting gaze. His one eye squinted and his manner implied that she should have been serving him tea. Perhaps not, Rosemary contradicted herself. It's just that men's eyes are so unpleasant here, all of them, Robbie's most of all. She preferred not to look.

'Did you manage to clean out the coffee machine, Mansour?'

'Coffee very clean, madam, very peautiful coffee.'

'Chris did mention a cockroach or two on the counter. They do get everywhere, I know.'

'Titcher Chris say my coffee no good? You don't like my coffee?'

'Please don't get upset, Mansour. Just one more thing. Do you think we could clean up the toilets before the police class starts on Sunday evening?'

'Tomorrow I must going to Ministry for visas.'

'Could you perhaps clean them this evening?'

'In my country this job for very low class people and womans.'

'I have done it for the last year, Mansour,' Rosemary said without thinking. And then in an attempt to regain face, 'I shall expect you to do them before the weekend.'

'*Inshallah,* madam.'

But God never willed. After Mansour left the room Rosemary stood up, her fists clenched at the end of her long, white arms. She was tall and, as a young girl, her slenderness and pallor had been willowy. Now, at thirty-two, she was merely scraggy and unhealthy, as Robbie constantly reminded her. In a way it was a relief to hide her body. She picked up her navy-blue cardigan: the air-conditioning, on the rare occasions it worked, shot out blasts of freezing air. Even a veil might be comforting, she thought – an extra layer to deflect all that hatred. Flinching, she knocked on the door of the staff-room. Once she had walked straight in and found Jonathan, the ex-Director of Studies, masturbating over a *Companion Guide to French Wines.*

Six teachers crowded round the notice-board, where the c.v. of the new Director of Studies was pinned up.

Rosemary smiled at them. 'He must be quite bright if he did a thesis on that Icelandic saga. I can't even pronounce it.'

'It wasn't his thesis we were speculating about.' Bertram's loathing of both Rosemary and her husband was so passionate that he couldn't speak to either of them without spitting.

Her eyes flickered, her smile was fixed now and she clasped her hands behind her back. Only Chris looked back at her with any friendliness. 'I expect you're wondering what his wife's like. She must be jolly clever too. Her thesis was on Minoan pottery.'

'Have you seen her?' Chris asked.

'No, Robbie did all the interviews. It'll be nice to have another woman around.' The teachers assented with an embarrassing chorus of moans and grunts. Rosemary turned to John and Peter, who were going away for Ramadan. An aura of beatitude surrounded them, like that of early saints whose penance was almost over. 'Mansour's going along in the morning to get your visas.'

Rosemary's smile was an agonized gash in her thin, white face, a direct appeal for someone to be nice to her. They hated her because she did Robbie's dirty work, but she did it so innocently. John and Peter looked at her with less hostility than usual, softened by the prospect of a walking holiday in the Himalayas and a brothel-crawl in Bangkok.

Too quickly, Rosemary turned to John. 'Did Robbie mention the change in the standby system?' At once they were on the defensive again, seething with anticipated insult and injury. 'We just thought, as classes will be so small during Ramadan, it might be a good idea to organize a rota of jobs. To make the school a pleasanter environment. After all, you do all sit around here doing nothing rather a lot of the time, don't you? I mean, if the coffee bar and the loos were a bit cleaner, we'd all appreciate it, wouldn't we? Of course nobody enjoys doing these jobs but....'

Bertram, who had almost as little sense of decency as Robbie, roared explosively, 'I'm not cleaning your fucking shithole for you! It's bad enough living in a shithole with a shit like Robbie. You cut one minute of our standby and I'll write to London about some of Robbie's goings on. I could get you both deported.'

After his attack of spleen Bertram felt drained. He would have to go to the Embassy official's house when he finished teaching and play Chopin until his equanimity was restored.

Rosemary backed towards the door, shaking. She didn't know how much any of them knew, how much listening at doors and snooping went on at the Villa Despair each night. All the teachers smirked silently, except Chris, who liked women and could never look at Rosemary without pitying her. Her passivity was a magnet for brutality; even the mildest people became bullies in her presence. She was the only woman who had ever made him feel domineering.

'Do you want a lift anywhere, Rosemary?'

'Oh yes – please – I have to go to French Corner.'

'The Prince is coming to supper, is he?'

'That's right. Do drop in, by the way, if you'd like to.'

Rosemary's eyes bulged with dread that one of them might

accept and there wouldn't be enough food. But since the night when Bertram had dangled Robbie over the parapet of the flat roof and threatened to drop him, the teachers had held their own parties at the Villa Despair.

Women weren't allowed to drive in Riyadh, Robbie wouldn't pay for a driver for her and the public buses were inadequate, so Rosemary was dependent on lifts from the teachers, who shared four cars between the ten of them. Robbie was hardly ever in the school, as he spent most of his time on mysterious business in ministries or the Prince's palace. When Rosemary wanted to go out, she either had to appeal to the teachers' non-existent goodwill or walk, in her flowing dress and huge Chinese straw hat, in temperatures of well over 100°.

She came out of French Corner with fragrant boxes full of stuffed quails, lobster quiche, avocado salad and a strawberry cake iced with the Saudi coat of arms, a palm tree over two crossed swords. A loaf shaped like an alligator poked out of another bag. She almost looked forward to the Prince's visits because those were the only times when she was allowed to deviate from Robbie's food budget. According to his five-year plan, on a diet of fish fingers, rice and porridge, combined with resistance to the follies of expensive clothes and holidays, they could save half a million pounds. Rosemary was puzzled by this figure, as it was nearly twenty times his annual salary, but she didn't question his financial wizardry.

'Do come in later, Chris. There'll be plenty.' She settled into the front seat beside him.

Alone with her, Chris was severe. He was afraid that if he was too sympathetic she would confide in him, drag him into the masochistic, penny-pinching grave she had dug for herself. 'Oh, I'll have a Kentucky Fried Chicken Takeaway, as usual.'

Chris was a large, square man in his late thirties, older than any of his colleagues. For him Riyadh was an endurance test which had to be passed so that he could save enough money to escape for ever from teaching English literature to adolescents and play the bagpipes in peace.

The air-conditioning in the second-hand car dribbled cold air on to their feet while the rest of their bodies baked in the hot, dry air. The Villa Despair was a twenty-minute drive from the school, near the vast Safeway Supermarket. Like most houses in Riyadh it was detached and surrounded by a high concrete wall which

was broken only by a steel gate. The Prince had built it eighteen
months before, one of a development of twenty whose blank walls
faced a sandy wasteland. On the fourth side of the square the
Prince's palace shimmered in the heat like a gigantic, tasteless
cake iced with pink and lime green. From the windows of their
communal sitting-room the teachers looked down on the palace
grounds and dreamed of harems, banquets, private aeroplanes
and perfumed, cockroach-free bathrooms. But the Prince had
misjudged the property boom, all the houses had remained unsold
and unrented, and he had been glad to present Robbie with one
when he came to Riyadh to open the school. The nineteen empty
houses made the teachers hate Robbie just a fraction more.

Inside the gate was an acre of shrivelled yellow and brown
weeds, sand and dusty paving-stones. A blue metal fence surrounded a small, deep swimming-pool, on the surface of which
floated dead leaves, scum, old tea-bags, empty bottles and dirty
tissues. Nobody had ever been able to agree on who was to clean
the pool or do the gardening. Now that they were in the war zone,
Chris nodded curtly and walked straight to the teachers' side door
which, in a Saudi household, would have been the entrance used
by women. The architectural apartheid of the house was probably
the only reason why murder or suicide had not yet been committed
in the Villa Despair.

Rosemary stood in the big hall with its dusty marble floor and
plastic chandelier. Her body was less rigid now she knew she was
really alone and could walk freely around the vast, ugly, neglected
rooms. In the sitting-room a second-hand orange couch and a red
leatherette armchair huddled with some old packing-cases in the
middle of acres of unwashed marble floor. In the bedroom clothes
were hung on nails on the wall and the only furniture was a double
mattress. In the corner Rosemary's collection of teddies, dogs and
other toys sat on the dusty floor. She straightened the riding-crop
of the fox in hunting clothes her parents had given her for her
birthday just before she had left Chichester. He looked so like
Robbie. She was sweating; all the rooms were the temperature of
warm tea. Crying again, too. It was absurd the way she cried
whenever she was alone. If it got too hot in the distillery the beer
and wine might explode. She hurried in there to turn on the air-
conditioning, which roared above the alchemical bubblings and
gurglings of three dozen jerrycans full of liquor. The curtains in all
the rooms were kept tightly drawn to keep out the sun, and the fine

yellow dust that fell on everything in Riyadh and into the teachers' eyes.

Still snuffling, her nose and eyes pink in her white, drawn face, Rosemary went into the kitchen; another huge, bare room. Apart from a sink, stove and fridge it contained only three plastic bins: one for rubbish, one for porridge and one for rice. The rice was crawling with weevils. Whenever she lifted the lid she saw their fat, obscene little bodies. But Robbie insisted that, boiled, they were harmless and even nutritious, and of course it would be wasteful to throw away all that rice. Thank God for tonight – Rosemary unpacked the Prince's feast. It would have to be served on paper plates with plastic knives and forks, as Robbie had decided it wasn't worth buying good crockery and cutlery just for five years. She wouldn't be able to sit down with the Prince, of course, but after they had eaten she would be able to eat the leftovers in the kitchen. Unable to resist the aroma from the boxes, Rosemary helped herself to a stuffed quail and a spoonful of avocado salad. The exquisite little bird was fat and juicy. It had probably been raised in Europe, frozen, then thawed and stuffed in Riyadh by a Tunisian chef. Anyway it was delicious and she couldn't cry and swallow at the same time. Rosemary took a handful of the cheese straws. She hoped the Prince wouldn't invite her to another of his female relatives' interminable weddings.

2

Rosemary sensed his anger before she saw or heard him.

'Fer Christ's sake, woman, Farouk'll be here in a few minutes. The house is like a greenhouse. Will ye poot the air-conditioning on and get me a drink.'

Robbie was half a head shorter than Rosemary, with red hair, a scrubby, reddish beard and skin that was boiled scarlet. His eyes were blue, quick, and saw nothing outside his own immediate self-interest. This gave him a juggernaut power which Rosemary had long ago been crushed by. He had the vitality of a man who can say to himself a dozen times a day, without boring himself, 'I used to be a primary school teacher in a small town near Glasgow but now I've got me own hoose and a BMW and one day I'll be a millionaire.' Rosemary's sense of well-being had always been fragile and was constructed of mild intimations of goodness – going

to evensong, passing exams and being nice to people. In Robbie's
presence it evaporated and she felt merely weak. I'm a jelly, she
reminded herself as she switched on the air-conditioning, poured
him a glass of murky, home-made beer and stood, her hands
clasped behind her back, waiting for further instructions.

'Ye're not going to wear that apron when he comes?'

It was pink with large yellow flowers on it.

'Do you think I should change?'

'And fer God's sake poot some colour in yer face. Ye look like
a ghost.'

The Prince, one of whose many names was Farouk, was a very
junior member of the vast royal family. He had no direct responsi-
bility for government but used his title and contacts to set up
lucrative business deals. The English school was a whim which, he
felt, made his other Western appetites respectable. He enjoyed
visiting Robbie because, in that shabby barn of a house, he felt like
a powerful benefactor whereas, at the dinners, weddings and *majlis*
of his relatives, he was treated as a lazy and not very intelligent
parasite. He had met Robbie in London, where he had studied
English, although Rosemary found his English almost
incomprehensible.

At ten – two hours late – Farouk billowed in, beaming fatly
above a huge expanse of virginal white robes. He was in a good
mood because he was leaving for London the following day. His
minder-driver, a highly educated young Sudanese, sat cross-
legged in a corner of the sitting-room.

'Bliz, madam, sitting with us,' Farouk insisted as Rosemary
hovered with dishes of tired delicacies. He patted the couch beside
him. Robbie had decided it would be wasteful to buy a dining-
table when it was more informal and friendly to eat on your knees.
Rosemary sat down and ate a piece of quiche, smiling at the Prince
as she frowned, trying to understand what he said.

'Today very happy night for me. Tomorrow, *inshallah*, London.
Oh, very happy London. I like London too much. I am going
every night to the Balham Bleach. You know the Balham Bleach,
madam?'

When she was faced with a direct question, Rosemary's frown
deepened. She pictured a punk launderette-cum-night-club in south
London. Perhaps he went there to keep his robes so beautifully white?
'The Balham Bleach?' she repeated encouragingly.

'The Palm Beach, woman. The casino!' Robbie glared at her

and turned to the Prince with leaden suggestiveness. 'Are any of yer wives going with ye?'

'One wifes she is going to Geneva for buying clothez. One she is going to New York for seeing children. One she is staying for Ramadan in Riyadh. Then Taif, this wife she likes God too much – no, no wifes coming tomorrow. Oh, English womans.' Farouk put his hand on the white folds somewhere in the region of his heart. 'Very nice. Last time I am in London I am meeting Mrs Cha-Cha. You know Mrs Cha-Cha? Peautiful English lady, very cliver.'

'No, I don't think we've met,' Rosemary said primly, imagining the madam of a brothel breaking into out-of-date dances.

'But yes! She is your brime minster.' Astounded by the ignorance of Western women, the Prince turned to Robbie and they discussed work. 'Next year this sgool is being very pig pisness, I am telling the Minster Edgecation. My cousin. No good little classes, maybe four, maybe five students. Much bitter twenty, thirty students, pig glasses, too much titchers.'

'Well, we are trying to expand,' Robbie said, pouring Farouk a glass of the liqueur his friend at an oil refinery brewed from desert shrubs. 'We do have a new Director of Studies coming oot on Sunday, as a matter of fact. And his wife.'

'More English womans living here?' Farouk asked with interest.

'They're coming in a few days. *Bukhrah,*' said Rosemary, pronouncing it so strangely, 'Book Hurrah', that the Prince thought it was an English phrase.

'In London I am having English titcher, woman, for bringing to my country.' Rosemary looked embarrassed, Robbie fascinated. 'For titching my childrens, wifes. This one wife too much religion. Always she braying, reading, crying. Niver happy. Much bitter English womans, laughing, dancing. Viry nice.' Rosemary wondered if she lived up to this joyful national stereotype. 'But also mans – why I am not meeting titchers at your house? They are living you? Very nice, like English poarding sgool. Your bublic sgools – I am sending my children there.'

'Well, yes, we did all decide to move in together. It saves so much bother, money and so on,' Robbie mumbled.

'And you not all eat together?' Farouk looked astonished.

'Shall we ask the teachers to come in, Robbie?' Rosemary asked nervously.

Robbie had had several glasses of distilled desert shrubs and

brandy made from tinned peaches. Chuckling, he staggered over
to the bell which, in a Saudi household, would summon the women
to the men's quarters. The bell squawked horribly, emitting a kind
of Woody Woodpecker mechanical guffaw calculated to annoy.

The teachers didn't hear the bell because they had disconnected
it months before. Bertram, Chris and Leo lay on mattresses on the
flat roof, drinking Seven Up mixed with sour home-made wine.
Even at night it was hotter outside the house than in, but the night
sky at least offered visual refreshment. Stars like lamps hung out
of a rich velvet ceiling embroidered with the thin crescent of the
Ramadan moon. Quietly, Leo focused his telescope on a star and
made notes. A seasoned English teacher, he made a point of
studying a different subject in each job: in Libya it was Arabic; in
Italy, art history. In each job he became more erudite and benign.
Bertram had just come back from practising on the piano at the
home of a British Embassy official, whose wife always listened
appreciatively and gave him an authentic gin and tonic. For a few
minutes the music, still pounding in his ears, soothed his furious
unhappiness. Usually John joined them on the roof, but he was
packing. Oh happy day, oh promised lands of milk and honey and
fun and decent wine that lie beyond Saudi air space....

'If Ramadan does begin on Saturday it'll take them hours to get
through Customs,' Chris said hopefully.

'And it'll be monsoon in India, won't it?' Bertram added.

'Peter will probably catch something in Bangkok.'

Aids loomed in all their imaginations, a monster that dwarfed
even Robbie and made some sense of their compulsory celibacy.

'Cockbang. He did at Christmas but it didn't put him off.'

'Shall we go to the desert tomorrow?'

'Might as well.'

'I haven't practised for weeks.'

Chris was a keen piper. His childhood had been spent in the
south of England but later, at Edinburgh University, he had
acquired the bagpipes which now dominated his life. Because of
them he had been thrown out of several flats and more than one
girl-friend had left him. When he first arrived in Saudi Arabia
Customs officials had confiscated them, under the impression they
were either explosive or alcoholic. Robbie had threatened to
sabotage them several times, until Chris stopped practising at the
Villa Despair and drove off into the wilderness instead. Often at
weekends the three of them camped in the desert, several hundred

yards apart: Leo with his telescope, Bertram with his Mozart operas and Chris with his bagpipes.

They heard noises downstairs. 'Move the telescope down a bit,' Bertram hissed, and snatched it from Leo. He could see the blackheads on the Prince's nose, the orange hairs plastered down thinly on Robbie's scalp, Rosemary's prominent, hopelessly honest teeth and the minder's bulging biceps, all uncomfortably big and close, illuminated by the light from behind the open front door. That man's a trained killer. Bertram thought. If he did look up and saw me pointing something he might – but the fascination was irresistible. Bertram hated Robbie more than he had ever loved anyone. His toenail parings and even his dreary wife were monstrous, repulsive, mesmerizing. Looking up from the confusing round eye, Bertram saw how huge and still the white figure below was, and how the smallest of the four bobbed and capered. They've been drinking, Bertram thought, as he heard Robbie's shrill giggle. Once, at a staff meeting, Robbie had boasted that the school could never be closed because he supplied the Prince with alcohol. Bertram often cited this as an example of Robbie's extraordinary mixture of megalomania and naïvety. Robbie really imagined that the Prince, who could have any of them deported or imprisoned at ten minutes' notice, lived in fear of him.

Chris pulled him back. 'You nearly fell over the parapet. Anyway, they'll see you, or hear you – what were you muttering to yourself?'

'I didn't know I was.' Ashamed, as he would have been if he had been secretly in love instead of openly in hate, Bertram crouched over his Seven Up cocktail.

The teachers brewed their booze in a room in their own quarters. Every night they split into groups and drank together, conspired against Robbie, planned how to spend the money they were saving, watched videos which in various ways offended against Islam, reminisced about past holidays and looked forward to future ones. Like prisoners, they fantasized about how they might escape. Every time one of them went on holiday he threatened not to come back.

John and Peter, the chosen ones, walked in and out of each other's rooms (mattress, chair, video, cassette player, paperbacks). Usually, John spent his evenings on the roof reading Dostoevsky, and he despised Peter, who played Rugby and wore a

gold chain. But tonight they were allies, alienated from the others
by their happiness as they packed and re-packed. The preparation
to leave was such a joy.

'Are you coming back the day before we start teaching?' John
asked.

'If I come back.'

'Really? D'you mean you'd break your contract and leave your
video and your share in the car?'

'I'm considering it. I've applied for a job in Bangkok. I'll just
have to see if it comes through.'

'Well, good luck. I think I'll just come back for one more year.
If only I can save twenty thousand I reckon I could leave teaching
for good.'

'What would you do instead?'

'Oh, write maybe.'

Returning from the Prince's limousine, Robbie looked up at
their windows malevolently. 'Bunch of pooftahs,' he muttered to
Rosemary as they opened their door.

'Oh Robbie, surely not. Not all of them.'

'Christ, woman, don't ye notice anything? They're in and oot
of each other's rooms all the time. I try to weed them oot at the
interviews in London but ye can't always tell. They're very good
at covering their tracks. Take Bertram. He mentioned a girl-
friend at the interview and said he'd played cricket at school. Hoo
was I to know he played the fucking piano all the time?'

'But it's nice that he's so musical. I really don't think ... I
mean Yehudi Menuhin got married and had children, didn't he?'

'Will ye stick to the point? They're up there noo, giggling and
whispering like a buncha Jessies. Those teachers are a decadent lot
and if the Prince knew aboot their goings on it'd be. . . .' He
mimed the *Shariah* punishment for sexual offences, his eyes
sparkling. 'Ye know, in many ways this is a healthier society than
our own. Men are men and women are women, and that's
probably why there's a good deal less crime than in the Yookay.'

'Well, I don't find it as difficult as I did at first. But we won't
have to spend much longer here, will we, Robbie?'

'We'll just have ter see.'

Ignoring her, Robbie sat down to the high point of his day, his
intimate conversation with the computer guardian of his treasure,
which wasn't buried but transferred speedily to the Isle of Man,
Luxembourg and anywhere else where interest rates were high.

Rosemary threw away the dirty paper plates, put on her pink gingham nightie and decided to take Benjamin Bear to bed instead of Reynard. The fox's face had grown sharper over the last year, his snout more leering and malevolent. He held his riding-crop against his jodhpurs as if he was about to lash out with it, pounce on her when she least expected pain and really hurt her. Rosemary huddled under the sheets, squeezed her eyes tight shut and rushed to get to sleep before Robbie came in and turned the air-conditioning on again. Every night there was this battle between them, between freezing or sweating, noise or peace, waking up with a cold or a headache. It was the only battle she fought and she always lost.

Her sister Jane had written to say she might be coming to stay and Rosemary prayed that she wouldn't get a visitor's visa. My prayers are all negative now, she thought miserably. Don't let me have a baby, don't let Jane come here, don't let him shout at me in front of the teachers. Jane would see it all so clearly and of course remark on the situation in her loud, confident voice, with the superiority of a single woman who thought marriage was atavistic and marriage to a man like Robbie cretinous. Ever since the evening Rosemary had met Robbie at a party in London, Jane had been advising her to leave him. With Jane in the house she wouldn't even be able to comfort herself with images of Chichester, of their parents' garden and the Close and sailing with friends. As it was, on Rosemary's brief visits home, when the school could spare her and Robbie could afford her air fare, Jane and her parents treated her like the survivor of an appalling ordeal. And she behaved like one: in their house she was able only to eat, sleep and tell curious anecdotes about life in Riyadh which, she hoped, were funny. She would drive to the detached Victorian house near the golf-course, which she and Robbie had bought, and try to envy herself.

Rosemary put in her ear-plugs, took a sleeping-pill and curled up to receive her nightly instalment of uneasy dreams.

3

On Sunday evening the police cadets poured into the school, devoured all the stale cakes in Mansour's coffee bar, swigged vast quantities of fizzy orange and Pepsi and looked around for further entertainment. There were about sixty of them, dressed in transparent white *thobes* which revealed their bony, adolescent bodies: narrow shoulders, backbones like fine knives, thighs hardly thicker than their ankles. On their neat, proud faces thin moustaches and beards sprouted like threads of black silk. Each of the young men carried either a swagger-cane or a revolver strapped to his waist. Five teachers and Rosemary wandered among them, trying to split them into classes.

All the police cadets were riveted by Rosemary, a Western woman and a blonde, and they tittered at the prospect of a woman teacher. She handed a list of their names to Chris and scurried into the office to work invisibly. She was breaking the law by working in this building full of men, but Robbie was too mean to pay for a male secretary and the Prince kept promising her the directorship of a new, separate school for the flower of Saudi womanhood.

John and Peter stood in the staff-room doorway. Over the weekend their faces had crumpled and aged. Their visas hadn't materialized, Ramadan would start tomorrow morning at the latest and they wouldn't be able to book alternative flights, as most of the Saudi and foreign population left the country for Ramadan. Robbie's school was one of the very few businesses to stay open throughout the month of fasting. The prospect of six weeks' holiday in the Villa Despair was so unbearable that John and Peter felt compelled to haunt the school in the hope that either Robbie or Mansour would feel guilty enough to bribe the right official. Robbie hadn't been seen in the school all day and Mansour had refused to leave his coffee bar while it was doing such good business. When the police cadets had at last been herded upstairs Peter approached him again, menacingly. He fingered the gold chain on his chest and stood in his most aggressive Rugby stance, muscles abulge.

Mansour stared at the angry pink and yellow face. Westerners were so brightly coloured that they seemed to him to be made of plastic. 'Viry sorry, titcher Beter. After tomorrow my friend in Ministry is giving you visa, *inshallah.*'

'After tomorrow?' Peter bellowed.

John shuffled beside him, a thin brown man who muttered in an agonized voice, 'Oh God! Oh my God!'

Both the celestial beauty of the Himalayas and the massage parlours of Bangkok receded with such speed that they felt ill. Mansour slipped downstairs and Peter became apoplectic. He looked around for something to destroy but the school was so bare, and so scarred by previous teachers' assaults, it was hard to know where to begin. The grey walls were pockmarked with blobs of Blu-tack where pictures had been ripped down. The only remaining decorations were a poster of Windsor Castle, drooping in two places, and a strip of green tinsel which Robbie had defiantly put up the previous Christmas (Christmas was illegal in Saudi Arabia). Mansour's coffee bar used only paper cups. Viciously, Peter kicked a crate of Pepsi and managed to break several bottles, while others rolled deafeningly down the concrete stairs.

Rosemary came rushing out of her office. 'Are you all right, Peter? Mansour shouldn't leave his drinks in such awkward places.'

Peter shouted something at her, but the sunset prayer call drowned his words. A new mosque had been built a hundred yards from the school and the stereophonic equipment on its roof was particularly effective. The muezzin began with the amplified clearing of a gigantic throat, then there was a blurred whoomph as if a dusty needle had been jerked on to a record and a nasal voice wailed, *God is most great,* so loud that He seemed to be fighting to get inside your head. Peter stopped shouting, crushed by his visaless state, by the repressive demands of a higher, noisier power and by Rosemary's surprised grey eyes. John sat in the grubby staff-room, his head buried in his arms, and sobbed to think he might have to listen to hundreds more muezzins before he could escape. Sometimes, at dawn, the distant call to prayer touched him by its mystical sadness. But now it was an intrusion, an insulting reminder of his helplessness.

The police cadets poured downstairs. Even if any of the teachers had wanted to blaspheme by continuing to work during prayer-time, he couldn't have made himself heard above the muezzin.

Shaking, the teachers helped themselves to Near Beer, developed in America during Prohibition, and staggered into the staff-room.

Bertram glared at John. 'Christ, you're so lucky, not having to teach that lot. They wanted to use the board for target practice.'

'I haven't got a visa. I'm not going on holiday.' Glazed with misery, John was unable to absorb any new ideas.

Chris lit cigarettes for them all. 'I hope I haven't offended them. I asked when Ramadan was going to start and they kept saying coyly. "We don't know, nobody knows, only God." I mean they

must know, mustn't they, otherwise how come they all rush out of
the country? By the way, John, you'll never get on a flight now,
even if your visa does come through.' John moaned. 'Anyway in
the end I picked up that toy telephone I use for dialogues and said,
"Hello? Allah? I ´was just wondering if Ramadan begins
tomorrow." They didn't think it was very funny.' He roared with
laughter.

Outside the door, in Mansour's coffee bar, two cadets with bare
feet and sandals had trodden on splinters of glass left over from
Peter's rampage and were hopping around in agony. Another
student had burst into Rosemary's office to complain about
Teacher Chris's disrespect for Islam. When Rosemary realized
that his uncle was a *mettahwah,* she apologized abjectly and begged
him not to report the school to the authorities.

After a meal of boiled rice and fish fingers Rosemary and
Robbie drove off to the airport to meet Christopher and Vivienne.
The airport was in the middle of the desert; a huge conglomeration
of vaulted white buildings including an enormous mosque, a
terminal that was for the use only of the royal family and a
plantation of carefully irrigated palm trees. Inside the departure
terminal was chaos. Saudis and foreign workers fought, shoved,
yelled and wept to get their luggage weighed in. Several Egyptians
whose planes didn't leave until the next morning lay asleep on the
marble floor, kicked and stumbled over by those desperate to leave
the country. Once their luggage, tickets and visas had been
accepted, the travellers were overcome by euphoria and floated up
the escalator to the departure lounge, where they celebrated with
Pepsi. As they drove past, Rosemary saw John and Peter standing
outside the plate-glass windows, looking in at the gates of Heaven.

'Goodness gracious! Did Mansour get their visas after all,
Robbie?'

'What? Oh, those two prats. No, I shouldn't think they'll get
visas till after Ramadan now.'

'Oh dear. I think they're rather upset.'

'I'll give them a couple of weeks in lieu at Christmas.
Meanwhile you'd better get them timetabled back in. I don't want
them stirring up any trouble.'

The arrivals terminal was more sedate. Few people arrived on
the eve of Ramadan and those who did were tight-lipped and
silent.

'Let's hope he's less of a Jessie than our last Dosser.'

Jonathan, the last Director of Studies, had had to be repatriated to England after he locked himself in the teaching materials room for two days and two nights and chewed the covers off all the copies of *Kernel Lessons*. Robbie was still sending him bills for replacement copies.

They stood with their arms around each other, a couple in their late twenties. Christopher was dark and good looking, in tight jeans. He carried a small leather handbag and several pieces of smart luggage. Vivienne was a redhead in a crisp green cotton dress with elbow-length sleeves. They emanated brightness and cleanliness. Rosemary was charmed, even before she had spoken to them, and smiled. 'That must be them. They do look nice. . . .'

But Robbie had already strode up to them, head forward and shoulders hunched. 'No need to introduce ourselves. When ye've been here as long as I have, ye'll realize ye can't hold hands or be lovey-dovey in a public place like this. It's all right between men but not between men and women. And I hope ye've brought some more suitable clothes.' He glared at Vivienne. 'Ye're asking for trouble if ye show off yer arms and legs like that. There were several British nurses raped last month – ye really can't be too careful. And while we're on the subject of clothes, d'ye normally carry a handbag?' He looked at Christopher, who hadn't said a word, although they were now loading their luggage into the boot of the car.

'Yes, as a matter of fact. In Rome, where we've been living for the last two years, most men do. I find it very convenient.'

'Well, ye can't do that here. They might like queers in Italy but over here it's a capital offence.'

As they got into the back of the car it occurred to Christopher and Vivienne that this boor might be, not the school's odd-job man but its director, Robert McTavish. Occasionally Rosemary turned round with the fixed grin she had worn since she met them.

'Did you have a good journey?'

'Yes, thanks,' said Vivienne.

'It's a pity yer name's Christopher,' Robbie continued.

'Oh? Why?'

'Well, we've already got one Christopher, we can't have two. The students have such difficulty with the teachers' names as it is. Ye'd better choose another name.'

'I'm perfectly happy with my own name.'

'How about Martin? We've not got a Martin jest now.'

'No, thank you.'

'Or Steven?'

'No!'

'Or Jonathan? That might be a good solution, as Jonathan was yer predecessor, so the students are used to having a DOS called Jonathan....'

'I've come here for a job, not a fucking rebaptism!'

'It's reelly not a good idea to use obscene language here, particularly not if ye're going to drag religion into it.'

'You're from Bournemouth, aren't you? My uncle lives near there. We're from Chichester.'

But Rosemary's gentility only made Christopher and Vivienne more uncomfortable. Furtively, on the back seat of Robbie's shabby bargain Nissan, they held hands and stiffened with the first intimations of paranoia: the phrases of the advertisement and interview, the free accommodation and tax-free salary and friendly team of graduates, already seemed barbed. After miles of flat desert road they were driving along a wide motorway through a vast suburb of new buildings and shops broken every few yards by wastelands and building sites. Everything was new, nothing quite finished. There was a total lack of exotic orientalism. Even the palm trees growing on the grassy strip that ran down the centre of the motorway looked as if they might be made of rubber.

Vivienne's first sight of the Villa Despair was of a high, reinforced concrete wall surrounded by a sandy void. Robbie helped her out of the car with an unctuous leer, but she couldn't bring herself to touch the thick, short arm, bristling with red hairs, he offered. She clung instead to Christopher's hand and Robbie glared at them pointedly. Rosemary helped them with their cases as Robbie opened the gate.

'There'll be a lot of excitement aboot yer arrival,' Robbie said, ogling Vivienne again. 'Ye're the first woman they've had aroond here.'

'Except me,' Rosemary said gently.

'Ye don't count.'

Rosemary laughed, as if Robbie's straight-faced insult had been an affectionate joke.

'How many people live here?' Christopher asked, looking up at the huge, hideous concrete villa.

'Fourteen of us, noo you're here.' Robbie led them round to the side door. 'Ye'll get a double room, as a couple.'

'But the man who interviewed us said we'd have our own flat. Anyway it's illegal, isn't it, for unmarried men and women to live in the same building?'

'We'll expect ye in at the school in the morning fer the induction course. And if ye've not brought proper clothes with ye, Vivienne, ye'll have to borrow some from Rosemary. We can't have ye turning up at the school looking like a trollop, particularly during Ramadan.'

'Do come and have a little chat in the morning,' Rosemary gushed before she and Robbie hurried back to their own territory.

Cautiously Vivienne and Christopher dragged their cases up a flight of bare concrete stairs. Christopher opened the door at the top and they found themselves in a huge bare room full of bottles, glasses and young males, all staring at him and at Vivienne behind him. Although the room was thirty feet long and had a ceiling fifteen feet high, the only furniture was a red leatherette couch, two hard wooden chairs, a video and a long table covered with yellow plastic. Vivienne was reminded of parties she had attended in her first year at university. She started to play with her long hair, accepted the foul-tasting drink that was put into her hand and smiled, embarrassed, flattered, as seven men paid her homage she had never been paid before.

Much later, Christopher and Vivienne stumbled into a tiny room which contained a double mattress and a wardrobe. Once they were inside the room with their luggage it was impossible to open the door. Unable to sit down, his head still buzzing with heat, travel fever and home-made beer, Christopher stumbled over to the window. It overlooked a complex of buildings and gardens illuminated by fairy lights.

'Must be a hotel. I wish we were staying there.'

She stood beside him and they clung to each other, rather desperately. 'No, it's the palace where the Prince lives, the one who owns the school. Don't you remember? Bertram told us.'

'Which one's Bertram?'

'The pianist, the one with the curly brown hair.'

'To think we've got to live with these people!'

'They seem very friendly.'

'A damned sight too friendly towards you.'

On the other side of their thin walls, strangers who were suddenly fellow inmates shuffled, whispered, splashed and creaked their way to bed. Christopher and Vivienne collapsed on to the mattress together, leaving their luggage against the door to act as a barricade. They had met in Rome, where they had worked for another ICBM school and lived in a room not much bigger than this one, near the Piazza Navona. For two years they had been mutually obsessed by each other, so that the intimacy imposed on them by poverty and lack of space had been a pleasure. They had made few friends during those years, when neighbours and colleagues had existed only as incidental music in the broader drama of their passion. When they tired of making love and talking in their room, they used to walk around Rome. Her piazzas, fountains and ruins, together with the ochres, pinks and creams of her crumbling façade, had been the third person in their love affair. Now when they shut their eyes they could still see the vistas and colours of the city they loved, the city which had invented their love. These images hovered above them and formed a bridge between them as they fell asleep in the dry, tepid room.

4

Three weeks into Ramadan the air-conditioning in the school broke down again. Christopher, whose name was now Jonathan, was trying to teach adjectives to a class of beginners. He usually prided himself on his talent for clowning and keeping students amused, but the heat paralysed him. He flopped on a chair and tried to think above the headache that thumped behind his dry, red eyes.

The small class-room was so hot that the plastic-covered chair burned through his trousers and his shirt was soaked. Mingled with the smell of his own sweat was the sour breath of fifteen students who hadn't had a drink since the previous night and who had slept until they were dragged out of bed to go to their English class. The acquisition of English was regarded by parents as a mystical virtue, rather like playing the piano for young English ladies in the nineteenth century. Christopher pressed the 'play' button on his tape recorder and, as if in harmony with his thoughts, a Chopin polonaise came galloping out. The students were supposed to sway and nod their heads as they chanted their English phrases in time to the music. But they were too tired even to stand up. They're even more bored than I am, Christopher thought as he chorally drilled them: 'What's he like? He's tall and thin.'

He held up various flashcards. Two of the students had fallen asleep on their desks and the eyelids of three more were drooping. Christopher gave way to a jaw-splitting yawn, turned up the music and then said apathetically, 'Now let's try something new. OK? You ask, I listen. First you, Abdul Rahman, ask Abdullah. Talk about Khalid, please.'

Abdul Rahman glared at him resentfully. Slowly, Jonathan repeated himself with painful teacherly gestures. A third student fell asleep and started to snore, his mouth open. Christopher bellowed above the music, 'Now, Abdul Rahman! Tell me about Khalid. What's he like?'

Abdul Rahman glared at the teacher and then at Khalid. With profound contempt and a perfect accent he said, 'He is fat, stupid and ugly.'

Christopher switched off the Chopin music and watched in horror as Khalid and one of his friends leaped up. Abdul Rahman jumped over his desk and fled to the door. The fight, which started between Abdul Rahman and Khalid, soon spread to all the students who were still awake. Those who were wearing their head-dresses, or *ghutras,* took them off and started to whack each other with the plaited cord that kept them in place. Khalid and Abdul Rahman rolled out on to the landing, down the concrete stairs and eventually on to the pavement, where the fight ended with a great deal of blood and vomiting. Christopher watched them from the window, horrified by the violence yet quite detached. He no longer felt he had any control over his students, his name or his wife. He looked at his watch and hoped they wouldn't come back for the second half of the lesson. He would let the others sleep until it was time to go home. Khalid and Abdul Rahman had their arms around each other now and were weeping. Friends pulled them into huge American limousines and drove them home, bounding at a hundred miles an hour over the deserted roads.

Christopher sat down and read *The Guardian Weekly,* hardly daring to rustle the thin pages in case he woke his remaining students. He could hardly breathe in the stifling atmosphere. Already English party politics seemed to be curious tribal rituals performed on a small, distant island. He looked at the job advertisements and tutted in derision at the salaries offered.

The sunset call to prayer rattled the windows, reverberated through the school and woke the students, who yelled with delight that their fast was over, rushed downstairs and roared off in their cars to feast all night. All over the city brakes squealed, tortured cars started in top gear and there were even more accidents than usual. Christopher ran downstairs after them. As it was illegal to eat, drink or smoke in public between dawn and sunset during Ramadan, the staff-room had been turned into a lockable canteen, with cartons of cigarettes, crates of Pepsi and Seven Up, boxes of dates and digestive biscuits. Christopher walked in and saw Vivienne surrounded by teachers. He thought with annoyance how all these taboos added savour to the most innocent social contact. Not that he had much faith in his colleagues' innocence. Peter's flirtation with Vivienne had become so obnoxious that Christopher had almost hit him, the night before Peter and John had been bundled off to Cyprus for a two-week package holiday.

Now Bertram, who thought Vivienne was the most attractive and indeed the only attractive woman whose face he had seen for months, was saying, 'Of course I could be arrested for giving you a lift to Safeway. You're only allowed to go in your husband's car with your husband. If a *mettahwah* saw you and me out together, he might demand to see our marriage certificate.'

'Ridiculous,' said Vivienne, who was now wearing a droopy black garment called an *abaya*. It was rather like the gown worn by English graduates at degree ceremonies and conferred a fake academic dignity on the foreign women of Riyadh, undermined by the fact they often wore jeans or sun-dresses underneath. 'Hello, Christopher. Good lesson?'

'No. Half the class fell asleep and the others tried to murder each other. I'll take you to Safeway. Come on.' Even in the car they were hardly ever alone, as these were shared.

'I'll come along too if you're going shopping,' Bertram said.

Vivienne resented Christopher's constant bad temper. She didn't like the uncertainty about his name either, and obstinately called him Christopher although the teachers all called him Jonathan to his face and Noggin the Nog, because of his Icelandic thesis, behind his back. They had all acquired such faintly malicious nicknames: Bertram was WAM, for Wolfgang Amadeus Mozart, Peter was Superstud, Robbie and Rosemary were Haggis and Hag and Chris was Peter Piper. Vivienne didn't know her own nickname but suspected it was obscene. She had changed her mind about the resemblance to student life. The teachers had regressed further back than that, to a sort of sniggering-in-the-dorm state. She wanted to keep her distance from them but also wanted them to like her.

That night, when they were at last alone in their thin-walled room, Christopher burst from a sulk to a whispered row.

'What's the matter with you now?'

'I just can't bear to see you cock-teasing all evening. You really encourage them.'

'What am I supposed to do, ignore them? Anyway, they're a lot nicer to me than you are.'

'It's an intolerable situation. It's like a volcano, one woman living with all these men. If Robbie doesn't give us our own flat soon, I'm going to leave.'

'What about the money for our deposit?'

'Sod that. There's no point in buying a house if we're not together to live in it.'

'It was your idea to apply for the job – "Teaching couple". I haven't taught one lesson – they can't find any woman students because Robbie's too mean to build a separate entrance for them. He has some loony plan to introduce aerobics classes for fat Saudi women. Learn English while you leap around to pop music. Meanwhile, all I do is to type the odd letter and sit around in that filthy staff-room cataloguing visual aids. I could have done that the first day. All they've got is ten sets of flashcards and some posters. You're working all the time, and whenever I do see you you're furious with me.'

'Don't cry. I know it's boring for you, but it's not a bundle of fun for me either. Do you realize we've only been here three weeks?'

'Feels like years.'

'I know what we could do – buy our own car. Then at least we'd have some privacy.'

'You mean you'll buy it. I'm not even allowed to drive. Anyway we can't afford it.'

'If we are going to stay in this cesspit, we'll have to find some way of enjoying it. Even if it's only driving round the desert in circles. We could buy a second-hand Jeep and go camping at weekends. Wind down.'

'On our own?'

'Well, I'm not likely to enjoy myself if all my bloody colleagues are there, am I?'

'They're really quite a likeable bunch.'

'It's only too clear you think so.'

'Don't start that again. I don't like all this You-Tarzan-Me-Jane rubbish any more than you do. I'm used to being friends with men, working with them. Here you can't talk to a man without his thinking that you're propositioning him.'

'I thought you just said they were a nice bunch?'

'They are, really. They're just so repressed and frustrated. It's not their fault. They can't open a can of Pepsi or light a cigarette without some infantile *double entendre*.'

'Which you usually laugh at.'

'Well, what am I supposed to do? Blush? Hide behind my veil?'

After two years together in Rome they had got married, just to make themselves eligible for the Saudi job, or so they had both said. But their wedding, celebrated in a pizzeria with a few friends and no relations, had been what they both wanted. We loved each other, she thought. That love must still be here, somewhere, like the images of cypress trees and cobbled streets floating behind my eyes. As if love and beauty, frowned on by Islam, don't dare to enter this country. Vivienne stuffed her knuckles into her mouth. It's so boring, crying all the time, I've forgotten how to be happy. Now they lay side by side, naked under the sheet, shivering because the air-conditioning was so ferocious and because their rhythms, which for years had been in harmony, were suddenly, chillingly dissonant. Christopher was inhibited by the invisible presence of his colleagues. There they were on all sides; listening, smirking, envying, whispering, burning to enjoy the thin, white body beside him. It was quite impossible to imagine any passion between Rosemary and Robbie, unless perhaps they held hands to look at their bank statements together. In this enormous house he was the only man with a woman to fuck, that word constantly, angrily, on the lips of the expatriates here. Perhaps that was where all the tension in Riyadh came from. Perhaps the foreigners, alone, or with their bored wives, all suffered from the same impotence. . . .

Vivienne was already asleep. He touched her creamy shoulder and the line where her freckled skin met her metallic wisps of red hair. She had grown more beautiful here, flourished under the beams of desire that shone on her from all directions. Yet at that moment he didn't want her. He was aroused only by the suspicion that one of the others would try to seduce her or that she would fall in love to relieve the tedium. Christopher, for whom sex had always been simple and monogamous, felt that the secrecy and repression all around him had turned the act of love into something rather nasty.

In the morning they caught Robbie at breakfast.

'Come in. Sit doón. Rosemary, give them some cold porridge. I've been meaning to have a talk with ye. How're ye settling in? How's yer marriage?' He ate very fast, leaning over his bowl. There were several glutinous lumps in his beard.

'All right. How's yours?' Vivienne asked coolly.

'No one's ever done a survey, but I'd estimate about eighty-five per cent of the expat marriages oot here break down.' He helped himself to another dollop of cold porridge. 'Ye see too much of each other and the women get too much attention. It goes to their heads. Though I can't say anybody bothers to chase after Rosemary.'

'Oh, Robbie!' She said mildly.

'Noo if I was to advise a young fellow coming oot here I'd tell him to find the plainest, stupidest woman and marry her. Like me. The pretty ones don't last long.' He stared at Vivienne.

Collectively insulted, the three other people in the room were silent. Then Vivienne and Christopher went on the attack.

'We've come to complain about the accommodation.' Christopher spoke very fast, his head and eyes lowered. 'It's not what we were promised and it's really not acceptable. If you can't provide us with our own flat, we'll have to leave. I shall be writing to London to complain.'

'Poor you, it must be awful,' Rosemary said vaguely.

'There's noo need to bother head office – there's nothing they can do aboot it. I'll ask the Prince when he comes back from holiday.'

'When's that?' Vivienne asked sharply.

'September. He'd love to meet ye.' Robbie stared at Vivienne again.

'That's two months away. We can't wait that long. I absolutely insist that we're given our own flat before then.' Christopher's throat was dry and his face burned. It cost him such an effort to make even a small scene.

Robbie chuckled. 'Is it that bad? It it's any comfort to ye, they have capital punishment here for adultery.'

Vivienne felt her temper zooming up like a rocket. His rudeness was so brutal that it disarmed you at first, took your breath away.

He reduced all of them to idiots or whores, he steamrollered over subtlety, kindness and poor Rosemary. This venomous red troll held their passports, decided where they slept and treated them with utter contempt. 'Come on, Christopher. He's obviously not going to help us. We'll write to London anyway, Robbie, see if they know about your wheeler-dealing.'

'Noo, don't go off in a huff like that. We'll see what we can do. Ye could always move in with us.'

'That would be nice,' Rosemary said, beaming at Vivienne.

'We want at least two rooms. And our own kitchen and bathroom.' When she was bargaining, Vivienne's face became tight and very hard. Beneath her prettiness Christopher could see the rapacious shell of another face.

'We do have two spare rooms, actually,' Rosemary pleaded. 'I'm afraid we'd have to share the kitchen and bathroom, but perhaps you could make do with that until we can find you your own place?'

The few yards between Robbie's front door and their own were so hot that thoughts and feelings baked dry in their brains. In their room they turned to each other and Vivienne saw with dismay that he was still angry with her.

'The thing that really amazes me about this place is the way you take all this shit from Robbie. All of you. At least I forced him to make us an offer.'

'And what an offer! I'd rather share a house with Stalin and Lucretia Borgia.'

'I don't think Rosemary would be any bother. She'd just be infuriatingly self-denying all the time. When we're in that office together she always insists on sitting in the draught and drinking out of the cracked cup. Robbie's a bastard of course, but you just have to stand up to him.'

Again he observed that expression of manipulation and raw egotism. They were qualities he disliked in her even when her manipulations were to his advantage. Coldly, he squatted in the corner with his back to her and busied himself tidying their bags. Most of their clothes and books were still packed because they couldn't bear to admit that they were going to spend a year in their cell.

This tendency of Christopher's to sulk had occasionally soured their relations in Rome. There, Vivienne had been able to leave him alone, go for a walk or visit a friend until he felt better. Here, she thought desperately, I've nowhere to go. If we do have a blood row – which would be a relief – twelve other people will be listening in. If I go out and talk to them, Christopher will be even angrier with me. He's probably right, I probably do flirt with them. Well, there's nothing else to do. I have to exist as an object of desire because I don't exist on any other level. Oh God, he's going to crouch like that for hours, pretending I'm not here. Well, since I can't please him, I might as well please myself and talk to one of the others.

Chris the piper was the only teacher she regarded as a friend, perhaps because he was older and more stable than the others, and never embarrassed her by schoolboy fits of giggling and leering. As she stood in the corridor, lonely and puzzled, Vivienne wondered if she could seek out a man without being misinterpreted. Here, life for women between puberty and menopause was one long chain of taboos and ambiguities.

As she hovered, the bathroom door opened and Chris seeped out. Water poured from his brown hair, streamed down his thick, square glasses and made his T-shirt and jeans cling to his large, thick body. He squelched down the corridor towards her, blinked at her wetly and said, without explaining why he had had a shower fully clothed, 'I'll be dry by the time I get to the school.' Then he oozed downstairs, his sneakers slapping the marble steps and leaving shiny prints in the dust. She heard him open the front door and wander out, steaming presumably. Vivienne sighed because friendship was impossible in this place. They were all mad and it was only a matter of time before the insanity she knew was hidden in corners of her and Christopher manifested itself.

She and Rosemary had their loneliness in common. In the afternoons while the others taught, the two women sat in the dim office. The air-conditioning replaced the weather as the main topic of conversation: if it was working, they complained about the cold and even lent each other cardigans. Such acts of casual kindness were the closest they came to intimacy. If, as was usual, the air-conditioning had broken down, Rosemary and Vivienne sweltered together, agreed it was too hot to do anything, that the dry heat was good for your skin but bad for your hair, that Mansour and all the other men were hopeless not to have mended it. Now it had been decided that Vivienne and Christopher were to move in with them Rosemary tried with clumsy generosity to make friends with her, to make her time in Riyadh less unhappy than her own.

'Don't feel you have to sit around in the school all day. I know you haven't really got a job at the moment.'

'There's nowhere else to go. Everything's shut for Ramadan, it's about 140 out there, and anyway I've no transport.'

With Rosemary, Vivienne was at her coolest. She spoke in a clipped voice and presented the strong, unbroken wall of her personality as an obstruction to Rosemary's crippled goodwill. Rosemary was reminded of the role she always played with her sister Jane.

'What about going to a meeting of the World-Wide Women's Group? I'm sure one of the teachers would take you there and pick you up. Those women do quite a lot, you know, at their meetings.'

'A feminist group? In Saudi Arabia?'

'Oh, they're not feminists. But they do organize lots of coffee mornings, bridge, macrame classes. That sort of thing.'

'Do you go?'

'I did go once, when I first arrived. It was very interesting really. They've produced the most lovely cookery book. But since then I've been busy working ... perhaps you might make some friends there?'

'I doubt it. And if I did, I wouldn't be able to communicate with them.'

'We are getting a telephone at the villa soon. Mansour's been a bit slow about the application.'

'I must say Mansour seems to be about as much use as a fixer as Robbie is as a principal. Is he coming in at all today?'

Rosemary never denied the incompetence with which the school was administered, and even seemed relieved when it was remarked on. 'He must have got held up at one of the ministries.'

Whenever Rosemary went out of the room, Vivienne opened the filing cabinet with the key she left in her desk drawer. Vivienne felt no guilt about snooping, as she considered she was defending herself against Robbie. Sooner or later, when the time came to attack him, she would need all this information. There was a file for each teacher, which contained surprisingly personal remarks, considering Robbie's complete failure to make any personal contact with them. Bertram was described as a 'neurotic homo-sexual with psychopathic tendencies', Christopher as 'negative and incapable of disciplining students' and she was 'self-centred and vain'. His behaviour to their faces was diplomacy itself compared with the insults flying back to London, for use in future references. Gleefully, Vivienne copied out all the juiciest remarks and gave them to the appropriate teachers. She tried to work out, from the other files and account books, exactly what Robbie was up to and whom he was swindling, but she couldn't prove he was dishonest. She read a bundle of cordial letters from the head office of the Intercontinental Choral Balletic Method and learned that Robbie had to give them fifty per cent of his profits, which were higher than in any of their other schools around the world.

Armed with this information, Vivienne joined the teachers on the roof that night, wearing a sleeveless, low-cut, white crêpe dress. On the high, walled roof she was free, the star of a timeless adolescent party, and the planets were as indifferent to the taboos of the Koran as to all other systems. Haram, happy, Vivienne waited for the circle of men to grow until it was an audience. Saudi champagne – home-made white wine with soda water – was distributed liberally.

'To your industrial espionage,' Leo toasted her.

'Anything new?' Bertram asked eagerly.

'He's making pots of money for ICBM, so they certainly won't want to get rid of him. Unless we can prove he's swindling them. I'm sure he is, aren't you? And the Prince, too. We just need something definite to put in that letter to London . . .'

'Get him deported,' Leo suggested.

'Imprisoned!' Bertram burst into manic laughter. 'Flogged in public! Then we could all watch.'

Christopher stayed outside the circle of which his wife was the centre. He thought of her as 'my wife' now, he felt at once more possessive of her and more remote from her. He sat against the wall and drank steadily, burping from the gassy drinks, savouring his contempt for their tawdry fantasies. Sooner or later, he thought, she'll sleep with one of them. We're already so far apart. I don't know if it would break my heart or provide me with a wonderful excuse to leave. We're not the same here, she's not the same, she even looks different. Harder, older, coarser. Flirting without charm or dignity. We've forgotten how to love each other.

'. . . and then we could form a co-operative,' Bertram was saying. 'Run it all ourselves, share the profits. How much does he make, Vivienne?'

'Thousands and thousands,' she said vaguely.

'We'd still need the Prince though. He'd have to be the

Director. You have to have your token Saudi when you form a
company here. You'll have to find evidence that Robbie's
cheating him, Vivienne. Have another look tomorrow.' Bertram
smiled. 'I could buy a really good piano, have it shipped out here.
Awful climate for it though.'

'We could all move into these empty villas,' Vivienne said.
'One each. It would be worth staying here for five years or even
ten, if we were making real money. A villa like this could be really
nice. We could have sprinklers in the garden and clean up the
swimming-pool, grow vines and bougainvillaea up here – you
could grow anything in this climate if you watered it enough.'

'I think I'd buy a really good telescope, have a proper
observatory on the roof. Then after a few years I'd go back to
Reigate, buy a house and retire,' said Leo.

'If I had a sound-proof room I could practise my pipes every
morning before work. We could have reel parties at the weekend
whenever the air conditioning was working. After all, there's a
group of morris dancers here.' Then feeling that, as the eldest, he
should contribute a note of sobriety, Chris said, 'We'll have to be
careful though. Robbie's crafty.'

Later Vivienne went downstairs to get some more wine and
soda and make sandwiches. Bertram came into the kitchen,
clasped her and kissed her, beginning on her shoulder and moving
up to her mouth.

'You shouldn't really.'

'When are you moving to Robbie's?'

'We're not moving very far, Bertram' She picked up two bottles
and stumbled upstairs. On the stairs she met Leo coming down.
He reached out and touched her small, high breasts.

'Sorry. They looked so nice,' he said and continued downstairs.

Vivienne thought, I ought to feel humiliated or embarrassed.
But somehow my reactions are never quite right in this place.
Things don't really happen here and so they don't seem
important. But what if it is all real? Then Christopher's right, I am
behaving badly, I'm destroying what we had together. Which was
real, I think. I can remember it, but I can't feel it any more.

On the roof Christopher still sat glaring at his toes, two empty
bottles in front of him. The personification of funlessness,
Vivienne thought. Really this place is bad for him, he's deterio-
rating so fast. Amazing to think we've only been here a month and
he's turned into a complete slob. Put on weight too – his

paunch is sticking out where his button's come undone. She smiled again as Bertram and Leo came upstairs with more bottles.

Rosemary lay in bed. The pounding feet above her head kept her awake despite her ear-plugs. Surely that was music, they must be dancing. Strange, with only one woman. Perhaps Robbie's right about them. There was an article in the *Mail* about a man who liked to wear frocks – well, here of course they all do, and hold hands in the street. I'm beginning to think I'll never tear Robbie away from this place. Now he wants to let our house in Chichester on a three-year lease.... Rosemary heard the door bang as Robbie went off to work. Often he stayed at the school until early morning, said he couldn't work there during the day with all those prats around.

Robbie let himself into the empty school. A brown cockroach three inches long scurried upstairs ahead of him and fled to its home in Mansour's coffee machine. The air was tepid, thick with the yellow dust that had settled with confidence on every surface in the school. Robbie went into the office, put his portable computer on the desk, turned on the air-conditioning, picked his nose, dug some wax out of his right ear, scratched his balls and got out the school accounts file. He compared the columns of figures on paper with the figures in the BINGO file in his computer, making adjustments where necessary. Perhaps Head Office won't believe I spent five thousand pounds on entertaining last year. When he had finished, he wandered round the school switching on all the lights. The stink from that bog is really disgusting, I'll have to speak to Rosemary about it.

Upstairs, Robbie went into each of the eight class-rooms, checked that the lights and the air-conditioning were working, straightened tables and went through the contents of the waste-paper baskets. He liked to pace the empty rooms, hear his sandals flap and shuffle on the concrete. Often he was able to catch the teachers out, little things he could mention later at staff meetings, show he knew what was going on. He pulled felt-tipped board pens out of the teachers' waste-paper baskets and tried them out on the board. They still had ink in them. Rosemary could refill them downstairs and they could be used for at least another week. John

had missed one of Abdul Rahman's spelling mistakes. That was
the trouble with holidays, they made people lazy and complacent.
Robbie crouched over Bertrams's waste-paper basket and tried to
piece together a letter to someone called Lizzie. Why was it written
on school paper? He would have to put Bertram's hours up if he
had time to sit around writing letters. Grinning, Robbie
scavenged for the scraps of paper, curious to see what Bertram had
to say about him.

The party on the roof ended with Leo strumming a guitar. Sad
eyed, they all sang 'Waltzing Matilda', 'Little Brown Jug' and
(subversively) 'Hark the Herald Angels Sing'. Then they drifted
back to their lonely rooms.

Christopher and Vivienne collapsed on to their mattress, as far
away from each other as was possible in such a confined space.

'Oh God!' he groaned theatrically.

She wanted to touch him but couldn't. She felt trapped inside all
the worst aspects of her personality: all the bits of herself she'd
never liked, growing like triffids here, smothering her, both of
them. With a huge effort, she moved a few inches and took
Christopher's hand. It was warm, heavy, real.

Christopher gripped her, relieved to feel the last of his rooftop
cynicism dissolving. They were both weeping.

'Something about the raw alcohol here. It gives you a hangover
the same night.'

'Don't let go of me.'

'Are we going mad here?'

'Let's just hope we go mad together,' she said.

They touched each other's tears, surprised. They had each
grown accustomed to thinking of the other as being thick-skinned.

In the Desert

It was nearly sunset when they turned off the motorway. They were both giggling with excitement and Christopher paused to kiss her before they bounced off over the unknown desert scrubland. Behind them the muezzin sounded from the nearest mosque, three miles away. Inside the car the voices of Callas and Tito Gobbi singing *Tosca* surged and billowed in a blast of counter-culture.

'Turn them up!' Vivienne shouted, still laughing.

'Did you see all those other cars turning off?'

'Yes. What d'you think they were up to?'

'Praying. Boozing. Screwing. Getting away from Riyadh like us. A lot of the urbanized Saudis camp out in the desert at weekends.'

'A cottage in the country?'

'Some of them have permanent tents here, so my students were telling me.'

'Careful! You nearly hit that camel. They're lying down all over the place. It must be their bedtime.'

Christopher drove straight down a wadi, or dried-up river-bed. He knew that you had to go fast to avoid getting stuck in the sand, so they cruised at forty miles an hour. The sun bled gold and pink over the sand and Vivienne felt as if she was flying deep into the heart of a vast water-melon. She turned the music off because it seemed offensive to make so much noise as they roared along in their second-hand Jeep.

'Look up there! It looks like the ruins of some great civilization!'

Over to their right, silhouetted against the dark-blue sky, was a high ridge dominated by bumps and zigzags of honey and rose-coloured stone.

But there wasn't any civilization here, great or otherwise.'

'There might have been,' Vivienne said hopefully. 'Perhaps

they left no trace – all buried beneath the sand, like Ozymandias.' She beamed at the desertscape because it was so pink and warm and old, unlike the terrible sterility and white newness of Riyadh.

They stopped where the wadi ended in a natural wall of soft rock honeycombed with holes like miniature caves, which made Vivienne feel nostalgic for childhood seaside holidays. 'It's like a rock pool that's been drained of water.'

'This was sea, millions of years ago. Let's camp here. It's a good place because it's sheltered.'

Vivienne had never camped before, had never in her life spent a night in a place where there were no hotels or plumbing. She opened the door and climbed down from the high Jeep, cautiously lowering herself into the dusk. The silence was broken only by the noises they made. Vivienne felt small and insignificant in the desert, but loud and unwieldy in relation to the creatures who lived there. As they had bounced down the dried-up river-bed she had worried about the thousands of insect, reptile and plant lives they were destroying: crushing, killing, then hurtling off in their tank. Yet now they were alone in the darkness their small noises – the rustle of the bag of charcoal, the clang of the metal grill and the flap of their sneakers on the hard sand – were comforting. There was also a faint background stir of desert creatures settling down for the night or coming out to hunt, now that the human earthquake was over.

Christopher gripped her shoulder and shone his torch down at a patch of sand. 'Look!'

A tiny round hole was being sucked out of the sand. Out of it darted a black whip, fluid as water and quick as flame. It lashed out a few yards over the sand and then disappeared into another neatly sucked hole. Looking around, Vivienne saw that the ground was riddled with identical holes.

Once the car headlights had been switched off, the darkness was like a bath in warm, black velvet. Inside their circle of firelight Vivienne and Christopher sat thigh to thigh, grilling steaks and sausages. In the two years she had lived with him, Vivienne had never felt so acutely aware of Christopher's warmth. When he disappeared to pee behind a rock she felt desolate.

'Imagine Chris with his bagpipes and Bertram with his Mozart, coming out here and sleeping on their own. Miles away from each other. I'd go crazy with fear.'

'I don't want to imagine them. We've come here to get away from them. Anyway, what is there to be afraid of?'

'Snakes, scorpions, breakdowns, other people ...'

'Good place for a murder.'

He said it matter-of-factly, staring at the foil-wrapped potatoes he was burying in the flames. She gasped, laughed as she perceived it was a joke and then shivered to think that it might not have been. Of course she could trust this large Boy Scout, who had so quickly established a domestic routine in the middle of the desert, not to be violent. She leaned her thigh and buttock against his with complete confidence. But she knew now that jealous murder, like poisonous snakes, could happen to her. She had already lost much of the vulnerability with which she had arrived in Riyadh.

Christopher was surprised by the face she turned to him. 'If you're really scared, we'll go back.'

'No!'

He looked at his watch. 'They'll be coming out on to the roof now. Opening bottles, lighting up cigarettes, talking about how to get rid of Robbie. And there'll be no queen bee, unless Peter managed to get hold of that nurse he was after.'

'Oh, shut up.' She sliced a melon, which was warm and swollen with juice. It had a slightly rotten smell, like nail varnish. As they buried their faces in its wet, yellow crescents of flesh, Vivienne flushed with embarrassment and annoyance. She felt she had fallen into a trap during her first few months there, a woman-eating trap of narcissism. But nothing happened, as she constantly reminded both of them. In fact, a lot had changed in her: she had known what it was to be the belle of a rather seedy ball as she had watched herself wound Christopher and chalk out the holes in his forehead where horns had never actually been planted. Now she was inclined to dismiss it all, to blame circumstances and his colleagues, from whom she kept aloof. But Christopher, triumphant to have her to himself again, knew how to sabotage her attempts to rewrite history. His anger and her guilt burned on a long fuse, making them both more passionate and unpredictable.

When the eating was over and the fire was a red, round cluster of fading rubies, they lay back on the blanket they had spread over a rock.

'Are you all right? You're very quiet,' she said anxiously. They had got into the habit of taking each other's emotional temperature twenty times a day.

'I'm fine. Very happy,' he added, astonished. 'It's so strange to be on our own like this. No walls, timetables, prayer-time or people banging on our door to offer us Saudi champagne or cold rice pudding ...'

'Don't keep talking about them!' She shut her eyes. Strange how hard it was genuinely to escape from the world. The night was so warm that she was sticky inside her jeans and T-shirt. No wind, hardly any air even on this vast plain. In England, she thought, it's autumn. The woods near my parents' house are turning golden brown, there's a smell of compost and wood-smoke and those warm blue skies that come as if summer has overslept. Then she opened her eyes and let them be, willed them to be, hypnotized by the dark vault circling above her. Stars seemed to congregate here, as if they migrated from more polluted skies, to swell up and ripen. At last she felt the tension of the previous week release its stranglehold on her. She rolled over towards Christopher and reached out for his hand.

'That's better,' he said. He held her very tightly and looked at her so hard that she wanted to shut her eyes again. Instead, they stared at each other. In the dark her red hair and his brown hair were the same colour. They each saw a young, pale, vulnerable face with eyes that at last acknowledged love and need. Silently they agreed to extract the poison from their hearts, then they kissed, touching and groping in greedy passion. On the flat rock exposed to a million unknown dangers, they pulled off each other's clothes and fingered and fucked each other into oblivion. But even oblivion couldn't satisfy them for long, so they got up and did a crazy dance together under the stars around the embers of the fire. Then they wrapped the blanket around them like a cloak and sat beside the fire, in which Vivienne saw the ancient desert cities of her fantasies rise and fall, and Christopher saw an arena where lust and dignity flickered and fought. He suspected lust would win. When the last fragment of charcoal grew dull, it was time to go to bed.

They slept in the car on a platform made by folding down the back seats. It was just uncomfortable enough to remind them they were there. Throughout the night Christopher woke up every hour, stared up at the miraculous sky, inhaled the emptiness and turned back to her. All the nerves and feelings that had become numb sparked in him again as he made plans frenetically: we'll stick it out in Riyadh for a few years and then go back to Italy, buy a house in Tuscany or Umbria and start our own school. He wanted to wake her up to tell her, to charge her with the optimism he suddenly felt. But sleep swept him away again, dreams of olive groves and Etruscan smiles jostled behind his eyes. The next time he woke up it was dawn. She was beside him pulling on her clothes and the scene beyond the car was beige and grey, drained of vitality.

When the sun had stained the landscape, so that beige became orange and grey warmed to brown, they went for a walk and found that they weren't on the vast empty plain they had imagined around them all night, but in a muddle of hillocks, scrub and shrivelled bushes. A hundred yards away there were two tents with goats and pick-up vans parked outside. As they walked away they stumbled over empty Pepsi cans, old tyres and sheep skulls.

'It's hideous!' Vivienne complained.

'We're too close to the road. Later we'll drive off over there, to the south. Bertram said they found some really beautiful, unspoilt valleys.'

'But we might get lost. We don't have maps or anything.'

'There aren't any.'

'But what if we break down? Who would ever know?'

'You can't have it both ways. Even if we do break down, we've got tools in the back and enough water and food for a few days.'

But she trod with distaste over the litter on the way back to the car. Vivienne didn't have much sense of adventure; a five-mile walk in the New Forest was as close to nature as she wanted to get. Driving off over uncharted sands, exploring alien squalor – it wasn't how she would choose to spend her weekends. Then she remembered how happy they had been the night before. She dropped his hand, ran back to the Jeep, climbed into the driving seat and turned the key in the ignition. The right to drive, which had never before seemed much of a privilege, made her dizzy with power now that it was denied her. She shot off towards Christopher and drove round him in wild circles.

Although at first she found the desert ugly, it soon engulfed all other landscapes in Vivienne's mind: the soft, flat glades in the New Forest, seaside cliffs and proms and the friendly, humane olive terraces of Tuscany. Underpinning them all were these bare bones of geology, harsh craters and desolate plains. Because she couldn't live without making stories, she kept trying to humanize the strange rock formations, to pretend this one was the ruins of a great fortress, that one the result of an ancient nuclear explosion. She could hardly bear to acknowledge that in the desert there had been no history because people hadn't been able to leave any mark on it.

Speeding along in their fast air-conditioned Jeep, they had an illusory sense of power. But whenever they stopped, Vivienne imagined clusters of people on foot struggling from one water-hole to the next. It sickened and depressed her to think that life could be so harsh. There seemed no point whatever to all that hardship, yet it made their own comfortable exploration appear trivial, an insult to all those others who had suffered there.

The prehistoric sea had left so many traces that sometimes when they stopped she felt it was still washing over them, invisible and imperceptible to the senses, like radiation. Beach everywhere, with rocks and caves where it would be low tide for the next few million years. Christopher found the fossilized skeleton of a complete fish and Vivienne picked up a shell fossil which, she insisted, still smelled of salt. Again and again they tried to photograph the strange, abstract beauty of the desert, which was so richly suggestive when you stood in the middle of it. But all their photographs looked crude, blobs of orange, red and yellow against a bland sky. The desert didn't want to be seen.

'Leo's given me a map to the Hidden Valley,' Christopher said one Friday morning as they set off.

'It can't be very well hidden or he wouldn't have found it.' Vivienne was still bad tempered after a week trapped in the office with Rosemary, unable to walk freely around the all-male school. 'I suppose we'll get there and find all your colleagues sitting around having a barbecue.'

'God forbid.'

They avoided other people to intensify their renewed closeness. *Tosca* blaring, Christopher zipped through the suburbs of the has-boomed city. All around them new apartment blocks and offices had been left half finished and untenanted, to crumble expensively back into the desert. Driving like this, so fast and unreal, Vivienne always expected to crash. Somehow it all went together: the opera, their new prosperity, the flashy car and their melodramatic death. She didn't think it would hurt, to die in Riyadh.

An hour later they were bumping and jolting over the stones. Every few minutes Vivienne's head slammed against the padded ceiling, and as the car lurched down into yet another trough in the sand she thought, he won't get out of this one. The track narrowed, and they just managed to squeeze through, past sheer rock on their left.

'Leo's map's probably wrong,' Vivienne said cheerfully.

They didn't really care where they were going; they only wanted to drive fast, away, over the top. The car was their horse and they rode it hard, flogged it over the impossible terrain, defied it to throw them off its back as they galloped into oblivion.

'I'll get brain damage if I bang my head again,' Vivienne said as she did. 'It would be easier to get out and walk. It's quite cool this morning.'

But the car was part of their identity in the desert and they both felt uneasy if they wandered out of sight of it. She took over at the wheel, charged with the energy it always gave her to drive in the desert. It was the only time she felt in control of her own destiny, which had come to seem such a flimsy thing in Saudi Arabia. She egged herself on to more and more daring feats; I've never been interested in cars yet here I am, acting out some macho fantasy, she thought as she hurtled round a bend and through a narrow opening in the rock. The Hidden Valley, it's really more like a rather grand canyon. As if American oil money's so charismatic that a little piece of the Wild West had spontaneously flown there. Like the holy household flying from Nazareth to Loreto in Italy.

Vivienne had the familiar sensation of guilt, because they were about to spoil this unspoilt landscape with the trappings of the city they were escaping from. Methodically, they lumbered between the car and the flat rock they had chosen to be their table. Soon their jerrycans, cold boxes, folding bed, Thermos flasks, grill, charcoal and blankets covered an area the size of a sitting-room. While they waited for the fire to heat up they lay back on their red and pink floral canvas sunbed. As Christopher had remarked, it brought a touch of Surbiton to the desert. He was both aroused and soothed by the way their bodies fitted together into the narrow space. He clasped her breasts from behind and pressed against her taut buttocks.

'Can't you see the fascination of the desert now? I think it must have been terribly romantic before cars and air-conditioning and motorways.'

'Romantic for who? You and I wouldn't have survived in it for very long.'

'You couldn't have done very much, of course . . .'

'I can't do much now. As for being a black bundle stuck in the women's half of the tent, my eyes glued together with sand and flies, with only camels and my twelve kids for company – that doesn't appeal to me at all.'

'How prosaic you are. I think it would have been wonderful to go out riding with the Bedu, fifty or a hundred years ago. I was reading Glubb Pasha's descriptions of their raids the other day. He says they were "a cross between Arthurian chivalry and county cricket". You weren't allowed to attack between midnight and dawn, or steal each other's sheep or goats or women . . .'

'In order of importance.'

'Then at night there'd be wonderful stories, poems around the fire about heroes who died in battles centuries before. Imagine how close you'd become, alone in the desert, sharing food and drink and knowing that was really all you had. Thesiger writes about it so beautifully. He came back, you know, years later when the Jeeps and helicopters and water-tankers had arrived, and loathed it.'

An ancient fury, which had become far more acute since her arrival in Riyadh, surged up in Vivienne. 'Of course he loved it all. Of course it appealed to their mystical, masochistic, public-school souls. All that discomfort, and no women, just lots of handsome men being *Boys' Own* heroes together. You slogged away on camelback for a few months, got enough material for a book, established your racial superiority and then buggered off home where everyone made a fuss of you. Whereas the poor Bedu were stuck here, from malnourished birth to early death. They must have thought those rich white men were crazy, savouring desert squalor as if it was a rare wine.'

'Nonsense. It wasn't like that at all. You should read Thesiger. He had a wonderful relationship with them, and so did Lawrence.'

'According to them. Tribesmen don't write travel books, do they? Anyway Lawrence knew he was swindling the Arabs. He kept telling them England would reward them for their help by giving them independence but he knew his government wouldn't keep its promises. And as for despising the Bedu because finally, after thousands of years of starvation and vendetta, they can choose how they live – that's outrageous.'

'It's a pity you're so determined to hate it all.' Hate me, I mean, he thought gloomily.

She smiled at him. 'But I don't. I am beginning to see beauty

in the desert. I quite enjoy these trips now. But it's much easier for
you to identify with Arab culture than it is for me. I think a lot of
your colleagues like it here, too, even though they moan all the
time. Some of them'll probably stay on for years. Whereas I'm
excluded from almost everything. Where else in the world would
I have to spend most of my time trapped in an office with a woman
like Rosemary? Though, as a matter of fact, I'm becoming quite
fond of her. Learning to love my slavery.'

'Well, you're not a slave here.'

'No, that's why I keep coming back.'

'It's hot enough to cook on now,' Christopher said hastily
before she had time to articulate any more grievances.

Despite the heat they ate heartily, devouring steak, sausages,
baked potatoes and onions, salad, bananas and dates as if they
were eating on behalf of all those who had starved there in the past.
Afterwards, they lay back in suburban splendour with their eyes
shut and nuzzled each other, too bloated with food to do anything
more energetic.

'Excuse me. Do you speak English?'

They shot up and glared at a man in an emerald-green track suit
who had just materialized in the valley. For a moment Vivienne
wondered why her mirage should be so ignoble.

'Please excuse that I disturb your picnic. Haf you seen vun,
two, maybe sree people? Running? Ze Hash Harriers?'

'No,' Christopher said resentfully.

The man jogged off, disappearing almost immediately behind
the rocks. But their afternoon had cracked down the middle. Their
peace of mind in the desert rested on the illusion that they were
alone in it, proprietors of whichever tract of sand they chose to
discover that day. They wanted to share it only with creatures,
Bedu and decorative weekenders who put up their tents at a safe
distance. All the charm evaporated from the Hidden Valley now
they knew that teams of international hearties were competing just
beyond it. So they packed up again, consulted their amateur map
and decided to squeeze the Jeep through the narrow gap at the far
end of the valley.

Vivienne drove very fast to avoid getting stuck in the soft sand.
As she lurched towards the sheer rock face she squinted at the small
patch of blue which was her target, thinking of herself and the car
as an armoured tank. Images of the upside-down car wrecks which
sprawled all over the desert flashed through her mind as the car

leaped through the gap and she braked. An inch away a rocky abyss spread itself wide to embrace more skeletons of cars and camels.

Soon they were both so jolted and bruised that they felt ill. The plain which, according to the map, led back to the motorway, stretched for miles. It was seemingly flat but ditches opened up ahead of them and boulders slashed at the chassis. It was fun for the driver, who identified totally with the car, but boring and painful for the passenger. Vivienne reluctantly handed over the wheel as they approached a more inhabited area where she counted as a woman again. She sat back, punch-drunk from the shaking her bones and brain had received.

On their right a ridge of blood-red hills, high as mountains, blocked out the sky. The plain ahead was silvery, washed over with bigger grained orange sand. The colour and variety of the desert surprised her. At first it seemed a void, harsh and monotonous. Then, as your eyes adjusted, you found almost every kind of landscape subtly alluded to. It left something to the imagination, as her father used to say of radio. In fact Vivienne felt this was the kingdom of the imagination. She knew the green parks and gardens of England would seem banal and predictable by comparison.

As darkness approached, the colours of the plain deepened to brick red and purple and the ridge of hills grew almost black. Fear of the desert, which was never far away from Christopher, gripped his stomach like a sexual charge and made him drive even faster. Everyone had warned them not to go off alone like this. People did disappear. Their obsessive need to be alone together made them so vulnerable. They had intended to be back on the motorway long before it was dark, but now they wouldn't make it. He didn't want to camp out here on the plain. It was too exposed, too bleak, too treacherously open.

'Look at the tree!' Vivienne said in a high, frightened voice. Straight ahead was a scraggy, thorny, grey tree. Something was swinging from a rope tied to one of its shrivelled branches.

Christopher stopped the car abruptly. They got out and stood in the hot wind, staring up at the dead wolf. It was a desert wolf, pale and small, like a dehydrated Alsatian. Hardly room for Little Red Riding Hood in its shrunken stomach. Its throat had been cut and it had been strung up by its hind legs, as a warning or as a boast. It was nearly sunset, when insects, snakes, vultures and, for all they knew, wolves came out to hunt.

Christopher made the car gallop over the plain. Beside him, Vivienne settled into her weekday mood of brooding loneliness. As the sun blazed deep rich pink, gold and orange she glanced over to her right and saw a flock of skinny, sharp-faced, dusty sheep. They were being herded by a shepherd in Old Testament robes, and he waved at them as they passed. For a moment she saw his face and wondered why he should look after them so benignly. Ten minutes later they were on the motorway with the rest of the traffic commuting between Bedu weekends and hi-tech apartments. That picture of the old man with his sheep in the sunset stayed with Vivienne always, as if she had been presented with two thousand years in addition to her own life.

At the end of one of those weekends they came to Dariyah. The groves of dusty palms looked lush and jungle bright after the desert tones of beige and terracotta that still played behind their eyes. The town was full of Saudi men holding sheep-killing picnics, and the smell of charred flesh rising from their bonfires reminded Vivienne that the Turks had razed Dariyah, the ancient capital of the region. Gangs of bewildered Korean building workers wandered through the sandy ruins, trying to enjoy a day off in the closest thing Riyadh possessed to a tourist attraction. Vivienne watched as the Koreans asked an American couple if they could borrow their two small children to pose for photographs. All the men carried cameras and were smiling. They shouldn't smile, she thought angrily. Like that poor old man with the sheep, they've got nothing to be happy about. The men took it in turns to pose in the rubble with the bored, pouting, flawlessly blond children. Men and children wore identical clothes, the cotton T-shirts and jeans with which America had colonized the world. The photographs would be sent home to real children, who had no other image of their fathers.

Vivienne wandered through the labyrinth of ruined houses, hoping to acquire a sense of the place by being alone in it. She fingered the walls and lintels of the houses which looked as if they had been destroyed in the Second World War, instead of over a century earlier. The dry air preserved all, decelerated history and desiccated ghosts. She heard Christopher calling her anxiously, his footsteps pounding after her with a solicitude which ought to have been flattering, but only added to her blankness.

Later they drove through the new, inhabited area of Dariyah, smaller and more sociable than Riyadh. Men and boys in white thobes congregated in the dusk. Outside small white houses, dusty carpets had been unrolled to make outdoor living-rooms where groups of friends sat, talked, lounged, smoked, drank mint tea and brewed coffee in brass pots with cruelly curved beaks. The women in black seemed to have melted away into the darkness, wished into oblivion. Driving past one of these outdoor parties, Vivienne stared at the men's thin, animated faces, illuminated by the lurid acetylene lamps beside them. She reached out, as if to feel their warmth and touch this confident, articulate civilization to which she would never have access.

During the week the foreigners exchanged inadequate maps like keys to a private mythology. All those who had experienced the desert intensely had something in common. They shared their Jack London gazetteer; the Hidden Valley, the Red Sands, the Petrified Forest, the Escarpment and the Limestone Gorge. The desertscape existed outside time. It had wormed outwards from their inner life, a manifestation of images they had dreamed.

The Red Sands were the colour of brick dust pulverized with dried blood. Their corrugated waves were voluptuous, like the long red hair of a Pre-Raphaelite beauty. The dunes rippled in diagonal slabs across the electric-blue sky, and opposite them an emerald-green circle of irrigated wheat sparkled as lazy sprinklers rained on it. The colours were so intense, the red the blue and the green, that it hurt the eyes to see them. Vivienne could feel the ruthless heat of the colours burn deep into her memory, where they scorched away the delicate halftones and pastels of her childhood.

At the wheel, Christopher was afflicted with the same colour madness. He crouched forward and slammed his foot down on the accelerator as they lurched off the road and swooped over the soft red mountain. The car, the sleek white symbol of their will, zigzagged wildly up and down the slithering dunes. They waltzed in huge circles, listening to Elizabethan madrigals as the colours whirled around them. They were both shouting with laughter, swept up in a dry red wave of exuberance.

At first when they realized they were stuck, it was part of the joke and they continued to laugh. The wheels spun helplessly in the trough, like legs in a nightmare which have no power. Their elation dropped slowly as the temperature rose and it occurred to

them that there was no AA, no phone, no one to call for help. It
was midday in early December, hot as the hottest summer day in
England. As the music and the air-conditioning cut out, they had
a taste of what it is really like in the desert. After swigging pints of
tepid water from a plastic jerrycan they felt their flesh grow tight
and itchy. Suddenly the car was a small tin box on inadequate
wheels and they were trapped in it, slowly cooking.

When the claustrophobia became unbearable Vivienne jumped
down and tried to run off over the sand. But her feet slid backwards
as the red velvet powder sucked her in. It was like treading water
in a swelling current, although the water had evaporated millions
of years before. The colours were so different, now that she was
inside them. The hot red sand was flecked with yellow and gold
and littered with pebbles, rocks, Pepsi cans, sheep skulls and tyres.
The brilliant green circle of wheat on the hill opposite made her
want to leap across and shower beneath its expensive sprinklers.
And the sky, which had seemed so benign, was ferocious now as it
beat a headache down on her and dried the spit in her throat. I feel
so small, she admitted to herself, a speck on cotton-wool legs.
People and cars are buried here under the dunes, Robbie's full of
horror stories – Christopher caught up with her, lolloping with
difficulty against the hot wind. His sneakers were weighed down
with fine sand, and there was sand in their nostrils, ears and eyes.
Sand was claiming them like dust and ashes.

They waded back to the car and sat in it. Huge flies buzzed
around the hot fig rolls and Barb-Y-Q Snax they ate from sweating
plastic containers. Lunch left them feeling stickier and drier than
ever. Their eyes were red, their skin and hair were dull. It was too
hot for them to sleep or talk or respond to each other. The colours
throbbed as their eyes flickered, exhausted by the orgy of light.
People hallucinate in the desert out of boredom, Vivienne
thought, too stupefied to try to talk.

When they heard the other engine they stumbled down and ran
towards the sound, flapping their arms and yelling. Their shadows
stretched, attenuated, flowing backwards over the dune. At first
they could perceive their rescuers only as human, oases of flesh in
a universe of sand. They were also French and very efficient,
towing their car out of the trough with ridiculous ease.

One morning they bounced over a plain of dreary beige, brown and yellow, littered with a few shrubs. The sky was an oppressive muddy yellow and all the sallow desert waited for the rains that hadn't come. Vivienne's spirits lifted as they climbed a hill that relieved the flatness. She remembered a similar hill where they had camped the previous summer and watched a magnificent display of summer lightning staged, it seemed, for their benefit. Perhaps it was the same hill: she still had very little sense of direction in the desert. On the other side of the hill dark sand was almost hidden beneath thousands of stones and boulders which had been glazed a deep ox-blood red, purple and black. Around the shattered plain a small range of hills rose.

Vivienne didn't want to break the beautiful stones with their wheels. 'Let's leave the car and walk.'

Mechanically, Christopher backed and braked. They got out and walked over the burnt-out plain, in silence, for they felt less and less need to talk on these excursions. All week they bickered, complained and entered into exhausting banter contests with the other teachers. In the desert they were content, most of the time, to listen to music and watch the alien beauty unfold. They felt almost porous, as if the sand had entered them and turned them into statues that absorbed impressions.

They stooped to examine the charred and broken stones. 'There's been an explosion here.' She still wanted to identify with the desert. 'Do you think there might have been a volcano here, ages ago?'

'I don't know. Maybe just the sun, burning down. All through Egyptian, Greek and Roman times, and for a few million years before that.' Christopher yawned. The desert's history or lack of it exhausted him.

'Look, there's a cave in the hill over there. Let's have lunch in it.' She was eager to possess this mysterious place by playing house for a few hours.

They trudged back to the car and hauled food, water and charcoal back across the plain, stumbling over the boulders which became bigger and more jagged where the ground rose towards the cave. Although it was only about thirty feet above the plain, in the flat, low landscape even that elevation gave them a sense of power.

Framed in the entrance to the cave, they watched the first heavy, rusty raindrops of the year plop on to the sand. If it rains for a few hours, Christopher thought, the sand will turn to mud and even our Jeep won't be able to get through. But again, the danger wasn't real. They stared out at the soggy desert with amused detachment as they ate lamb chops and baked potatoes.

'In pre-Islamic times the people here used to worship caves. And wells and trees.'

'You can see their point.'

'They had goddesses before they had gods. And polyandry, it was a matriarchy. The mother's blood, not the father's, was what counted. Like with the Jews.'

'Until Muhammad came along and spoilt all the fun?'

'I think they were scared of women's power. That's why they had to cover them up and destroy their sexuality and hide them away from life. So, before that dreary misogynistic Bedu life you find so romantic, there were powerful women living in these caves. Choosing men and discarding them and having babies by anyone they liked.'

'Sounds just like expatriate life.'

'Ha ha.'

'I'd still like a few weeks on camelback, crossing the Empty Quarter with my *Boys' Own* gang, starving and suffering together. Shall I sing you a Bedu chant?'

'If you must.'

He cleared his throat and droned:

> 'God endures for ever
> The life of man is short,
> The Pleiades are overhead,
> The moon's among the stars.'

His voice, a light tenor, echoed backwards into the dark cave and out over the saturated plain. Vivienne was moved; the human voice raised in song seemed appropriate there, as conversation wasn't. After their toasted marshmallows and cardamom coffee they sat together and sang, Vivienne's flat contralto weaving in and out of his more tuneful voice. They sang hymns, carols, folk-songs, pop songs and madrigals. The rain washed the rocks a shinier black, a deeper purple, a more voluptuous shade of burgundy, and the sands beneath were ochre. A rich smell of vegetation waiting to burst back into life rose up to their cave. The wet desertscape looked and smelled familiar to their English senses. When the ponderous rain stopped, Vivienne leaped down

over the boulders, which were slippery now. The sand wasn't
slimy, as they had expected, but firmer than before. Her sandals
slapped down on crisp slabs of it, the texture of a beach at low tide.
She ran to a twisted pile of black stones she had been staring at
from the cave. At the top she stood and waved to Christopher,
wishing he could share in her exultation. By the time she had run
back to him this moment of release, of pure uncomplicated
happiness, would have passed.

That night the moon turned the sand into snow wedged under
lumps of coal. In the cave Vivienne had a dream that showed she
wasn't really unaware of the dangers around them. She was alone
in the desert at night. Christopher had driven off without her, his
headlights had been swallowed up by the blackness and she had no
voice with which to call out to him. Without him, the desert was
suddenly vast and terrifyingly alien. She had no place here and the
sands and stones and creatures hated her, wanted revenge for her
blundering invasion of their territory. They were combined
against her in a vendetta, the laws of which she couldn't
understand. Vivienne's impulse to run after the car weakened as
she felt their combined venom drain her of energy. All her
weaknesses were present in the dream, too, every incident that had
ever shamed or embarrassed her, a personal hell that joined forces
with the army of unknowable desert powers; snakesouls,
bouldersouls, scorpionsouls and beetlesouls. She crouched behind
one of the rocks and tried to hide until morning. But there was no
chance of rest. The night was sending out an emissary of its
hatred, some creature was approaching, snarling and grunting,
sniffing for the sacrifice that had been left out for it. . . .

When Vivienne woke up she was sobbing with terror. She
squeezed Christopher in the sleeping-bag they shared and sucked
the sleeping flesh of his shoulder. For the first time in months she
acknowledged how much she needed him. Then she opened her
eyes and gazed around the cave, which suddenly looked like a dark
mouth ready to spew out terror. An insane place to camp. She
guarded Christopher until dawn and then let him snore and
rumble for three more hours. Perhaps he was more attuned than
her to the spirits of the place. At breakfast, as if the night was
teasing her with evidence, they discovered huge jagged
toothmarks in the plastic top of a cylinder of crisps that had been
beside their bed all night.

During the short rainy season a yellow malaise settled over Riyadh. The teachers, trapped in the school and the Villa Despair, resorted to desperate measures to entertain themselves. They set up a dartboard with the face of Robbie, the school's director, on it; they sat at their windows lobbing empty bottles down into the Prince's compound; and spent hours rolling marbles at the huge brown cockroaches, the shape of lobsters, which now infested the Villa Despair. Not even the Hash Harriers ventured into the desert during the rainy season.

Three weekends in a row Christopher and Vivienne mouldered in the Villa Despair. They breathed in bitterness and frustration and bickered all the time, as they had at the beginning. Vivienne stayed in bed for three days with an illness Rosemary called flu. Distemper, Vivienne called it to herself: her eyes and skin grew dull, her red hair mangy.

One Saturday they woke up after a particularly hectic night of cockroach baiting.

'Let's get out, let's get back,' she mumbled.

'To the desert?'

'Yes. If there's a flood, we'll turn back.'

The streets they drove through were shallow rivers where barefoot children paddled and splashed. They passed two little boys who sat in the middle of the road, calmly fishing with sticks. Twenty minutes out of Riyadh they turned off the main road and passed a ruined mud village, a remnant of pre-Opec civilization, which was slithering back into the sand.

They drove past The Dam, as it was marked on all the expatriate maps. Usually it was a big, dry, muddy hole to the left of the track. But today it was churning with khaki waves, which had the hallucinatory power that water has in the desert. Vivienne thought, people from wet countries fantasize about desert islands and palm trees, and Arabs have invented a paradise of grass, trees, flowers and fountains. Now it's as if the two ideal landscapes are merging.

Past the dam, shrubs appeared, and small, tough wild flowers. Camels placidly chomped their new pasture with enormous teeth and leather gums. Vivienne wandered among them and examined the shrubs, which were the same withered bundles of brown and yellow they had passed before, now suddenly glossy and sleekly green. The wild flowers seemed to be distantly related to European ones. There were hefty buttercups and roses and primroses wearing heavy crowns of thorns, gripping on to life by tough roots that drove far down under the ground. From the car Christopher sat and watched her, listening to Kathleen Ferrier sing about places where wetness and fertility were taken for granted:

> 'Is it not sweet to hear the breeze singing
> As lightly it comes o'er the deep rolling sea?'

They drove alongside the wadi which they had so often crossed, walked down and picnicked on. The water had changed all its contours. They got out of the car to explore the rocks at the end of the wadi, which had filled up to become rock pools. In one of them some sort of tadpole was swimming. How miraculous, Vivienne thought. Where did he come from? How can eggs survive, let alone hatch, in the ovens these rocks are, eleven months of the year? But I suppose he just feels like any other tadpole. If tadpoles feel. They walked beside the wadi, trying not to destroy any of the life that seethed at their feet. Armies of insects were fleeing between the newly sprouted plants.

Then, in the distance, they heard a great roar, the uncontrollable noise of a natural disaster. The desert should have been silent except when they chose to break the silence. Oh God, Vivienne thought, an earthquake. And the insects knew it was coming, of course. They stopped the car and looked around, suddenly aware of their vulnerability. The roar pressed down on their eardrums, coming nearer.

Then Christopher pointed to a long finger of water trickling towards them down the dried-up river-bed. In fear and excitement they ran to meet it. The roar of the water was so loud now that it pounded in their brains and hearts, their blood surged with it. On their right the brown river insatiably filled every crevice of the wadi and lapped the sandy banks at their feet. Within minutes the plain was transformed into embryo meadows. The river swept along thousands of plants and insects, while thousands more escaped over the sand. Vivienne wondered if all the other wadis had been resurrected as well, so that they were now standing on one of a series of islands.

They took off their shoes and socks and dipped their feet in the water. Then, when they found the wild new river came only up to their knees, they became more reckless. They splashed and laughed and danced and squelched, giving themselves willingly to the vital waters.

A Thousand and One Coffee Mornings

My dear Andrew,

What a pity you couldn't manage to get to the airport on time. Luckily Poppy came to see me off, and Sylvia, both of them much amused by the fact that one of the Prince's 'heavies' met me at the Saudia desk and ushered me into the VIP waiting area, where women have to sit behind screens. Peeping out, we saw a number of men, aged between twenty and sixty, dressed in long white robes. Poppy, whose views have always been somewhat racist, nudged me and said, 'Don't come back married to one of them, will you?' I was about to explain that I am at least forty years too old to appeal to any of them, but they were staring at us and I disliked the view we presented to them – three elderly English women giggling like schoolgirls. I'm afraid Poppy is too deeply rooted in colonial India, where she grew up, ever to change. She seemed convinced that I was going to teach some 'Raja, Sheikh or whatever' table manners, and kept advising me to join the English Club and order a mosquito-net from Lillywhites. It won't be like that, I kept explaining. But of course I had no idea what it would be like.

Sylvia was more tactful, although she also seemed incredulous that I was really going. She pressed books into my hands – Freya Stark and Thesiger and several contemporary studies of Saudi Arabia, the covers of which she had ripped off. They were all inscribed meticulously, *For my dear friend Barbara to read in her harem.* With the possible exception of myself, Sylvia is the most passionate

105

advocate I know of books as a panacea. When it became clear that you weren't going to turn up (the 'heavy' was sent off to look for you), I had a craving for some bacon. As Poppy said, rather like a condemned prisoner's last wish. So we went off to a sordid eating area, full of litter, screaming children and nauseating technicolour photographs of hamburgers and chips. I devoured eggs, bacon, sausages, toast and marmalade while the other two gaped at me. As you know I rarely eat breakfast, but somehow my apprehension and excitement had gone to my stomach and gnawed a great hole there.

I nearly phoned you before going through passport control. Then I thought, he's probably still in bed and I'm tired of worrying about with whom. Sylvia and Poppy hugged me warmly and compassionately. I haven't been so generally pitied since your father died. As our ways diverged I remembered that they were returning to that most unenviable existence, stranded gentlewomanhood in a seaside town on a small pension. Whereas I might be able to afford something more stylish in a few years. Perhaps a little flat in London, if you could put up with having me so near? You know that in our circles we don't talk much about money. However, the subject does cross our minds occasionally and, as I boarded the plane, the prospect of quadrupling my income made my old friends' pity a little easier to bear.

I must say this VIP nonsense has something to recommend it. I was given a most comfortable window seat next to a delightful young man who is studying to be a pilot in Scotland. He was returning to his family in Riyadh for the Easter holidays. Ahmed isn't a bit like one of our students, I'm glad to say. Terribly well dressed and polite, with the kind of deference to an older person which is sadly out of fashion nowadays. Before we reached Paris he had invited me to meet his mother and sisters and had practically adopted me as an honorary grandmother. I remember how Sylvia always used to say, 'The worse one gets on with one's own children, the easier it is to get on with other people's.'

As the only non-Arab woman travelling first class I caused a mild sensation. Half my fellow travellers turned out to be related to my Prince (when I finally managed to pronounce his name). The food was very pleasant, a considerable improvement on Skyways Pennywise Ecoclass. No alcohol, of course, but prayers on taking off and landing, which I thought a charming touch. The lack of alcohol is not going to present many problems for me, as it doubtless would for you. But we won't go into that again. Ahmed showed me a gold watch he had bought in Switzerland which, in addition to showing the time and the date, bleeps insistently five times a day when it is prayer-time in Mecca.

After chatting to Ahmed for a while I found myself longing to read but terrified of offending my companion by my choice of reading material. The briefing notes the British Council sent me were so full of Don'ts that I still have no idea what is permissible. I took off my shoes to relax and then worried that I might unwittingly point the soles of my feet at someone (an unforgivable insult). I thought of reading one of the books Sylvia had given me, but it might contain sympathetic references to Israel – marked on Saudi maps as occupied Palestine – or criticisms of the Saudi royal family. The other books in my hand-luggage were *Tess of the D'Urbervilles*, a dishonoured trollop, and *Anna Karenina*, who would have been publicly stoned (hardly worse than her actual fate). While I agonized over what to read, my companion told me what he thought of life in a small Scottish town. He was absolutely bewildered by the inhospitality, the weather, the consumption of alcohol and the callousness shown towards ageing parents and grandparents.

'You are putting them in zoos. Why you are calling them homes? My home is my family, mother, father, sister. Not this locking up in big house, everybody old, everybody sad. Very bad. Same same prison.'

'Yes,' I said sadly, thinking of the fate that awaits us all on the Costa Geriatrica.

'How much babies have you got?'

'One son. He's not a baby, he's older than you.'

'He is putting you in this prison home?'

'I hope not. I'm coming to your country to make enough money to be able to choose my life when I am old.'

He looked disgusted at this. I was dying to ask questions about his culture but didn't know where to begin. Before we reached Cairo I was calling him Ahmed and he was making valiant attempts to pronounce my surname, which came out sounding like Fairy Clugg. So I became Mrs Barbara.

The lights were dimmed and all around us substantial figures lay back in their seats, substituted leather sandals for Gucci shoes, relaxed and expanded inside their Old Testament robes. There was a smell of aftershave, coffee and leather. Arab men of all ages

pay great attention to their appearance. They were all plucked and
perfumed and spent ages adjusting their *ghutras* when they woke up
after their naps. It seems to me that their obsession with
masculinity is mixed up with a strong streak of narcissism and
effeminacy. I couldn't help noticing several pairs of men wandering up the ramp hand in hand as we were boarding! Ahmed
slept for an hour, while I read a stirring account of how King
Abdul Aziz recaptured the fortress in Riyadh as a young man in
1903 and gradually unified the whole country behind his family.
It's a marvellous story, and many of the international business
men snoring on the plane were old enough to remember some of
it. The older ones must have been born in mud palaces, had little
formal education and no experience of the outside world until they
were adult. But the boys Ahmed's age radiate faith and confidence
in the sophisticated technology they've grown up with. They are
about a thousand years beyond their fathers and grandfathers.
However, it seemed to me, looking around the plane, that the
older men have a more regal air. My prince, during that
formidable interview I told you about, strode around the drawing-
room in Sunningdale like a not very benevolent despot. The
younger ones like Ahmed have felt the shadow of Western neurosis
and are not quite so certain about things. I felt some tenderness as
Ahmed's head slid down on to my shoulder, and I turned the pages
carefully so as not to jolt him. I couldn't imagine an English boy
whom I had just met treating me with such unconscious
trustfulness. Indeed I wouldn't want most young English heads on
my shoulder. I would be afraid of catching something, or of some
unsavoury dye or chemical rubbing off.

When Ahmed woke up, I asked if he had many friends in
Scotland.

'Girl-friends, very many. Too much girls. Boy-friends, never.'

I tried to ask whether he had encountered a lot of racism.

'At first, before I left Riyadh, my uncle he said: "In England,
never say you are coming from Saudi Arabia. They will steal your
money." So I am saying always I am from Kuwait or Dubai. But
for these people there is no difference. All Arabs are rich and
stupid for them. I have a flat, a car, money to go to clubs and
restaurants. The girls chase after me, the boys start fights. They
hate me, really. When there is holiday I am going always back to
Riyadh because there are my friends.'

I made foolish apologetic noises. As we approached Saudi

Arabia I felt that we were, increasingly, formal representatives of our cultures. He gave me his telephone number, having told me that he had never been invited inside an English house. I wondered if I should be able to visit him, or only his female relatives. I was on my way to a society even more exclusively female than Palatine Hill. Looking around, I noticed that there were only two other women in first class, both draped in black from head to foot and courteously ignored by all the men. It was quite impossible to tell whether either of the women was married to any of the men. All the seats around the two women were empty, as if they had been deliberately isolated. I kept staring at them. They talked and giggled in high-pitched voices and I caught glimpses of earrings, bracelets and necklaces flashing as they moved their arms. One of them had a little girl of about three who ran all over the plane and was hugged, fed and played with by all the men, including Ahmed.

About half an hour before we were due to land, I felt a wave of panic. The aeroplane was neutral territory, but soon I would belong to the Prince. He would hold my passport, his minder would meet me and drive me off into the night. Of course a woman like me has no fears for her virtue and it was clear from Ahmed's behaviour that I don't really count as a woman. Still, I felt unpleasantly helpless. I noticed that as we approached Riyadh the men became more relaxed. The sight of a bearded man in robes and sandals shuffling down Oxford Street has always made me want to titter, and this faint aura of buffoonery was still attached to them until just before we landed. Then I realized how their dignity increased as they approached a world where nobody dared to laugh at them. The women, however, grew less animated, their voices sharper as they scolded the exhausted child.

When the plane landed, people disgorged from the cheaper seats on the other side of the curtain. I got up and reached for my hand-luggage but the minder, who had ignored me throughout the journey, indicated that I was to sit down again. Ahmed said mysteriously, 'Waiting for next terminal.' Only three or four of the first-class passengers got off. Then the doors shut again, the plane taxied a few hundred yards, stopped, and the doors opened once more. 'This, Royal Terminal,' Ahmed explained, pronouncing it 'Real'. I realized that all these twenty-odd men were princes. This appealed to my snobbery and my sense of humour in about equal proportions. It was rather glamorous and

Arabian Nights to have have all these members of the royal (real) family jostling one another to help me carry my bag and help me and the other two women off the plane. But it was also ludicrous. If twenty princes happened to be travelling from London to Riyadh on one day, how many must there be altogether? Hundreds? Thousands?

The terminal was the closest thing I have ever seen to a palace built by one of the later, nastier Roman emperors. All gold plated pillars, marble, gaudy mosaics, flowers and fountains. At Palatine Hill we had, for obvious reasons, models of the palaces on the original Palatine, which we used for ancient history projects with the girls. I can assure you Nero and Caligula were quite tasteful compared with these people.

My bags weren't searched, as I had feared. I glided through – bags magically carried, doors magically opened, passport quietly pocketed by the minder – to a disgustingly big car, which brought me here. And I really have no idea where I am! Behind quite a few locked gates and doors, in a large room with a balcony and a very flashy bathroom. You will laugh and call me a fussy old insomniac when I tell you I sat down right away and started to write this.

Now it's six o'clock in the morning and a wonderful golden pink dawn is breaking over the roofs of a large complex of buildings, in one of which I seem to be living. I shall try to get some sleep now, although I really feel too excited. I shall write again soon, and expect to hear from you. Please don't use the post as an excuse as you did when I went to Greece on the field trip. I hope you are managing better for money. It seems to me your salary should be quite adequate.

> Your affectionate mother,
> Barbara Fairclough

November 25

My dear Andrew,
   I was surprised and touched to receive your telex. Thank you. Although I would remind you that words like 'pissed' are offensive to Islamic sensibilities. Most things are. And your reference to the articles was most unwise. After all the palace has its own telex machine. Somebody received your message and he (I'm sure it wasn't a she) must understand English, as there are no mistakes. I don't think you have any idea how precarious my situation here is or how seriously one must take all these taboos, which you persist in treating as a joke. It is probable that almost everything is censored – including my letters, for all I know, although I can't bring myself to write them as if they were. Now that I'm here I realize I couldn't possibly write the articles we discussed. It would be too dangerous and, frankly, I can't think what I would have to write about. Perhaps, after a few months, I will come to feel I have gained some insight into life here, but at the moment I have only a bewildering string of impressions.
   That first morning I didn't sleep, but lay down fully clothed on my bed and listened to the sounds of the palace awakening. I felt as if I was staying in a very big and expensive hotel, but wasn't sure whether I was there as a guest or as a servant. Dozens of feet padded down corridors, and pans clattered in a kitchen that seemed to be just beneath my room. By seven, when I went out on to my balcony, there was a glaring blue sky. The palace compound consists of four large buildings, linked by lawns, flower-beds and gravel paths, all too neat and symmetrical to be attractive. The building I am living in is a particularly nauseating shade of pink, with pale-green window-frames and shutters. In the gardens I could see several concrete fountains and lamp-posts, and a green and white striped awning beneath which, I hoped, there might be a swimming-pool. A high green metal wall surrounds the complex of buildings, and I could see beyond it only by leaning suicidally over the balustrade of my balcony. Then I caught a glimpse of a road, a sandy wasteland and more ugly new buildings behind high walls. In the gardens male servants dressed in long white nightshirts moved around with the characteristic gait of the place, which I would describe as a slow rush. The backless sandals which most people wear make them shuffle and shamble, so that running is largely symbolic. Just under my balcony eight young men sat in

a circle, laughing and chatting as they dipped bread into big dishes and poured coffee from a pot with a curved beak into tiny china cups. They looked so relaxed and intimate that I smiled enviously. Then one of them looked up, saw me and cried out in alarm. They cleared up their delightful picnic and disappeared.

Rather sad at having ruined their party, I went inside and closed the french windows and shutters, so that stripes fell across my white bed. On the table beside it was a telephone which I half expected to ring with a summons from the Prince. I thought of phoning Ahmed, the only person in the whole city I could think of as a friend. But he was a man, and young. Taboos which had not existed when we chatted on the plane surrounded him now. I was in a thwarted holiday mood. My room looked as if it was in a luxurious Mediterranean hotel, and it would have been wonderful to go downstairs, have breakfast in a bar and spend the day sunbathing on a beach. But I had no idea how much freedom of movement, if any, I had. In the distance I could hear nasal pop music, a child crying, a car starting. Nobody had told me to stay in my room, yet I felt compelled to.

I washed, changed and tried to read. At about nine a pretty Arab maid knocked on my door with some breakfast on a tray. She smiled and said 'Welcome' (pronounced 'will come'), and disappeared before I could talk to her. I laid out my breakfast on my desk – a pot of strong coffee and two excellent croissants. Again, traces of the Riviera holiday I wasn't having. I ate nervously and too fast, suffered a terrible scourge of indigestion, took a couple of Rennies and had to lie down again. I must have fallen asleep for a couple of hours.

I was woken by a noise outside my door, a hard click followed by a slurping thud, repeated again and again. I couldn't get back to sleep and the sound began to alarm me because I could find no explanation for it. At last I tiptoed to the door, opened it and found myself staring down at a man with a squint wearing a striped nightshirt which was rucked up most indecently around his thighs! I'm afraid I panicked. I ran down the white marble corridor to escape my attacker. But while I ran, I rationalized. I remembered there had been a bucket of water and a mop beside the man and he had not in fact attacked me. It occurred to me that I didn't really want to make my first public appearance in the palace in the role of a hysterical elderly woman fleeing from an imaginary assault. Before I reached the stairs I stopped, turned, and walked slowly back down the corridor. The cleaner smiled encouragingly, as if relieved that my impulse to jog had worn off. As I shut my door again I saw his hairy, knobbly knees sink to the floor again as the poor man scrubbed a new patch of floor. I sat on my bed and giggled, wishing I had someone to share the joke with and imagined him telling the other servants and laying the foundations for the inevitable myth of the crazy English woman upstairs.

I stayed in my room for days. Delicious meals came on trays. I slept a great deal, wrote letters and read the whole of *Anna Karenina* and *Tess*. The arrival of your telex this morning was most salutary. A call to duty, not that my duties here are at all clear. You oblige me to live up to the idea of my personality that you have, and I hear myself over the years telling you what you should or shouldn't do, not that my interference seems to have made the slightest difference to you. Yet I feel I must not give up. I can hear your voice too, sneering at me because I'm too puritanical. I hear so many voices here. I've always known that solitude was dangerous and designed the timetable at Palatine Hill to avoid it, both for myself and for the girls. In the absence of real people one populates the air with memories, dreams, the dead – this paragraph is quite shapeless so I shall start a new one.

Finally, this morning I ventured out of my room. This corridor is vast. I counted six doors beyond my room and eight more before I reached the top of the stairs. The scale of this building – of all palaces, I suppose – is absurd. It precludes all intimacy, beauty and utility. To judge by the silence most of these rooms are not used at all. At the top of the stairs I discovered another corridor, equally long and pompous looking, leading off in the opposite direction. Downstairs I found myself in a cavernous marble lobby, which was also deserted, and turned into a vast reception-room furnished with gaudy carpets and vulgar, oversized reproduction antiques. The shutters and double doors were closed and the room was extraordinarily gloomy and cold. The air-conditioning in all the rooms hits one like a wave of frost-bite whenever one opens a door.

I hadn't the heart to explore any further. Shivering, I went back into the lobby and sat on the stairs, where I decided to stay until some sign of human life reached me. Facing me was a door which led to the gardens I had seen from my balcony, but the door was locked, and out there were men, that alien race who would run away from me. I cursed myself for not having asked more

questions when I met the Prince that day in Sunningdale. I was so
bowled over by the salary he offered me that I was in a state of
shock. I realize now I should have interrogated him for hours,
demanding a map of the palace, a detailed job description and
volumes on etiquette.

After nearly an hour an Indian maid approached, carrying a
tray on which, I suspected, was my lunch.

'Today I shall eat in my room, thank you.'

'Madam not eat upstairs?'

'No.'

She looked puzzled but led me through several morgue-like
reception-rooms until we came to a smaller room full of books. She
laid my tray on a table which was only big enough for about six
people, and fled. This room was almost friendly, although I still
had nobody to talk to. I went over to the bookcase and tried to read
the titles through the locked wicker doors. But I could only
distinguish rows of beautifully bound leather volumes.

'Welcome.'

A woman with long, thick, black wavy hair and a beautiful,
melancholy face stood in the doorway. She wore a long blue satin
dress with long sleeves and a high neck and held herself very
straight. Her eyes were black, enormous, dignified and very sad.
She clasped her small pink hands under her chin and gesticulated
nervously with them. Unlike our British royals, she does look like
a princess, but one beneath a cruel nocturnal spell. Her name,
Aisha, means evening.

She made me feel awkward, old and grey. I apologized for being
there but she welcomed me in good, clipped, dreadfully polite
English. We had a slow conversation, like two sleepwalkers who
cannot quite wake up. I realized that this was her room, the only
mark she had been able to leave on the palace. She unlocked the
bookcase and proudly showed me the rows of Dickens, Melville,
Shakespeare and Agatha Christie as well as French and Arabic
books. 'Please, use my library,' she said.

A maid kept bringing tiny cups of coffee which I didn't know
how to refuse and, in my polite frenzy, I drank about ten of them
until my heart raced. I failed, just as I had done with the Prince,
to ask the right questions. The only information I managed to
extract was that she has four children and had grown up in a place
called Ta'if. The conversation swirled around us, formal,
repetitive and obsessively complimentary. I had no idea where the

Prince was or whether I was supposed to mention him. I had read somewhere that if you admire any object in an Arab house, your host or hostess is obliged to give it to you, so I tried not to be specific in my admiration. I marvelled at the beauty of her house, longed to see her children and almost swooned with pleasure to think how much I was going to enjoy Riyadh. I don't think I have suddenly become a compulsive liar but something about her, the place and the situation demanded this artificial behaviour. All the time I was thinking, she's an intelligent girl, serious, she must be as curious about me as I am about her. I told her how good her English was and she looked delighted.

'I came here to teach your husband.'

'My husband is very busy. He comes only sometimes to my house.'

'Your palace is very big.'

'Yes. Too big, too many houses.'

I wondered if the other houses contained other wives. If I was teaching her, I thought, I could ask some of the questions I don't dare ask in normal conversation. So I offered to teach her for an hour a day. Aisha responded with great warmth, suddenly looking young instead of matronly. Soon after, a driver knocked on the door and swept her off to some social engagement. I had to ask a maid to guide me back to my room! Altogether, in my travels around the palace this morning, I counted three staircases, five corridors and four reception-rooms.

It was a relief to have something to do. I looked through the textbooks I brought with me and planned a test and lesson for Aisha. Then I wrote this letter – but now I'm in a state about posting it. I gave the first one to a maid but immediately regretted it. What if there is an official censor inside the palace, or if the girl simply lost it? I shall have to post my letters myself, although I haven't yet left the palace and have no idea how to do so. I have spent a great deal of time watching cars go in and out of the gates, and tomorrow I shall venture out in one of them. I have been afraid to go out on my balcony again since I had such an alarming effect on the boys downstairs, but if I sit on my bed at a certain angle I can see over the walls. I have seen young men going in and out of the house on the corner. They are Europeans and I like to imagine they are English, just down from university. I expect they are learning Arabic and enjoying themselves here – I dare say this is a marvellous city if you're young, male and free.

In view of what I was saying I don't think it would be wise for you to write to me here again. I will obtain a post-restante address.

Your affectionate mother,
,   Barbara Fairclough

December 5

PO Box 2745
Riyadh
Saudi Aradia
(My address in future. To think
that I should end up in a PO box!)

My dear Andrew
   The mornings here start early and are very long. Before my lesson with Aisha at eleven I read voraciously – I have already finished most of the books I brought with me. I try to save letter writing to fill the evenings, which are even longer. Every night the windows of the central palace, over to my right, are ablaze. Huge black cars with tinted windows disgorge black silk women and Omo white men who disappear inside (separate entrances, of course). I also hear music, which comes I think from the servants, who sleep behind the kitchen on the floor beneath mine. At least they are part of a group, clearly identified, and are not isolated as I am. Not that I really envy them. It seems to me they're treated abominably. Even Aisha screams orders at them, and I've seen her eight-year-old son viciously kick and bite a maid, who of course could do nothing to retaliate. Slavery was only abolished here in the 1960s. I don't know on what basis these young men and women are here, but I suspect their wages are very low and they have little if any freedom of movement. Even less than me – but before I go into that I must tell you about my lessons with Aisha, the only event which could be of any possible interest to your newspaper. We'll talk about that when I see you next summer, although I still feel it would be rather tasteless to 'sell my story'. More to the point, do I have one?
   Aisha arrived at her first lesson on the dot of eleven. This punctuality of hers is most unSaudi, a habit she must have picked

up in Switzerland. Normally, appointments here are infuriatingly vague, and it is considered presumptuous to assume you will be anywhere at a fixed point in the future. She was wearing a long, green silk dress and looked radiant, as if something far more thrilling then *Kernel Lessons* was in store for her. Whenever I am in the same room as she is, I feel very old and dull. Shyly, that first morning, she shook her head when I held out my right hand to her. She spread out her hands, which are plump and pink with tapered fingers, and indicated that I should do the same. Sourly, I contrasted her exquisite hands with my yellow talons. Then she made my fingertips touch hers, gracefully, as if she was teaching my fingers to dance. She raised my index finger to her lips and kissed it (I didn't know whether I was supposed to kiss hers). Then she laughed at my confusion, sat down and waited demurely for her lesson.

We have quickly fallen into a teacher – pupil relationship – which is, perhaps, the only basis on which I can relate to young women. I think that's why I've failed to get on with your endless stream of girl-friends. There was nothing I could teach them. Aisha has a great thirst for knowledge and her passionate desire to obtain her First Certificate illuminates her like a vocation. The sticky politeness of our first meeting has vanished and she is quick and responsive now, overjoyed to be using her mind again. Although she obviously enjoys lessons, she rarely laughs and has no sense of irony. My little jokes fall quite flat.

Her children were away on holiday for the first week I was here, otherwise I would certainly have noticed them. There are four boys aged between four and eight – one a year, poor girl, and she can't be much over thirty. They are extremely noisy, destructive, barefoot louts who are rude to everyone, particularly their mother. I have been unable to think of anything complimentary to say about them, and Aisha's only boast about them is that they are boys, which is of course quite an achievement here. It probably consolidates her position with her husband (whom I still haven't seen). Every lesson we have is interrupted by some tantrum or fight. Their mother tells me they are going to Eton, although I think Borstal would give them a more fitting education. After a particularly unpleasant scene when Fouad, the eldest, beat up his four-year-old brother so savagely that the little one had to be rushed to hospital (all dealt with by the servants while Aisha looked on helplessly), Aisha said to me, 'In one year or maybe two

years, Fouad stays with his father.' She did not look heart-broken.
In fact I've seen no signs of any strong maternal feeling in her, which
might of course account for the boys' disturbed behaviour. I have
to keep my door looked as the boys appear to think I am a kind of
human trampoline. Their rooms are in the corridor near mine –
miles away from their mother – so I am rather at their mercy. Aisha
has suggested a children's English class, but I have been extremely
evasive and have no intention of letting myself in for anything of the
kind. Who knows how many more obnoxious little princes, princesses
and royal by-blows there are hidden away in these palaces? My days
of coping with children are past, and not regretted. Our girls at
Palatine Hill were really quite well behaved, although at the time
I often referred to them as spoilt brats. I can only say that, if this had
been my first experience of children, I would never have become a
schoolteacher and would probably not have conceived you either.

At the end of our first lesson, as Aisha got ready for one of her
mysterious social engagements, I asked about going out.

'Where?' She looked mildly surprised, as if she couldn't imagine
any reason to leave the palace compound.

'Well, to shops or to the post office, or just to explore Riyadh.
I haven't been anywhere yet, you know, or met anybody.'

I felt it was outrageous that I should have to justify my desire to
walk out of the palace gates. Yet I had just done so.

'If there is something you need, the maids will go to the shops.
And of course they will post your letters. They do not help you?'

Her face coarsened with the primitive bad temper I had already
seen her display towards servants and I hastened to defend them.

'Not at all, they've been most helpful. I should just like to go out
sometimes, walk around, have a look at the city.'

'It is not possible for ladies to walk alone in Riyadh. In England
the ladies are walking?'

'Yes. Sometimes I used to walk for hours.'

'Alone?'

'Usually. You've been to England. You know how we live.'

'I have been only one time to England. To Sunningdale.'

She made it sound wonderful – 'Sunn-eng-del'. She pronounces
Haslemere, 'Izmire'.

'There, the ladies did not walk because there was only mud.
Please, if you wish to leave my palace you must only telling me what
time you want the driver, where you are going and at what time you
are wanting to return.'

It seemed rather a lot. But by then letters to you and Sylvia were burning a hole in my bag and the prospect of returning to my empty room seemed unbearable. Still, it's most frustrating that I can't just go 'out for a stroll'. How I envy the young men over the wall, who wander freely in and out of their villa, jump into cars and drive away.

When at last I sat in the back of a hearse-like vehicle and glided through the gates, I felt absurd, as if I had chartered a helicopter to pick apples. Really all these restrictions aimed at protecting female virtue and beauty are ludicrous when applied to a tough old thing like me. I can't tell you how my sense of personal unattractivess has increased here – I shan't, it's too humiliating. One shouldn't revel in one's ugliness, it's a form of narcissism.

'Where to, madam?' Jamal, the Sudanese driver, asked.

'I would like to go to a post office and a bookshop.'

Almost immediately we were on a motorway, driving very fast past high modern buildings, American-style supermarkets and leftover patches of desert that reminded me of bomb-sites in London after the war. I had told Aisha that I would be gone for three hours, but after fifteen minutes racing through this hideous suburb I was ready to go home.

Jamal stopped outside a post office where I posted my letters and obtained my box number. But do be discreet, Andrew. No silly telexes like that one about the pygmy paedophiles you tried to embarrass me with at Palatine Hill. Then I was dropped off at a big, modern bookshop – I've no idea where. There was a large section of English books, which I fell upon: *The Mayor of Casterbridge*, *Moby Dick*, my dear *Portrait of a Lady* – even in paperback they looked so friendly and reassuring. I chose a dozen, at twice the price I would have paid at home. But since they are my only luxury I feel no qualms. I considered ordering a box of books every couple of weeks, as I am reading between one and two novels a day at the moment. But I decided that this would not match the pleasure of being able to go out myself to browse in a real bookshop.

I looked around, drinking in my first impressions of Saudi life. It was extraordinarily dull. Most of the customers were Saudi men buying stationery and calculators. I suppose they use them up fast. A black-veiled woman, utterly unapproachable, was looking at French books. It occurred to me that Aisha looks like this whenever she leaves the palace compound (if she does). A young woman barged through the glass doors with a push-chair and several bags of shopping. She wore a curious droopy black garment I'd noticed on several other women. It flapped over her jeans. Her face shiny from the heat, she came straight over to the English books and I was embarrassed by my relief at meeting a type I recognized.

'What a nice baby,' I said insincerely, as it slid out of its push-chair and crawled around on the floor, dribbling all over the Penguin Modern Poets. The male shop assistant came over to cuddle the child, something that would never happen in an English bookshop.

'I come here every day,' the girl said as the shop assistant carried the baby off to be admired by his colleagues and customers. 'It's the only break I get from being alone with Peter.'

'They do love children,' I said wonderingly.

'Yep. Pity they don't like women.'

'I also spend a lot of time here feeling isolated. I wish I could meet more people. I'm living in a palace, you know. I'm supposed to be teaching the Prince, but he's never there and I have nothing to do. . . .' I spoke very fast, eyeing the door as if I thought Jamal might burst in waving a scimitar to execute me for my disloyalty.

The girl cooled and I realized that I had sounded too desperate, that I represented too much of a threat to her precious reading time.

'If you really want to meet people, there are millions of coffee mornings you could go to. Haven't you been to the women's meetings at the Grand Festival Palace?'

'No. Do they really have that sort of thing here? I'd love to. Do you know this is the first time I've been out. When are these meetings?'

'The first Tuesday of each month. I went to one of them. I thought it was ghastly, but you might enjoy them.'

As I carried my pile of chosen opiates over to the cash desk, the noon call to prayer sounded. I was almost pushed out of the shop, and all around me on the pavement hot, flustered women in black rushed home. The Saudi women were solidly veiled and parcelled while the foreigners wore tattered fragments of black. Above them all boomed the voice of God the Father, the old killjoy with a beard as you used to call him when you were refusing to be confirmed. Some of the women were on foot, but most of them disappeared into cars driven by men. All over this city you see solitary women enthroned on the back seats of vast cars. On the way home we glided past each other and I wondered if they had anywhere to go or anything to do, or whether, like me, they visited the post office or a shop and swooped home again in ritualistic indolence.

I had a letter from Poppy, giving me the low-down on my successor at Palatine Hill. 'A' level results are worse for the second year in succession, fees are up and uniforms have been abolished. For the school trip last year they went to Amsterdam – an odd choice. As Poppy wickedly remarked, they probably left a few of the sixth-form girls behind in the massage parlours. I am heartened to see that in Torquay it is perpetually raining and 42. England feels very close and very remote. I feel a little as if I have not merely retired but passed away to a comfortable purgatory in which I float above my previous existence – even you my dear. Please write soon,

Your affectionate mother,
Barbara Fairclough

December 10

My dear Andrew,

Something most upsetting has just happened. I had just finished *What Maisie Knew*, about an hour before my lesson with Aisha, when I felt a craving for a cup of coffee – instant, sweet and creamy, just as we used to drink it in the staff-room at about the same time. I have at last acquired all the ingredients – Gold Blend, demerara sugar, Coffee Mate and digestive biscuits – which I keep in my room together with some attractive pink and gold cups and saucers. I was on my way down to the kitchen to borrow a kettle when Fouad, the eldest and nastiest of Aisha's four sons, launched himself at me across one of the vast reception-rooms. He is a fat, moist child whose expression is either sulky or insolently gleeful. If flies were permitted inside their air-conditioned rooms, I'm sure he would pull their wings off. He nearly knocked me over, sent my jar of coffee crashing to the floor, where it shattered, and then grinned at me fatuously. It is hard to convey the degree of masculine arrogance already present in this eight-year-old boy. His smile said, you're a woman, you have to do what I tell you, this is my house, my country, my world.

'Where are you going?'

'I was going to make myself some coffee. But now I shall go straight to your mother, to give her her lesson.'

'English lesson at ten o'clock,' he said, checking his gold watch. He was wearing sneakers and a blue track-suit which looked odd on his pear-shaped, unathletic body. 'Why you no give me English lessons? I am good pupil, very clever.'

'Are you indeed? I'm afraid I don't teach children.'

Although I dislike him so much, I'm sure he really is an intelligent boy. He took my hand, commanding rather than confiding, and dragged me through the sad marble halls to a room where his three brothers sat with two nannies, who were (I think) Sudanese. The room was the size of a normal European bedroom, and looked tiny compared to the grandiose proportions of the rest of the palace. There was a jumble of expensive toys – motor bikes, computers and train sets. The two women sat on a bed sewing and they, together with the children on the floor, were watching a colour television. They hardly looked up when I came in with Fouad. He made me sit on the floor, with an air of triumph, and I wondered why he wanted me there. To show off his toys? To give him some particular kind of attention? I looked away from his big, dark, insistent eyes and we all watched TV in silence – Mickey Mouse, Donald Duck, Tom and Jerry. I think the cartoons must have been recorded on video, as they changed very abruptly. The words, such as they were, were in English. Nobody laughed or spoke as the demonic cute creatures tricked, kissed, whacked and guffawed at each other. The women and children regarded all this manic activity quite passively, mouths open, eyes glazed. The atmosphere in the room was comatose, as if they had been dosing themselves with visual drugs all morning.

Quite suddenly the picture changed. Instead of cats and ducks we were watching the antics of human beings. Two gangs of youths, one wearing black leather and the other Neanderthal skins, were fighting with knives. One gang captured the other and proceeded to torture their prisoners. In close-up, we saw skin being peeled off, human meat filleted like fish, raw, bloody flesh streaming like rags down a man's back – the images were so horrific and so realistic that I felt sick. I feel ill now writing about them. I wanted to turn it off, but I had no authority over these children. In the end I jumped up, unable to bear the images, and before I left the room I stared at the others. Their expressions hadn't changed.

I couldn't bear to think of this filth being poured into the children's heads. I had to say something to Aisha, and this wasn't easy because although she is in many ways more shy and more submissive than Western women, she is after all a princess, in control of a large and complex household, in which my own position is ambivalent. I didn't think she would welcome any criticism of her children's upbringing – who does? But I was sure that she would want to know they were watching this awful stuff. She is after all a devout Muslim who prays five times a day, blushes at the mention of alcohol and dresses so demurely that I've no idea what shape she is. After great anxiety, I sneaked it into the lesson by giving her a reading comprehension about a Victorian schoolroom.

'In England we used to be very strict with children. But now we let them do what they like.'

'No good. In my country we make children work very hard. Only babies do what they like. Fouad is working very hard. Very clever boy.'

'I saw him this morning.'

'He is wanting so much to learn English. Why you cannot teach him?'

I could hardly claim that I hadn't enough time.

'Perhaps next month. He showed me the room where he and his brothers play.'

'Very nice room. We have very good nannies, from Sudan. My children are very happy,' she said with a kind of indifferent pride.

'They were watching a video.'

'My children have video – Fisher-Price, football table, transformer. Everything. Every year my husband is going to big shop in London – Harrods. You know? He buys everything.'

I don't think she was born a princess. She insists too much on her status.

'They were watching a very unpleasant film. What we call a video nasty.'

'What film? Cartoon?'

'No, not a cartoon. Real people, doing . . . very bad things to each other.'

'Not possible.'

'But I saw it.'

Fouad came bursting into the room to demand something. My Arabic is still very bad but I could understand enough to know that he was insisting he should do something and Aisha kept refusing to let him, with less and less conviction.

'Fouad, would you mind telling your mother about that film you were watching?'

'What film?' He glared at me.

'A very nasty film. Men were hurting each other with knives.'

Fouad turned to his mother, and made some dismissive remark, which made her smile. The smile was between them, against me, and again I felt the weakness of my position. In the end Fouad got what he wanted and, as he stormed out, I thought, if I agree to teach this little monster he'll be even ruder to me than he is to his mother.

She sighed peevishly. 'He wants to drive his car.'

'A real car?'

'Of course. My husband is buying all the children real cars – small, you know. A big toy. From Harrods. Very good shop.'

From what I've seen of Riyadh traffic it's quite bad enough, without eight-year-old thugs on the roads.

'You said no, of course?'

'What, no? He is like his father, he doesn't understand no.'

'You mean he'll be allowed to drive it in the street?'

'At first, only practising in gardens.'

I was flabbergasted. But I am rapidly learning not to say what I think.

'Your gardens are so pretty. Tell me, am I allowed to walk in them?'

'My gardens, your gardens. Please,' she said with a charming smile and a gesture of giving. This culture is such a mixture of exquisite courtesy and extreme rudeness.

Later this morning (our lessons now last between two and three hours), Aisha became more confiding. She told me her husband wants to send the boys to English boarding-schools but that she wants them to go to school in Switzerland.

'When I was fifteen, I went to school in Lausanne. For one year I was there. I was so happy.' Her face was suffused with the memory of joy, and she looked very beautiful and very sad.

'Did you learn French?'

'French. English. Music. Painting. Skiing. Everthing. I loved to learn. My teachers said I was very clever.'

'You are. Where did you go after Lausanne?'

'When I was sixteen I must return to Riyadh. For marriage,' she said matter-of-factly. 'After that, babies. When Fouad was born I am eighteen.'

So she can't be more than twenty-six now. Yet there is nothing young about her. Her youth must have ended when she was sixteen. I imagined how she might have continued her education, focused her intelligence and energy on something more demanding than her First Certificate. In another age, on another continent, she might have been a nun, a competent and scholarly Mother Superior. But here there is no tradition of women who work and do not marry. Women are property and bearing children is their function, as it was in ours until very recently. At that moment I saw Aisha as a tragic figure, a woman born in the wrong time and place with capacities she has no chance of developing. I know you'll say it's absurd to feel sorry for a woman with such glaringly obvious material advantages but I did, and Aisha caught my sadness.

After lunch she took my hand, slipped on her veil and guided me through the labyrinthine mausoleum to a locked door, which she opened.

I stood at last in the gardens I had seen from my window. They are enormous and virtually public, full of servants I'd never seen before, shuffling between the palaces. Gravel paths wind between banks of beautifully maintained flowers and palm trees – I suppose one can grow anything in this climate, if you water it enough. Seen close up, the fountains are ugly, huge reinforced concrete tubs like municipal rubbish-bins.

'What's that?' I asked, pointing to the striped awning.

'Swimming-pool.'

'Can I . . . can women swim there?'

'Sometimes,' she said vaguely. 'My gardens are very beautiful,' she added with that unconscious arrogance which makes it impossible to pay her compliments. One can only concur that she, her children and her house are beautiful, wonderful, etc. Yet in her innermost self she is a modest woman.

Perched on a red velvet pedestal, its hooded eyes malevolent, a falcon watched us. On the other side of a palm tree a mangy goat was eating shrubs voraciously. I had looked forward so much to wandering freely in these gardens. But, now I was in them, they gave me the same feeling of claustrophobia as the house. They were too big and too formal. We came upon a rose tree, wonderfully trimmed, like the head of a fashionable woman. It chilled me rather, but I admired it.

'Please. For your room.' But instead of just picking the flowers, Aisha stood helplessly on the path, looking around.

'Shall I do it for you?' I asked, thinking that she hesitated from some aristocratic feat of pricking or dirtying her fingers.

She wandered off along the gravel paths and soon reappeared with a small man wearing what looked like a very grubby nightshirt. I'm afraid I find myself the victim of what you would call racial stereotypes. All the men in menial positions here remind me of the villains in films that were made before you were born – *Sinbad the Sailor*, *The Thief of Baghdad*, etc. The Saudi men in their white robes take me back even further, to Rudolph Valentino. The women, somehow, seem to have more individuality, once you see their faces. Or perhaps this is just because I have made friends with Aisha, and because I trust my own sex. Anyway, this particular fellow looked furious and was shouting and arguing with Aisha, who was apologetic. In her veil she looked so meek, more nunlike than ever. The whole scene struck me as being quite extraordinary – would the Queen have to grovel to a gardener for ten minutes before she was allowed to cut her own flowers at Windsor?

When at last the gardener reached in his pocket for a ferocious-looking knife, I screamed and leaped forward to protect Aisha. The man glared at me, muttered a few curses and cut a single rose, which he almost threw at Aisha before disappearing back into his film archive. I was glad that, because of her veil, I was unable to see her face as she handed me the flower, which had drooped already, exhausted by the controversy it had caused.

I spent a peaceful afternoon with Jane Austen. One knows where one is in nineteenth-century Surrey.

Your affectionate mother is stuck in a time machine somewhere between medieval Baghdad and Silicone Valley. Please write soon.

Barbara Fairclough

December 20

My dear Andrew,

Many thanks for your letter which appears to be a reply to my first! Are my letters arriving? You should have had four by now. Please let me know about this.

Of course it was nice to hear from you. Although it is hardly reassuring to be told that you and Susie have split up and that you are also considering leaving your job. Is her name really Bim de Koch? I have cut out a most interesting article on celibacy from the *Guardian Weekly*, which I enclose. Frankly I was not impressed by the photographs of you both gambolling on the beach in Crete and I wish Ms de Koch would dress more sensibly. What if your letter had been opened by the censor? Sending me the draft contract was also, to say the least, unwise. In any case it's written in impenetrable English – what if they give me all this money and I then decide not to write the articles or the book? And what precisely is your role in all this? I fail to see what you have done to earn 15 per cent of my theoretical earnings. I am of course flattered by what you say about my writing, although I don't know what you mean by an injection of *pzazz*. I really don't think I can get involved in such a risky deal from this distance. I'm reminded of all your other 'money-making' deals – double glazing, the pizzeria franchise, the pet hire agency and so many others. All of which involved my capital or time and none of which materialized into any money for either of us. I'm so tired, Andrew. I don't want to turn this job with Aisha into a slick story for some meretricious newspaper. If you need money again you had better go out and get yourself a proper job. I'm puzzled by your objections to your present one. Since when were your sensibilities so easily offended?

As to my being titillated by all this luxury – I'm afraid that soon wore off. My life here is not exotic or even convenient. As Christmas draws near, the impossibility of celebrating it frustrates me immensely. I had thought of putting a discreet little tree in my room, but the white-robed officers of the Society for the Encouragement of Virtue and the Elimination of Vice have just been round all the supermarkets, confiscating trees, shiny baubles, holly, etc. Only 'seasonal greetings' cards and 'holiday puddings' remain. Although my Christianity has always been moderate, this place may yet make a zealot of me! It's so outrageous, this national conspiracy to behave as if Christ wasn't born, when his birth and life are authenticated in the Koran itself! Do we prevent Muslims from observing Ramadan or any of their other religious festivals? If I knew of an underground carol service, I would rush over to it – I believe I would even take communion again, after all these years. This country would make a dissident out of anyone. It's so bad for the spirit to be constantly told, you can't, you musn't, you're not allowed. Worst of all I still don't know exactly what the rules are. They're not written or clearly defined anywhere, as far as I can discover.

By late morning it is boiling hot. Downstairs, Aisha's rooms are dark and gloomy, but when I come up here after lunch the sun blazes through the open shutters. The sky shouts with blue and gold, an expression of joy which, it seems to me, is found nowhere else in this country. There doesn't seem to be any winter here. It hasn't rained since I arrived and the skies are uniformly clear, night and day. As far as climate goes, this is a most celestial part of the world. Perhaps that is why three major religions were born here. But the other day as I lay on my bed in the early afternoon (I rest far too much here), my thoughts were not so metaphysical. I only wanted to enjoy the sun, go swimming and have a holiday from Allah and his miserable definition of female purity.

I even considered climbing down from my balcony. All this authority makes one regress, I'm afraid. In the end I wrapped up my swimming-costume in a towel and went to find Aisha, to ask her permission to use the pool. I knocked on her door, in a remote and grandiose corridor, and entered a kind of Golders Green Renaissance throne-room with a vast pink satin bed as its centrepiece. Aisha, surrounded by maids, was having her long, dark, beautiful hair brushed and being zipped into a particularly hideous lime-green spangled kimono. She seemed embarrassed to see me there, as if afraid I would dismiss her as a frivolous, superficial woman. (In fact it is Aisha's total lack of frivolity and superficiality which is her tragedy.) Beside her, on a brocade chair, was a large present elaborately wrapped with a big yellow velvet bow. She looked rather forlorn, like an overdressed child going to a birthday party.

'I am going to the tea-party of the wife of the Minister for External Affairs,' she said without enthusiasm.

'I just popped in to ask if I might use the swimming-pool?'

'Of course. No problem.' But she looked distraught and screamed a high-pitched tirade of orders at one of the maids, who led me from the room.

As I went out I said to Aisha. 'Try and have another look at that list of prefixes and suffixes before tomorrow morning, will you, my dear? Enjoy your party.'

Although my Palatine Hill manner survives, I am less and less convinced by it. As the maid (a very young Indian girl) led me downstairs I felt, as I so often do here, that three of us were descending – a brusque, hatchet-faced old woman, a gentle, black-haired young girl and another young girl, whose heart thumped and whose legs wobbled with anxiety as she blundered through the maze of Islam.

The girl unlocked the door – the same one I had passed through with Aisha – and fled. I stood alone on the hot gravel, shut my eyes and lifted my face to the sun that had eluded me for so long. All around me the plants baked, dozed, breathed out their collective perfume. It was silent. Most of the household was sleeping off lunch and even the goat lay sprawled in the shade. When I opened my eyes again, the sun had painted dark, speckled mosaics all over the flat, bright garden. I felt dizzy and absent-minded and walked very fast to the swimming-pool. I was extremely annoyed to find its dark-green metal door locked, and thumped on it hard. There was a noise like a gong which clanged through the sun-drained garden and gave me a certain primitive satisfaction. I liked to think that my anger and frustration could wake a few people up so I bashed the gate again. Two men came running up and screamed at me in Arabic and (I think) some Indian language.

'Princess Aisha has given me permission to use the pool.'

More screaming, I wasn't sure whether or not one of the men was the gardener who was so unpleasant to Aisha. To my embarrassment, I can't tell the difference between most of the men here, with their black hair, black eyes, inevitable moustaches or beards and uniform night-shirts and sandals. They were still screaming at me.

'Please open the gate,' I demanded. 'Open the gate!'

The taller of the two shook his large bunch of keys at me defiantly and strode off, followed by the other. I was reduced to peeping through the keyhole at an inaccessible paradise of turquoise water and emerald-green Astroturf. I took a large pin out of my hair and jiggled it around in the keyhole, which swallowed it up. Then I glanced up at the high metal wall – but there was no gap betwen the top of the wall and the striped awning.

By now the sun had branded a headache deep into the back of my
neck, from where arrows of pain shot up behind my eyes. I
staggered back to the door of the house, only to find that the maid
had shut it behind her! I rattled the handle and shouted, but
nobody came. By now I was feeling really ill and also, to my
shame, afraid that the men would come back to shout at me again.

Looking up at the ugly pink and green building, I identified my
balcony on the first floor, and found a ladder which I dragged
over. All the time I was worrying: Is it illegal for women to climb
ladders? To wish to swim? To approach bedrooms by the balcony
instead of the door? Upstairs, I collapsed on to my bed, trembling
and weeping, and almost immediately fell asleep. I know you'll
laugh. I laughed myself, when the headache had worn off and I
had washed away some of my sense of failure with a shower and
two bottles of mineral water.

I've just received a letter from Sylvia, who reminds me what a
strict disciplinarian I used to be. She went along to an Old Girls'
Dinner at which, she says, I was toasted: To Barbara Fairclough,
who kept us all in order. When there was an order to keep. Here
of course there is a most rigid order, but I have no place in it.

I'm reading *The Thousand and One Nights*, which in its
bowdlerized version was a great favourite of mine when I was a
child. I'm afraid it's responsible for many of my preconceptions
about this place. I know it's silly, but somewhere at the back of my
mind I expected twentieth-century Riyadh to contain eleventh-
century Baghdad. These stories are great fun but not really a great
deal of use as a guide to etiquette in Aisha's household. Do you
remember my reading them to you when you were a little boy?
Well, the reason Aladdin was so bowled over by the Princess Badr-
Al-Budur was that he thought all women looked like his mother!
Can you imagine the thrill when a veil is at last lifted to reveal a
beautiful face? Certainly the accounts of female beauty are
sumptuous. This is how one of the girls in 'The Porter and the
Three Girls of Baghdad' is described: '. . . her forehead was white
as a lily and her eyes were more lustrous than a gazelle's. Her
brows were crescent moons, her cheeks anemones, and her mouth
like the crimson ruby on King Solomon's ring. Her teeth were
whiter than a string of pearls, and like twin pomegranates were her
breasts.' In the same story a poor girl is bumped off by a jinnee
who says, 'Know, son of Adam, that among us jinn the penalty of
adultery is death. . . . But I have now killed her because I found her

unfaithful: even if it was only with her eyes.' Which makes the Koran ('the adulterer and adulteress shall be given a hundred lashes') seem quite liberal.

The morality in the stories is decidedly one-sided. Ma'arf the cobbler flees from his wife Fatimah on the back of a jinnee. When the 'old shrew' at last catches up with him and observes he 'sought his pleasure with other women, she became jealous and her evil soul prompted her to seek his ruin'. Just as Fatimah is about to enjoy a magic ring, the Prince, her stepson, kills her. Ma'arf the cobbler, now a merry widower instead of a bigamist, 'praised his son for his bravery' and 'reigned through many joyful years'. But the women are not passive. They often make fools of the men and fight with the weapon of all slave races: guile. A kind of obsessive respect for this quality echoes through the stories. How nice it would be if there were still public baths here, where one could go for gossip and massage. But there is only the inaccessible swimming-pool and my all-too-private bathroom.

I suppose I must wish you a merry Christmas. There seems little prospect that mine will be anything of the sort. I enclose a cheque, Andrew, although I want to make it quite clear that this is not something you can expect more than once a year. I hope I haven't replied ungraciously to your letter. I would appreciate it if you wrote more often. I am really very isolated here.

Your affectionate mother,
Barbara Fairclough

December 29

My dear Andrew,

Christmas can hardly be said to be over, as it never began. On the evening of the 24th I fell asleep on my bed listening to the sublime voices from King's on my VHF radio. When I woke up on Christmas morning the radio was still crackling beside me, my only link with the outside world. Then, as I was getting up, I heard a man shouting downstairs – a vocal storm accompanied by bangs and crashes. His anger echoed through the palace in a way that was almost supernatural, as if a vengeful Old Testament God, offended that His son's birthday had been ignored, was unleashing His fury.

When I went down a few hours later to teach Aisha, the palace was even more silent than usual. I was tense with the effort of remembering not to mention Christmas, and as I passed through the dull, empty rooms, trumpets and inappropriately jubilant voices sounded in my head: Christ was born on Christmas Day. . . . Oh the holly and the ivy/when they are fully grown/Of all the trees that are in the wood/the holly bears the crown./ The running of the deer. . . . After taking sixty-four English Christmases for granted, I find that there is more to all this than turkey and habit.

Aisha was extremely pale and nervous, more melancholy than I had ever seen her. She stared down at the floor as if she wanted to entomb herself in the marble, and the lesson began miserably. I set her some written exercises so that we could legitimately avoid speaking to each other. Then as she wrote the date she raised her eyes to me and smiled.

'It is your Noël!'

'Christmas.'

'How do I say? Many Happy Christmas?'

'Just Happy Christmas.'

'I'm sorry – I am forgetting – please excuse me.'

She got up and ran from the room. All her poise and most of her English seemed to have deserted her. I wondered if the thunderous-voiced man had been the Prince on one of his rare visits. Certainly it was possible to imagine the man I had met in Sunningdale as a tyrant.

Ten minutes later Aisha returned with a small, beautifully wrapped package, which she gave to me. As I unwrapped it she watched eagerly, some of her confidence restored now that she was again my patroness. Inside was a gold Swiss watch in a dark-red suede case. I thanked her, wondering how on earth she had conjured it up so quickly. Does she have drawers full of expensive, ready-wrapped presents to distribute? I took off my battered old brown leather Rolex and strapped on her magnificent gift, which sat on my wrist like a tiara on a sausage.

'This morning very early my husband came. You heard him?'

'Well, yes. I thought I. . . .'

She almost spat with anger and contempt. Her face was transformed, as if I had suddenly opened a fire door and flames had leaped out. Then she said, with her usual quiet dignity, 'My husband is very busy. Do you know he has even an English school for himself, here in Riyadh? Also other business, all the time he is travelling, working, visiting his wifes.... Wifes?'

'Wives.'

'I am the smallest wife.'

'Youngest,' I said, irritated by the sound of my own voice correcting her. I wanted to be her friend but I couldn't stop being her teacher.

'The others are more important.'

'I see.'

'He is visiting them every night. For their children he is really a father. Every month he is taking them on holidays to Geneva, Sunningdale – my house is the smallest, and this is not right. It is written in the Koran that all wives must be equal.'

It seemed to me that her house was quite big enough. I have known English couples for twenty years or more without learning anything about their intimate relations. Yet Aisha, after only a few weeks of formal acquaintanceship, volunteered all this information. It seems that marriage, which in England is a sealed chamber until separation or a third person breaks the door down, is here an openly published list of material rights and grievances. I couldn't resist probing a little.

'I wonder, would it be possible to speak to your husband while he is here? About his English lessons? You see, when I met him in England he did say he wanted me to teach him.'

Aisha laughed. 'His English is terrible. Maybe for five minutes he wanted to speak properly, so he bought an English teacher. Then he forgot. Like his English school, for one week it was a big passion. Now he says the best language is Japanese. Before you came on the aeroplane he forgot you. You came to my house because here are all the things he no longer wants – old cars, old furniture, very bad servants. Also me.'

At lunch – we nearly always eat together now at midday – we were both very quiet, each wrapped in her separate loneliness. Since hers was thicker than mine, I tried to penetrate it with words. As I described our Christmas celebrations at home she looked almost faint with boredom. It was impossible to communicate the pain of my homesickness to a woman who was so obviously sick of her own home.

'... after Christmas we celebrate the New Year. We have parties, lots of food ...', get drunk, kiss each other. It's almost impossible to avoid moral misunderstandings. I felt like a rather stilted tape: English Small Talk, a total immersion course.

After another silence I said, 'In a few days I'm going to a meeting of the World-Wide Women's Group. I am looking forward to it, I must say. Perhaps I'll make some new friends.'

At last she showed some interest. 'What is it, this meeting?'

As I described it, 'or rather my stilted projection of it, a kind of greed suffused her face. I saw how hungry she is for company, even hungrier than I.

'Only foreign ladies are going there?'

'I don't really know. Any nationality, I suppose. Why, would you . . .?'

She giggled and became very coy. For a moment I saw her as an exquisite fifteen-year-old on the threshold of a world she never entered, making passionate friendships with girls from international rich families, flirting with male teachers and waiters, intoxicated by language and knowledge, mountains and lakes.

'Please come to the meeting with me, Aisha. I should like that.'

But a premature matron sat beside me again.

'No. Not possible. But maybe, if you are going there and making friends, you will invite some ladies to my house? For tea-party? It would be a great pleasure to me.'

It has become our chief topic of conversation, this meeting, what I'll wear and whom I'll meet and how I'll lure my new friends back to Aisha. The car to take me there was ordered ten days in advance and I've had to coach Aisha in conversation suitable for a ladies' tea-party (although, as you will have gathered, she does it only too naturally). The main problem is explaining that ladies, in the sense she means, are few and far between. A spontaneous conversation between most Western women would appal her. Or would it? I'm afraid she expects far too much from this glorified coffee morning. Perhaps I do too.

Just to amuse myself this morning I asked her to coach me in appropriate Arabic greetings at a gathering of women. She has often invited me to tea-parties and weddings and I've always been too ashamed of my bad Arabic to accept. This is what I can look forward to, if I ever do go:

'God welcome you.'

'May God give you long life.'

'God save you, very well, thanks be to the Almighty.'

'And your husband and the children, are they well?'

'Thanks be to God, they are well and kiss your hand.'

And so on, until the hostess and her guest have inquired about the health of their most remote connections. Don't you think it has a certain archaic charm? But I'm not sure whether I could face six hours of it – the weddings apparently go on for most of the night.

In two days the year will end, leaving me here in the fourteenth century (even the calendar is different here). I notice that Aisha hardly ever invites friends back here, and yesterday, after a particularly friendly lesson, I ventured to ask whether she had chosen such a lonely life. She replied, very bitterly, that as the least favourite wife she has no choice. The other wives, she said, don't like her and she is often not invited to functions. If she continues to displease her husband he has the right to divorce her instantly and take away her children over seven. I don't think the loss of Fouad would break her heart, but of course she would lose all status. I asked her where she would go if this happened.

'To my family. But they will be very angry. My father will say I am not his daughter. When my other boys will be seven years old, my husband will be taking them also. All. But the money that my father gave when I married . . .'

'Your dowry?'

'My dowry, it is mine. But it is not a lot of money, too small to go to live in Switzerland.'

I saw that this was her dream, a false one perhaps. For Aisha would be even more of an outsider in Europe than she is here. I wasn't sure whether her use of the future tense was deliberate or accidental. Then she started to talk about her family. Her father is some kind of prince but not a very rich one. She grew up on the edge of a small town, just outside its walls, in an old palace, of which she showed me photographs. It was so beautiful, this palace! As I looked at the photos and listened to her description I recognized the Arabia of Thesiger, of the Anglo-Arab love affair to which I have remained so dreadfully unsusceptible.

The palace had crumbling mud walls melting into the sand. There were overhanging, enclosed balconies made of delicately carved wood where the women, she told me, used to sit and watch the all-male festivities below. The courtyards were encrusted with Ottoman tiles and the only water supply came from the fountains and wells. All the doors and gates were ornately carved, and inside the house each dark room was a mysterious box fitted with organic shutters, beds, couches and cupboards, all carved out of the same wood at the same time. The women lived very close together in their quarters and they were busy. They looked after each other's children, sewed, embroidered, cured, preserved, baked, gossiped and prayed together. Here, in the sixties, in this extended, all-female family, Aisha grew up. She remembers the first fly-killing programme, the first refrigerator, the first cars and private aeroplanes to come to their town. Although it was a traditional household, her father educated his daughters as well as his sons and, until puberty, boys and girls played freely together.

'Is your father's palace still there?' I asked longingly. It occurred to me that, if her husband does divorce her, I might return with her to this wonderful place where at last I would be at peace. I saw myself ensconced in one of those darkly carved, womblike rooms, padded with silk rugs and perfumed with incense, listening to a half-understood conversation between Aisha and her sisters in the next room, and to the splash of a tiled fountain in the courtyard below . . .

'No. Of course we don't live in that, now, it was very old.' Aisha sounded irritated, as if I had accused her of having dirty fingernails. She showed me a more recent, colour photograph – a collection of humpy, muddy ruins in the desert beside a motorway. 'This is the old palace. When I am thirteen, my father understood it was not possible to continue to live in such an old house. Already he was travelling to United States, Switzerland. He wanted a house where he could invite business men. Very important men. So he built our new palace.' She showed me a smaller replica of her own house – concrete and marble surrounded by geometric gardens and high walls. 'Very beautiful,' she said rather aggressively.

'But you loved your old palace?'

'I was happy there.'

She started to talk about the women's meeting next Tuesday, yet again. Again I assured her that I would try to procure some foreign women friends for her. It is a little alarming, this frenzied expectation of hers. I am reminded of one of Poppy's silly stories. An old lady worked as a volunteer in a lunatic asylum, where she was on the governing board. One day she had a chat with one of the inmates, who was laying bricks outside the building. She found him charming and perfectly rational, and agreed with him that he really shouldn't be in the asylum at all. She promised to speak up on his behalf at the next board meeting, the following Tuesday. As she turned to leave, a brick hit her on the head and the man shouted, 'Don't forget next Tuesday!'

I hope my letters are arriving, my dear Andrew. I wish you would write more frequently. Poppy and Sylvia are both extremely busy with their charity work but they manage to reply to all my letters.

Your affectionate mother,
Barbara Fairclough

January 6

My dear Andrew,

I'm afraid I can't have made myself clear. Let me repeat once more that I have no intention of writing anything of the kind and, if you exploit my letters in the way you hint at, I shall cut you out of my will. Incidentally, I think you vastly overestimate the commercial value of my experience here. You seem to imagine yourself as the impresario of some Hollywood musical – 'The Prince and I'. Well I haven't set eyes on the blasted Prince since I arrived here and my lessons with Aisha are hardly sensational.

I thought your Christmas card was in questionable taste. However, I received welcome packages from Sylvia and Poppy, who actually managed to get a tin of mince pies through Customs. It's odd that I write to them less freely than I do to you. Not that I deliberately misrepresent my situation here to them – but I am conscious of massaging the facts. Perhaps it is because they are critical and curious about my life here, whereas you are quite indifferent. Also, despite your many failings, you have never been secretive with me. Indeed, your frankness has often embarrassed me. I don't know why you find it necessary to inform me of the slaughter of yet another of my unborn grandchildren. If Ms de Koch's life-style is as immoderate as you say, she should take more precautions. Fortunately I am feeling particularly unmaternal and ungrandmaternal after Fouad and his apprentice thugs burst into my room at six o'clock this morning on their motor bikes.

For the women's meeting, Aisha insisted that I borrow one of her evening dresses, a yellow satin horror embellished with brown velvet bows. She sent along one of her maids at eight to do curious things to my hair and face and then insisted on lending me a gold necklace and six gold bangles. I suppose this was her way of going to the meeting vicariously. As I stared at myself in the mirror, I thought I had rarely seen mutton dressed so unconvincingly as lamb, and certainly not before 9 a.m. Aisha came in, followed by a servant carrying a coffee-pot, tiny cups and sweet cakes. I have at last discovered how to say 'no' to coffee or tea. Simply saying 'no' only results in the servant smiling at your coyness and filling your cup for the fifth time. You have to cover your cup with the index finger and waggle it as you return it to the servant. The acquisition of this trick has saved me from at least one major coronary. But that morning I was so nervous that I drank at least ten thimble cups before I was escorted to the waiting hearse by Aisha and several servants. Even the boys came out of their room to see me off. The Korean driver played deafening pop cassettes as the motorways, flashy new buildings and wastelands flashed past the tinted windows. However long I live here, I don't think Riyadh will ever seem real or familiar. Perhaps it is only when we walk or drive in new places that we make solid relationships with them. Here, I am always a passenger.

I wasn't prepared for the splendour of the meeting. The Grand Festival Palace, where it was held, fronts a sandy wasteland. It is one of the most attractive buildings I have seen here, a reproduction of a classical Arab fort, very plain, with slit windows and well-kept gardens all around it. Women were converging on it from all directions – old ones, young ones, tall ones, fat ones. Like Browning's rats they came in all shapes and sizes. They all wore long skirts, and most of them would not have been out of place in the crush bar at Covent Garden. At the door an American woman handed me a ballot-book with 'Election of Officers for 1987' printed on its cover. It gave me a sense of power and security, to be a part of this tidal wave of English-speaking women, most of whom were as overdressed as I was. This, I realized, meant that I was appropriately dressed for what must be a very grand cup of coffee.

Inside the magnificent doors the style of the building changed from dignified neo-Baghdad to what I can only call Dallas Bordello. The velvety, emerald-green carpet came half-way up to my ankles, and the chandeliers were so big that they almost became entangled in the elaborate hair styles of the taller women (some of whom were wearing tiaras!). I drifted into a cloakroom which had – honestly – solid gold taps. Women were queuing up, not to go to the loo, but to take photographs of the taps, this being one of the few places in Riyadh where photography is allowed.

I found myself in another vast hall where white-jacketed waiters, the only men I saw inside the palace, served coffee from enormous urns. An alien might have supposed that this was the temple of an exclusively female cult dedicated to instant coffee. All around me pairs and clusters of women chatted, some of them old friends, but many of them newcomers like me. Someone came up to me and asked me which company my husband worked for, to which I replied testily that I had been a widow for twenty years. She turned away and I at once regretted my sharp tongue. Such a remark was out of place amid the prevailing graciousness. Most of the women were American and indicated by each inflection of their cooling voices, by their hostess smiles and loud clunks as their bracelets and rings clashed during embraces, that functions such as this were their natural habitat. The presidential atmosphere was accentuated by the candidates, who paraded with numbers on their chests like racehorses, twirling and frisking. In my booklet I inspected their pedigrees and saw that their qualifications included bridge, gourmet cooking, embroidery, macrame, racquet ball and even mahjong.

After a while I became aware of two distinct styles: the American imperial look, which elevates to the level of a cult the traditional activities of the Women's Institute; and the Shabby British Depression, which wasn't a style at all but an obstinate rejection of one. Sullen, dressed to look horribly natural, their faces unmade up or awkwardly daubed, my compatriots stood on the perimeter of the inner circle inside which the expatriate princesses of Riyadh sparkled. Thanks to the attentions of Aisha's maid, I belonged physically to the first category, but spiritually to the second.

I backed away towards the walls, which were lined with tables spread with leaflets about kindergartens, sewing circles, baby-sitting circles, Arabic classes, tennis clubs and golf clubs. I thought how much effort had gone into all this organization in a place where women have every incentive to be passive, and I was touched. These were the women who ran things, and I had always been one of them. Yet the problem remained that I didn't want to sew or baby-sit or compete for office. I wanted a quiet, literary friendship, and that was not offered on any of the tables.

One of the presidential candidates announced (without needing to raise her voice) that it was time to go and vote. I began to panic, as if I was a young girl at a dance again, waiting for the partner who rarely approached. Your father was the first man who was not scared off by the fact that I had no charm and too much nose, and we met considerably later. Anyway, as I drank my fourth cup of coffee I was amazed at my vulnerability. I felt as awkward and lonely as when I was seventeen, although I was only too aware that I didn't look seventeen. At my age friendship is not a magic carpet that comes to waft you away, but buried treasure that has to be dug up.

I had been staring for some time at the long golden hair of a woman standing with her back to me. When she turned, I saw to my surprise that her face was almost as old as my own, although she had obviously been very pretty and her youthful looks were still reflected in her extraordinary hair and slight figure. We smiled at each other, exchanged names and flashed sympathetic signals behind our glasses. Six weeks of words were dammed up in my head and they flooded out all over poor Iona, who listened, nodded and smiled. She has the voice as well as the hair of a girl, a schoolgirl of my generation, clipped and very English, although she said she was Irish and had spent most of her adult life abroad. She listened to my monologue until we were left alone in the coffee hall.

'I think we should go and vote now,' she said gently.

'Don't you think it's rather ludicrous, all this fuss about who organizes coffee mornings and bridge lunches?'

'I think Americans like all this razzmatazz – don't you, dear?'

We sat together near the back of another vast hall. There were long curved benches like those in an amphitheatre, covered in a velvety green fabric, and soft walls which changed colour disconcertingly. On a stage was a big screen, in front of which the candidates paraded like mannequins. In the audience hundreds of women were filling in their ballot-books, whispering excitedly to each other. I had no idea whom to vote for, but Iona has been here two years and seems to know every foreign woman in Riyadh.

'Oh no, not her. She's as hard as nails. And I wouldn't vote for her either. They say she cheats at bridge. And she snubbed Mavis once at a garage sale.'

'That only leaves number three for President.'

'Cynthia's not bad. We have a drink with her sometimes at the golf club.'

The lights were dimmed and the candidates began to make their final campaign speeches, which were fervent and extremely long. The outgoing President, who was on her way to Kuwait, threw out her arms to her audience like a diva giving her farewell performance. The chairwoman jumped up, hugged her, insisted that we give her a standing ovation and then hinted darkly at evil deeds afoot. Apparently an anonymous leaflet libelling one of the candidates had been handed out at the door. (not to me, unfortunately). Iona dashed off to find out what was in it.

'Well! According to Bunty it's absolute dynamite. It says number six has been having an affair with number eighteen's husband! Of course I don't suppose there's any truth in it, but let's just have a look and see who they are.... Oh, Jenny – well, she is rather attractive and Debbie isn't, poor thing....'

The elections were interminable, but I was impressed by the amount of energy poured into them by all these women, who insisted on referring to themselves as ladies. Of course, when I was young there was a valid distinction between the two – 'lady' meant breeding, gentility and virtue whereas 'woman' meant coarseness and low status. In the intervening years the words have changed their meaning, and I am glad of it. At Palatine Hill I tried to turn out young women, well-educated, active and capable of survival, not helpless, effete young ladies. But the ripples of this semantic revolution do not seem to have reached Riyadh, where we are all ladies and the word 'woman' is considered an insult. Sitting in that hall, I felt that expatriate life has sealed most of us up in a time capsule. It has turned the Americans into eternal cheer-leaders, forming sororities around the world, while the English women go on and on being shy, gauche prefects. All their intelligence and energy, which could have been chanelled outwards into careers or even real politics, just go round and round in circles, turning eventually into something rather sour. As Poppy used to say of our richer girls when they went off to be 'finished', how many flowers can one arrange? Of course the situation of the women here curiously resembles that of the heroines of my beloved nineteenth-century novels. They are totally dependent on their husbands and crushed by the burden of having too much leisure. Few of them work and most of their children are at boarding-schools.

'Pity the Brit didn't win,' mutterd Iona, who has not lived in the British Isles for fifteen years. The new President stood up to address us. 'I would just like to welcome any newcomers amongst us. We have a little custom at our meetings, which I think is kind of adorable. We try to find the newest lady in the audience and give her a little gift to show how much we appreciate her. We all know how lonely it can be here. But please, if you have just arrived, don't let yourself be left out. There's so much going on – why, I'm busier here than I was at home. Buy a ticket for our new arrivals' dinner at the Regency Hyatt – husbands are allowed to attend as well. Or join one of the clubs or just go along to your local coffee mornings.

'Now! Stand up, please, all those ladies who have arrived in Riyadh during the last month.' Shyly, a dozen women rose amidst giggles and applause. Iona nudged me but I couldn't bring myself to stand up. After all, I've been here six weeks, so I'm not a newcomer, although I shall always feel like one. At last they hunted down the newest of all, a petrified-looking English girl who was handed a present.

'And for all of you who are dying to know,' the President cooed into the microphone, 'Patricia's gift is a hand-chased, silverplated manicure set in an embossed leather case.'

A few women in the audience gasped obligingly, but most of us were getting up to go by then. I felt in danger of being suffocated by the syrupy graciousness of it all, and rushed out of the building into the luminous, golden, blue noon. The climate here is a great comfort. I was about to search for Aisha's driver in the traffic jam outside the palace when I remembered that I hadn't asked Iona for her telephone number. I stood in the doorway as the monstrous regiment of ladies (it doesn't have the same ring, does it?) swept out in their ill-assorted evening dresses.

I don't think I've ever felt so isolated. One of the candidates – I think it was the new Second Vice-President in the orange lace – had boasted that there were fifteen hundred woman at the meeting. I knew that among them must be quite a few who shared my interests. After all, I've spent much of my life getting on with a wide variety of human beings, most of them female, and I am not a leper. Yet I felt like one as they flowed past, not ignoring me but simply not seeing me.

At last Iona came out, surrounded by friends. Seeing her from a distance I was struck by her birdlike grace and chirpy voice.

'Barbara lives with a princess. Isn't that super?'

Six of them crowded around me, asking which school I had been headmistress of and whether I had managed to learn any Arabic (a rare accomplishment among the foreign community here). I was accredited with a profound knowledge of Saudi life and at last I felt visible. On impulse I said, 'Why don't you all come to tea at the palace? My princéss would love to meet you. How about Thursday afternoon?'

'We don't have a driver,' Iona said, eyeing the hearse which my driver had manoeuvred through the jumble of cars. He sat in it, glaring at me, honking and listening to loud pop music. I must say, Aisha's servants do lack a certain style. But Iona and her friends were obviously impressed, and it was so long since I had impressed anybody that I didn't want to lose them. I scribbled down Iona's phone number and gave her mine – the first time I had used it! I offered to give them a lift to the palace on Thursday and asked where they lived. Iona pointed to some white villas which I stared at enviously as I drove away in my air-conditioned cage. I imagined how companionable the lives of those women must be, as they pop in and out of each other's houses and go on shopping expeditions together. I suppose they are never alone unless they want to be.

I wonder if they'll come on Thursday? Aisha was delighted that I had obtained six foreign friends instead of one. Quantity matters a great deal in this culture. She at once cancelled a previous engagement on Thursday and I have had to tell her about my adventures at the meeting again and again. Rather less frankly than I have done to you, as Aisha doesn't appreciate irony. When she asks me to describe her future friends in detail, the only one I remember clearly is Iona. The others blur into a large fiftyish woman called Doris or Mavis, and I must admit I'm a little apprehensive about our tea-party. I spent an hour in the kitchen this afternoon trying to teach the girls how to make cucumber sandwiches and nice light fairy cakes.

I hope to receive a more sensible letter from you soon.

You affectionate mother,
Barbara Fairclough

January 15

My dear Andrew,

I haven't heard from you for weeks. I hope you didn't find the tone of my last letter too harsh. In hindsight I do regret the will-waiving – something my own mother did incessantly for the last years of her life and which I've always vowed not to indulge in. I'm afraid, in moments of stress, one reverts to patterns set by parents years before, for better or worse, usually the latter. A pleasure in store for you. However, I shall not apologize for my anger at the devious way in which you have tried to exploit my situation here. I would like a written assurance that you will stop putting pressure on me to write those wretched articles and will not use my letters. I am after all quite unable to come and stop you myself, as I'm not entitled to any holiday until June. I live in dread that Poppy or Sylvia will send me a cutting from your paper – some lurid nonsense concocted by you. If I didn't feel so embarrassed by the whole business I'd ask them to keep a watch on it for me (I'm sure they wouldn't normally read it). I certainly can't obtain it here. There is something to be said for Islamic sensibilities.

The tea-party would have amused you. Aisha sent her maid along to me again and I emerged in the early afternoon looking like an overwrapped Christmas present. Bows and frills really do look absurd on somebody my age and size.

Iona was waiting alone outside the Grand Festival Palace, wearing a long blue dress and an *abaya*. With her anxious face, long golden hair and black cloak she looked like a fairy godmother in front of a pantomime castle. She even carried a foil-wrapped stick as a magic wand.

'I'm awfully sorry the others couldn't come. They were dying to, but they remembered they'd promised Betty to do some crewel embroidery.'

'Oh dear.'

'Not C-R-U, you know. What a super car. I brought along some wholemeal garlic bread. Does your princess eat a lot? I've been asked to organize yoga classes in one of the big hotels here for Saudi ladies. Apparently they get dreadfully overweight, having babies every five minutes and comfort eating, poor things.'

'Aisha is quite slim. But I'm sure she would enjoy some activity like that, to distract her.'

'Bored out of her mind, is she, like most of them?'

'We – she – has so little to do.'

Iona and I get on so well, I'm sure we could spend weeks chatting. When I'm with her I'm afraid I just can't stop talking, I've been so starved of congenial company. Although Aisha has of course become a friend, I'm always on my guard with her. But with Iona I can talk quite freely. She has lived in South America, Papua New Guinea, America, New Zealand and Italy, following her husband, who works for a big oil company, around the world. She still retains the mannerisms of post-war Kensington, where she grew up. Despite six children and numerous grandchildren she still has the figure of a young girl, plays golf and tennis, swims, runs and teaches yoga. Her health and vitality are almost intimidating and she proselytizes shamelessly. On the way back to the palace she told me my posture was appalling and the state of my skin and hair showed I was deficient in vitamins C and E. She describes people, rather heartlessly, in terms of their physical defects. Her eldest daughter is prematurely aged by lack of exercise and vitamins, her best friend in Riyadh can't breathe properly because she smokes, and her husband suffers from high blood pressure and anxiety because he won't stick to a low-fat vegetarian diet. Apart from her zeal for health, I find her kind and wise – the white witch, I call her to myself. I admire her talent for putting down roots in new places. In all these different countries she has organized yoga classes, made friends and done her best to stay sane and cheerful. She has assimilated Riyadh's complex public bus system (women have to travel in a separate, unventilated compartment at the back of the bus) and she manages to get around here as she did in Papua New Guinea, where she learned to ride a motor bike. Meeting her has cheered me up no end.

Iona marched through the palace and handed Aisha the leaking, buttery parcel of garlic bread.

'Thank you. Only one lady?' Aisha tried to sound polite but her voice was petulant. Distastefully she opened the greasy, silver parcel. 'For eating?'

Iona launched into a eulogy of garlic, admired Aisha's glossy hair and peachlike skin and marvelled at the size of the rooms. This barrage of personal remarks must have been an astonishing experience for Aisha. But she realized that Iona was benign and struggled not to be offended by her. I think by then she was glad I had procured only one friend.

'Do you always use white flour? Really? This salt's awfully bad for you too, you know. I was reading about it in this month's *Health by Stealth*. Is this your throne-room?'

'My sitting-room.'

It was curious that, because of their respective tones, Iona's tactless remarks sounded friendly, whereas Aisha's polite replies sounded distinctly abrupt.

'And are men allowed in here? You don't mind my asking, do you, only I am so fascinated. My husband always says I go barging in where angels fear to tread.'

To my surprise Aisha tried to answer all her questions (many of which I had been dying to ask myself). But Aisha can't really explain her world to us, because she starts out from such different premises. She can describe the geography of the palace but not her relationship with her husband and sons and the other wives. As she talked to Iona I again had the impression that she is ashamed of her situation and pretends, even to herself, that her family life is more successful and warmer than I know to be the case. She plied Iona with presents and begged her to come again, to bring her friends and teach her yoga.

'Jolly sad, isn't it?' Iona said cheerfully in the car on the way home. 'I've never been in a country where the women had such a dismal time. Although they do say Jedda's a bit more lively, being a port and so on. Riyadh's the most puritanical place of all, you know. What a life, and she's so young – those women in New Guinea had to work like the clappers – head-hunting, I suppose – but they had a lot more life about them. Aren't you glad you're not a princess?'

On Wednesday morning we're having our first yoga class here. Iona is bringing some friends along to join in. I am looking forward to it, but at the same time I feel protective towards Aisha. I know she will be gawped at and gossiped about. For all her dignity she has no social armour.

So things are improving here. Perhaps your old mother will end her days in Riyadh instead of Torquay, with annual excursions back to London to sue you for libel. Seriously, Andrew, I must ask you again to be discreet. And please write soon.

> Your affectionate mother,
> Barbara Fairclough

January 23

My dear Andrew,

After reading your letter several times I am most unhappy. In fact I've arranged to take my leave next month so I can come back and see for myself exactly what you are up to. I shall be arriving in London on 10 February (*Inshallah*), and I can assure you I shall make my way straight from Heathrow to whichever seedy tabloid you are currently working for. I can think of many more pleasant ways of spending my hard-earned holiday than in chastising you, but your letter is so menacing that you leave me no choice. What on earth do you mean by 'edited extracts'? And how can I possibly remain anonymous? How many retired headmistresses with journalist sons do you think are currently living in Saudi palaces? I am astonished that any publisher would even consider such a proposition and I'm shocked that you've used your power of attorney so callously. I gave it to you only because my solicitor advised it. I notice you omit to name the publisher or mention the amount of money you have already wheedled out of them. My only satisfaction is that my letters are so unsensational, although they are probably enough to offend a regime which regards anything less than unqualified admiration as an insult.

I am so annoyed and upset that I've written to Poppy and Sylvia to tell them what you've done. I've even written to your Uncle Stephen, who may very well have something to say to you, and I've written to James telling him to withdraw your power of attorney. Your father often used to say to me, 'Andrew's an unknown quantity.' I must say I'm glad he died before your quantity and quality became so despicably transparent.

My first response to your letter was to rush downstairs to beg Aisha for a visa to go home. I was going to say you were desperately ill (wishful thinking, of course). I wept, Andrew. And as you may have noticed, I am a tough old boot who does not weep easily. Then I was forced to recognize my helplessness: *vis-à-vis* you, at this distance, and also *vis-à-vis* the Prince, who holds my passport.

Then I heard a great banging and shouting above the usual morning noises of screaming children and clattering plates. I lay on my bed, still sobbing angrily, and listened. I recognized the Prince's violent, megalomanic voice. The palace grew silent around him as his temper swelled and rose in a poisonous cloud. I head a deafening crash, then Aisha's high-pitched yelp of terror, followed by the ranting cruelty of his rage. The man is mad, I thought. Then I remembered: he's entitled to be both mad and bad, because there are no controls on his behaviour. If he decides to murder a wife or imprison an insignificant foreign woman, nobody would interfere or even report it. The newspapers here do not carry stories which are critical of the royal family, and I've heard that the British diplomats here are too nervous of jeopardizing trade relations to squabble over mere individuals. As it dawned on me that, between your stupidity and his omnipotence, my life and liberty were in danger, I began to hate both of you. Not very Christian, I know, but at that moment, if I had known of some black magic rite older than Christianity or Islam and abhorred by both, I would have made use of it to destroy both you and the Prince. And it's hard to say which of your funerals I would have danced at with more pleasure.

There was a terrible silence downstairs. I rushed to my window, raised the blinds and strained to see out. I had some idea that her limp body might be carried out of the garden door to be disposed of secretly. But all I saw was the Prince, elegant and affable. He came out accompanied by several other men in white *thobes* and *ghutras* and they all strode chatting and laughing across the gardens. I rushed downstairs to see if Aisha was all right. As I passed the children's corridor and the kitchen I heard voices, machines and other normal sounds cautiously returning. Dozens of people must have heard the scene between them and none of them, including me, would have lifted a finger against him to help her. Ashamed, I went into Aisha's library.

Aisha sat at her table, less erect than usual, and although it was obvious she had been crying, her face was composed. She has a psychological veil which makes her black one almost superfluous. Some maids were clearing up a pile of torn books, smashed ornaments and a broken chair. Aisha's eyes, which look younger than the rest of her, were bloodshot and surrounded by bruises. She was staring straight ahead and held out her left arm as if it hurt. We looked at each other like two slaves full of impotent hatred for absent masters. Then a maid rushed in with a veil, which Aisha flung over herself.

A few days before, I would have been appalled by Aisha's passivity. No man has ever pushed me around like that, I would have muttered with contempt as I barged in with disinfectant and bandages. Now I realized that she was lucky to be alive, that other women, royal or not, had probably not survived such attacks, and that this was not the moment to demonstrate my pity for her or ask for my visa. Pitying both of us, I went upstairs.

This afternoon I met Iona at French Corner, an agreeable café where women don't have to be too furtive. They even have a secret exit through the kitchen so that you can sneak out if you don't want to get locked in for prayer-time! Desperate to talk to somebody, I told Iona what had happened.

'Doris was saying to me only this morning over coffee, isn't it awful what the women here put up with? Maybe I should teach them karate instead of yoga.'

'But what could she do? She has no power. If he does divorce her, all she can do is go back to her father's house and be despised for the rest of her life. If her husband had killed her, I suppose he would have said he'd found her in bed with someone. Every servant in the palace would have backed up his story.'

'Well, we don't know how lucky we are.'

I showed her your letter.

'Silly boy. You pop over and sort it out. They're awfully materialistic, the young, don't you think? Mind you, wouldn't it be rather fun to be an author? You might make a fortune out of a book like that.'

I stared at her. We were eating delicious almond croissants and drinking fragrant black coffee. Nearby two other pairs of middle-aged women were discussing the price of gold and a Teddy Bear Conference in Montreal. I suddenly felt I wasn't living in the same city as they are or as Iona. I perceived tragedy, betrayal and cruelty where she saw only farce and food for gossip. She and those other women are protected by their husbands, sealed in the vacuum of expatriate life. I don't think they realize what a monster Arab masculine dignity is and perhaps they don't realize how closely related it is to the demanding egos of their own menfolk. I thought of my favourite story in *The Thousand and One Nights*, 'The Historic Fart' – do you remember it? After a sumptuous wedding feast Abu Hasan is summoned to the couch of his beautiful young bride. As he gets up he farts resoundingly. His guests pretend not to hear, but the man is so mortified that, instead of going to his bride, he saddles his horse and rides off, weeping, into the night. For ten years he travels abroad, trying to forget his shame, then at last he returns, disguised, to his native town, where he overhears a girl ask her mother when she was born. The mother replies, 'You were born on the véry night of Abu Hasan's fart.' I think it's a wonderfully subversive metaphor for the idiocy of masculine vanity, don't you?

Talking of which, I still feel extremely bitter about what you have done. I hope you realize that when I get off that plane I shall give you hell! I did in the end tell Aisha that I have to go back because you are ill, and she has promised me my visa tomorrow. I may not return here. Of course there would be problems – my bungalow is let until next autumn and I will have had only three pay cheques. I just don't know whether I shall be able to let go of what I complacently call normal life. Seen from here, peaceful retirement on a low pension in a green and grey seaside town looks awfully attractive. Do you know, I constantly dream of rain, mud, mist, frost, wood-smoke and clouds? February is the one month when the monotony of perfect weather is broken by a few days of rain – and I shall miss it. Yet I think I could have managed here for a few years and put away quite a useful sum. I wonder if you realize what you have done, Andrew? No, of course not. You never do.

> Your mother,
> Barbara Fairclough

February 1

Dear Andrew,

Now that 90 per cent of me has decided to leave, I am enjoying myself here. But don't take any credit for this as the rest of me is in turmoil. I feel guilty towards Aisha, who believes I am coming back here after a month, and yet I can't bring myself to tell her the truth. I imagine terrible repercussions if I do leave – Saudi secret police following me around Torquay, reading about Aisha's death in the newspapers – and yet I feel I must get away to become 'my self' again. Perhaps a certain amount of insecurity is salutary, but I think I have had enough for the time being. In England, you will let me down differently. I shall be closer to my ex-persona and perhaps better at impersonating her. Or so I hope.

We did have fun at our yoga class! Iona turned up with a suitcase full of leotards, matching tights and hair-bands for us and, to my surprise, Aisha tried them on with relish. She finally chose a bright-red leotard with green stripes, and I chose navy blue. Trying them on, giggling together in front of the mirror, we all relaxed. Aisha looked years younger and more casual and I was surprised by the difference this made to my own behaviour. Suddenly we were all girls together in the changing-room. Her dignity thawed, she became quite silly and for a few minutes I caught sight of what true harem life must be like. Then Iona made us lie on the floor, where we rolled about like brightly coloured spiders in distress. Aisha and I were as stiff as boards but Iona is quite disgustingly flexible. As we grunted and creaked she gyred and gimbled like the slithy toves. Gasping for breath, I watched us all in the mirror. I looked pear shaped and ungainly with frizzy grey hair and a red face, Aisha like some luscious fruit, a peach or a nectarine lost on the wrong tree, and Iona was perfectly composed and graceful. With her hair in a neat bun, wearing a black leotard and black tights, she was as fascinating to watch as a great dancer. Slowly, effortlessly, she made of her body a metaphysical instrument (although she is dismissive of the spiritual side of yoga).

'I don't think I'm really cut out for meditation,' she admitted when I mentioned the subject. 'I find I keep thinking of shopping-lists and nursery rhymes and getting the giggles – do you want us to try some, though?'

But it was enough of a revelation to me that I had been breathing wrong for sixty-four years and that a woman only a few years younger than I could still look marvellous. After forty minutes, Aisha and I collapsed. We rang the bell for coffee (I have taught one of the girls in the kitchen to make it just the way I like it, with Coffeemate and sugar). Aisha looked on, too polite to voice her distaste, and while Iona and I drank buckets of it she sipped a thimbleful of green Arabic coffee. I ached – but I felt so well! For years I've chosen to ignore what goes on beneath my chin and suddenly my body seemed to be flickering back to life. We smiled, chatted and felt good together.

Later Aisha said, 'English ladies are very nice.'

'Some of them.'

'You are free, happy.'

'Unhappy in different ways.'

Despite my protests I couldn't deny that, compared with her, we are in many ways blessed creatures. Under Islamic law men and women do have equal opportunity to enter Paradise, but until that happy moment there is, it seems to me, very little justice for women here.

This evening I telephoned Iona to ask whether she would carry on teaching Aisha if 'by any chance' I didn't return from my holiday. She agreed, which eases my conscience a little. And she told me a hilarious – or is it tragic? – story. All the women on their compound are in a tizzy because this morning, when Mavis went out shopping, she was stopped by a man in a car. Kerb-crawling, she thought, not knowing whether to be shocked or flattered. He said something incomprehensible, pointing to the villas where she and the others live.

'Pardon?'

'Activities with womans,' he mumbled with ambiguous gestures.

Oh God, he thinks it's a brothel, Mavis thought, terrified. We're going to be raided. 'No!' She shrieked. 'Only respectable ladies. Children. Grandchildren.'

He looked puzzled and again caressed the air with his hands. 'Activities, um, exercising. My wife she is wanting teaching. Same same dancing. Jane Fonda?'

'Yoga?' Mavis almost fainted with relief. 'You wife wants to learn yoga? Yes, we do have some classes.'

But they're still terrified he might be a secret policeman after all. You see, you never really know what's illegal here. Virtually everything. A group of women prancing around in leotards might be interpreted as immoral.

The more I read about this country's past, the more I regret having missed it. I really wish I had seen Riyadh when it was still a cluster of mud houses in the desert. I should have enjoyed sitting around a fire drinking coffee and listening to endless stories and poetry (*sihr halal* or 'lawful magic'). I should love to have seen the desert before the motorways cut across it, when the only way to get to Jedda or Mecca was to travel for weeks by camel in a huge straggling caravan. This past is so recent – just thirty or forty years ago – yet it's as dead as Elizabethan England. Perhaps my nostalgia for it is based on ignorance and presumption. I suppose

I wouldn't really want to live in a crumbling mud palace without air-conditioning or running water, pestered by flies and mosquitoes. And yet. There has been a murder of the spirit here, and I'm sure it has something to do with the way they treat women. There must be as many lively, talented girl children here as anywhere else, and what happens to them?

I've been reading about Queen Iffat, King Faisal's wife, who introduced educations for girls here. In the fifties she founded the 'House of Affection' and the 'Saudi Renaissance Movement', which runs free literacy classes and clinics for women. Renaissance of what, I wonder? Some pre-Islamic golden age? Queen Iffat was a real twentieth-century heroine, yet I've not been able to find any photographs of her, she gave no newspaper interviews and when she died there was no public tribute. As late as 1963 there were riots to protest against girls' education and the first headmistresses had to be installed by force.

Intelligent women here have no opportunity to develop beyond the level of basic literacy unless their fathers or husbands are exceptional or they themselves are fighters. Recently it has become illegal for girls to study abroad, so even Aisha's innocuous year in Switzerland wouldn't be possible now. Iona told me about a talk she had attended given by a young Saudi woman who had done a PhD at an American university on the life of women in the Empty Quarter. Apparently they are much freer than the urban women. Their menfolk disappear to work in the cities, leaving them alone, surrounded by hundreds of square miles of sand. There is nobody to tell them they can't drive or show their faces and so they run a kind of matriarchy. Even when the men are around, and go to their separate quarters inside the tent, the post-menopausal women are regarded as honorary men and need not segregate or veil. Iona said the lecture was interrupted by an American woman who asked, 'What about commerce? Do these women sell camel meat to supermarkets or something?' To which the lecturer replied, 'They don't have supermarkets.'

I laughed at the foolish question but secretly I thought I might have asked it. I don't know how it feels to be Aisha, let alone some desert queen of a kingdom of trucks, goats and camels. My ignorance and lack of sympathetic imagination are thicker than any veil.

Still no word from you. I wake up in the middle of the night imagining what new horrors you have in store for me. Have you

taken out a second mortgage on my bungalow or arranged for a
newspaper interview for me at the airport? I dreamed you came
here with your tape recorder and cameras. You crept all over the
palace asking people questions they didn't understand. 'I want to
be a fly on the wall,' you kept saying. And all of a sudden you
really were some kind of insect, not as harmless as a fly, a green,
stinging creature with transparent wings and many legs.
Interesting that my unconscious is so much more frankly
malicious than the rest of me. I often wish I'd had a girl. Sylvia
always says they're so much nicer, although I must say I saw little
evidence of that at Palatine Hill.

Well, soon we'll be together again, or at least in the same
country, so I suppose we'll have to tolerate each other.

Your affectionate mother,
BF (rather appropriate initials, I feel)

February 8

Dear Andrew,

I realize I shall be in London before this arrives. My passport
with its precious exit visa and Saudia ticket are in front of me on
the desk and I touch them nervously as I write. My Arabic is just
good enough to enable me to check that the visa is right. It allows
me to 're-enter'. But I shan't, I've decided now, although I
haven't told Iona, my only close friend here. I know she won't be
particularly surprised — every time someone goes on holiday here
there's the possibility that they won't come back. It's only that
possibility that makes life bearable for most of the women here,
who have so few reasons to stay. Now that I'm meeting other
foreign women I find I'm the object of envy because I have a job.
Well, in two days I shan't.

I have checked that my telex, giving you my flight number and
time of arrival, reached your office, so I don't want any excuses,
Andrew. If both you and the plane are on time I'll leave my
luggage at that little hotel near Kensington High Street and take
you out to dinner. Somewhere good — Simpson's, I think. There
won't be much to celebrate with, but I feel a strong impulse to
spend what I have. I've always thought of myself as rather a

puritan – I know you think I am – but after three months here I feel quite Bacchanalian. I want to get a bit drunk, buy some really good clothes in the sales if they're still on and go to Christie's to buy a set of flower prints for my sitting-room.

The only real problem is Aisha. She has said many times she will miss me and I know it's true. Our last few lessons have consisted of question-and-answer sessions about my life in England – the colour of my walls and curtains, the food I eat, your age and life-style. (And, I can assure you, an unmarried, childless man of thirty-six who drinks too much and writes for 'bad' newspapers takes some explaining here.) She keeps wanting to see your photograph, but the only one I have is of you and Bim (What is she up to now, by the way?) cavorting on the beach. I can see it dawning on her that sons can be worse than Fouad. All my preparations to leave are preparations to let Aisha down, and I do feel guilty. I am sneaking away from her and I can only do it by replacing the blinkers I have struggled to remove. I have had to make my skin thicker, my eyes cooler and harder. If the Prince comes to menace her again between now and Thursday night, I shall most certainly not hear him, because he could withdraw my visa. In my room I calculate just how many books and possessions I should leave here to make it look as if I shall return. I've already packed, and spend the hours I used to spend gossiping with Aisha sitting on my bed. Sometimes I imagine her, a black silk ghost, gliding up to my bungalow in Torquay in a chauffeur-driven hearse. I try to think of her as a young woman like my other ex-pupils who, I hope, will come to visit me. But the tragedy is that Aisha isn't young, has never been young except for those few months in Switzerland when she was sixteen. When the Prince finally tires of her she won't be free to choose another man or work or travel. She will be thrown on a kind of family scrap-heap until she is really old, and then forgotten. In my heart I'm sure I'll never see her again, although she will haunt me.

I shall have to remind Sylvia, who believes in these things, not to get herself reincarnated as a Saudi woman.

> Your affectionate mother,
> Barbara Fairclough

Memsahib, Inshallah

1

For the first hours of the flight Mona didn't even notice who was sitting next to her. She was moving towards Eric, as fast as possible, and after six months' absence that was all she wanted. In most of her memories he was young; walking on the moors, dancing in Leeds, waiting at bus-stops on cold nights when his beery, nicotiny warmth were the only reality she wanted. His face then was clean edged like a carving, his crinkly brown hair and cleft chin were freshly minted. The chin had lengthened since and curved, and the face folded around it reminded Mona of a goat's. Her own, fine boned and long jawed, combined with her gangly (once coltish) body to give her a horsy look. Still, they really had been a handsome couple, before they became a menagerie. In between, Eric's image became blurred by the girls'. He had been jealous of them, had felt pushed out, and she could see why. Though he never left. But he had stayed on the periphery of the circle Mona had formed with her two daughters, and when they left home he was still there, amiable, a good husband everybody said, but not quite in the room with her most of the time. Mona hadn't expected to miss him so much when he went off to Riyadh. So many couples they knew were separated now because of their work, and Mona had expected to enjoy having the house to herself, had said so to all her friends. She still had plenty of friends. But the visa took so long, Eric's letters were like shopping-lists and on the phone they couldn't talk, somehow. They were embarrassed in case the operator understood English and was listening in, and anxious because of the bill.

When the plane stopped, Mona stared out. Cairo, where Tutankhamun came from, where her dad had been in the war. He

156

used to tell rude stories about camels and belly-dancers when her mum was out of the room. It must be quite near Riyadh because there was sand everywhere and it was warm. When she left England that morning the roads and houses had been upholstered with Easter snow.

Then Mona became aware of the voice of the woman behind her, which had been monologuing for most of the flight, blocked out by Mona's memories.

'. . . and I'm not going Air France again, I can tell you. It's a disgrace, stopping at Cairo when they already made us wait for hours in Paris. As for the food – a tin of tuna, a soggy bit of rabbit food and a pudding you could bounce. Say what you like about the Arabs, on Saudia they treat you like a queen. And Gulf Air too. When I lived in Dubai I always travelled Gulf. They're very rude, the French, I've always said so. And the toilets. Have you seen the state they're in? Now Saudia toilets are always nice and tidy, with good quality perfume you can help yourself to. Mind you, it always gets pinched by the end of the flight. I don't know how people can be so mean. When you think what their husbands are earning! I've had some gorgeous food on Saudia. Kebabs and little cakes with almonds and honey. And smoked salmon – it really was, not just tinned. They come along with these little snacks in case you get peckish before you land. And such friendly hostesses! These girls, you'd think they'd swallowed a lemon and a pint of vinegar. . . .'

The voice was so near and so relentless that at first Mona thought she was being addressed. She looked back nervously and saw a woman of about her own age, in a white dress and sandals, standing in the aisle. She had yellow, frizzy hair and her face, arms and legs were dark brown, sprinkled liberally with liver spots and freckles. With one beefy arm she gesticulated as she talked, though her loud voice was emphatic enough, and Mona stared, fascinated, at her huge gold charm bracelet. The woman was talking, Mona now realized, to a group of women, all of whom looked English and apprehensive. Occasionally one of them asked a question. Mona decided to join them and, turning towards the bracelet, watched it swing and rattle as she waited for an opportunity to interrupt.

'. . . I know you do get the free champagne, but mine wasn't even chilled – and such tiddly little bottles. I don't know why they don't just give us a half-bottle each and have done with it. I

promised my husband I'd give it a try because of course it is
cheaper, but I always say you get what you pay for and, after all,
'tisn't us paying, it's the company. That's one thing I do like
about being out here – out there, I mean. You do get looked after.
What with the maid and the air-conditioning and the swimming-
pool. I don't think I've had to so much as change a light bulb since
I came out. I mean I love going home, of course, but it's quite
squalid really, the Yookay now. I went into Altrincham to shop the
other day and there was a group of young lads terrorizing
Mothercare, smashing the windows and scaring all the kiddies.
Now in Riyadh they wouldn't have any of that. That sort of
behaviour would not be tolerated, and a good thing too if you . . . . '

Breathless from her long wait for a break which never came,
Mona panicked and burst out in her soft voice, 'What about the
clothes? What are we allowed to wear there?'

The bracelet paused in mid-air and came down to a point just
above Mona's nose.

'Are you going to be on a compound?'

'Yes.'

'With a pool?'

'Yes.'

'Oh, that's all right then. Which company does your husband
work for?'

'International Oil Products.'

'Oh.' The woman became quite friendly. 'Oh, you'll be all
right then, love. The IOP compounds are very nice, specially the
new one. They've tennis-courts and heated pools. The reason I
asked, was that on a compound you can do pretty much as you
please. Shorts, bikinis – I wear the lot. And if I do go down the
gold *souk* with the girls, I put on my *abaya* or my kaftan. Where are
you from, by the way?'

'Nelson. And you?'

'We've just moved to Bramhall. We were in Northenden, near
the council estate. Do you know it there? But I must say it's not a
patch on Bramhall. Our new house is smashing.'

'Oh yes, I know Bramhall. Very nice. Have you travelled a lot
then?'

'Well, you know. Dubai, Cyprus, Kuwait, Portugal. Quite a
bit, really.'

'Oh. I've only been to Spain.'

'Never mind. You'll soon settle in. It's very pleasant over at

IOP. Give us your phone number, love, and I'll give you a ring, come and see you. You will have a driver, won't you?'

'I think so.'

'I'm Betty, by the way, Betty Grantham.' The charm bracelet was thrust out again to seal their friendship.

'I'm not going to a compound, I'm going to live in a block of flats. And I won't have a pool, or a driver, or a maid,' one of the younger women said miserably.

'Which company does your husband work for, dear?' Betty asked brusquely.

'CGL. They're a small computer firm.'

'They're very tight, some of these little firms. You want to be careful.' Betty turned back to Mona. 'D'you play bridge?'

'No.'

'Golf?'

'No. They never play golf out in the desert?'

'Oh yes, there's a lovely course. It is very sandy, you can imagine, and you get the odd Arab asleep in the bunkers, but you meet a nice crowd down there. You'll have to learn.'

On the short flight from Cairo to Riyadh all seven women established that they came from places within fifty miles of each other. The newcomers were comforted by this, repeating the familiar names like mantras.

Mona wasn't prepared for the magnificence of Riyadh Airport. She had assumed that, compared with Heathrow, most of the world's airports were a come-down. A few tents and camels were what I expected, she remembered as she glided down an escalator, past marble steps planted with trees. Real ones, where birds twittered, though it was past midnight and a bit late for birds, even foreign ones. Over there was a vast fountain with flowers planted all around it, they looked real too. 'Esther Williams,' Mona murmured to herself.

'You what, love?' said Betty.

'D'you remember her? Me dad used to be crazy about her. She used to make these swimming musicals, diving in and out of fountains like this one. Sort of underwater ballet, it was. Donkey's years ago now.'

'Oh, you'll be amazed by the luxury out here. A million pounds on marble is nothing to them.'

The queue for passport control was very long and slow. Documents were checked in a leisurely way by tall young men wearing red and white tea-towels on their heads and long white robes. Mona thought them very handsome, like silent film stars. Funny how I keep thinking of the cinema when it isn't allowed here.

As they inched nearer to the glamorous officials Betty paused in her monologue to hiss, 'Oh, look at that! They've got new computers. That's why it's taking so long. You don't mean to tell me these people can actually use those things!'

'I'm sure I couldn't,' said Mona.

'Yes, but it's supposed to be their job. They're not very bright, you know, the Arabs. Me 'usband always says about Saudis, if he's warm to the touch, they'll promote him. Oooh, you wouldn't believe the corruption. . . .'

Mona collected her luggage, which was copious because Eric hadn't given her any information about the shops. So she had stocked up with six months' supply of everything, even tights and toothpaste and Nivea cream. Betty was still beside her.

' . . . of course, if your husband's not here to collect you, you'll have to go into a separate room and wait for him. They don't let married women out of the airport on their own. You see, a few years ago there was this Egyptian girl, ever so beautiful she was, married to a Saudi, and she came out here to join him. He couldn't come to meet her, so he sends his best friend along, but the best friend takes one look at her and takes this pooor girl back to his flat. Well, he rapes her, you know, chops her up. They got him in the end and chopped his head off. They do it in public, too. A lot of the expats go and watch, though I wouldn't fancy it meself. . . .'

Mona was relieved to see Eric, waving both arms at her, on the other side of the glass barrier. He was very tanned. His face looked harder and he was wearing a wide-brimmed, dark-blue hat like their grandson's cowboy hat, a red and green check shirt and jeans. Mona threw her cases on to a trolley and rushed towards him.

'Are you off, then? Be seeing you.' Betty said.

'Yes!' Mona smiled, and her thin, pale face crinkled with joy.

Watching her, Eric thought, she's always had a nice smile. Pleased to see me too. He thought he was pleased to see her, thought he had missed her more than not, hoped she would fit in. It was odd to hold her angular body again and smell that very clean, hospital smell that always clung to her hair, which was greyer than his own.

'They don't allow that here.'

'What, love?' Mona held him, burying her face in his sweaty shirt, weeping with happiness.

'Kissing and cuddling. You'll have to wait until we get home, we've a bed the size of a football pitch.' Grinning wolfishly, he pushed the trolley. 'What've you brought all this for?'

'I didn't know what to pack. You didn't say . . . .'

'Oh, they've everything in the supermarkets here.'

Eric stopped in front of a very large, shiny black car with a big red wheel on the back. Mona thought it looked like a cross between a hearse and a Jeep.

'That's never your car, Eric?'

'Yours, too.'

'What's all the pictures on the back window?'

'That's the Rockies. You can see out but not in. So all those darkies can't stare at you when you're riding in the back. Gives it a bit of character too. D'you like it?'

'I don't know really.' Grunting, Mona hauled herself up on to the high front seat beside him. She couldn't lose the sense of unreality that had swathed her as soon as she got off the plane. Pale buildings drifted past as Eric in his strange hat and familiar voice talked, using alien words: *Sallah, sediki, abaya, mettahwah, souk*. The streets were silent and new, lined with palm trees like a vast, urbanized desert island. The car stopped, Eric got out and unlocked a gate in a high white wall. Up some steps Mona smelt flowers and rosemary. Eric let them into a hallway and Mona, suddenly excited, ran to look at a big sitting-room with a picture window, a dining-room, a bathroom with bidet and shower, a bedroom with the massive bed Eric had described. 'Oh, it's a bungalow. I always wanted to live in a bungalow!' Then, in the kitchen, Mona saw a strange woman. She stood smiling at her. The woman was dark brown, nearly black, with dark-red scars cut deep into her cheeks.

'And this is Seiko.' Eric said.

'Psycho?' Mona asked nervously, suddenly awkward, wringing her hands and staring at the woman.

'You can go to bed now, Seiko,' Eric said, and the woman disappeared. 'I thought it'd do you good to have a rest, love.'

'But what's she for?'

'She'll do all your cooking and cleaning. You don't have to lift a finger, just enjoy your holiday and the pool – have you seen it?'

Outside the dining-room window a dark rectangle of water
gleamed. 'It's even heated. You can go straight out in the morning
and meet the other girls. They're mostly Americans on this
compound. Very open, they are. And tomorrow night I'm taking
you out for a meal. Come on, let's try that bed out. I've been lost
in it all these months.'

2

The next night they went to a cavernous hotel, deserted except for
rows of uniformed, smiling, bowing men. Flunkeys, Mona
thought. One of them told her to have a nice day, although it was
dark outside. Mona caught sight of her reflection in the pink
mirrors on the walls and on the highly polished marble floors. She
looked tall, in her best beaded mauve kaftan, and felt almost as
glamorous as her surroundings. They passed a tickertape
machine, spitting out the prices on the stock exchanges around the
world, and crossed another deserted marble hall with an
illuminated green fountain and dozens of empty wicker chairs. It's
like a palace where they're all asleep, Mona thought, maybe I'm
sleepwalking. Music, too. They passed a grand piano where a
Korean pianist in a dinner-jacket tinkled away at 'A Nightingale
Sang in Berkeley Square'. That was Dad's favourite during the
war. They used to play it on the radio and he'd wisk me around the
front room. First time I ever danced.

'Are you allowed to dance here?' she whispered to Eric.

'You must be joking! They're worse than the Plymouth
Brethren and the Methodists put together out here – what d'you
think of that, then?'

They entered a huge pale-blue tent of a restaurant. Gleaming
brass rods supported the pleated canopy of the roof, in the centre
of which an enormous palm tree made of brass and green enamel
rose up. Banks of plastic flowers divided the tables, at which Mona
saw at once there were no other women.

'Signora! Signor!' Three immaculate waiters showed them to a
table.

'There were angels dancing at the Ritz,' Mona hummed
nervously, glancing over the vase of plastic flowers at Eric, who
was still grinning proudly. The waiter handed her a huge menu
which she frowned at, anxious to choose the right thing. On the

cover was a big, colour picture of cowboys on horseback rounding up cattle: AMERICAN BEEF * * * THE PRIME ONE. Inside, before you even got to the food, there was practically a whole chapter on steak. Mona had never realized it was so complicated, so many cuts.

'The rich American grainlands – secret of the unsurpassed flavour. America is a land overflowing with wheat and barley and all the other grains that help make up for the famines of the rest of the world. It's natural, therefore, that while Europe tends to feed its cattle on cheap grass, Americans can afford what to us would be a luxury diet of grain ... '

'What are you going to have, then?' Eric asked in the conciliatory, talking-to-an-invalid voice he used with her now.

'Oh ... I don't know.' She searched desperately for the page with the food on it.

'We'll have the avocados and two of the Turf and Surf, please. And a jug of *sangría.*'

'Are we allowed?' she gasped.

'It's not real. Just grape juice and soda and fruit salad on top.'

'Oh.' She was silenced by his air of belonging there, his familiarity with this exotic restaurant. She found the food page at last, and calculated that the meal would cost more than she used to earn in a week teaching dressmaking. 'I'll have to keep the menu, send it to Andy. He's wild about cowboys. He was four on the twenty-first. You didn't send him a card.'

They discussed their daughters, Bev and Lorraine, and their three grandchildren. Mona had spent the weekend before she left with them all and had unpacked their photos before anything else. She had said all along, I'm only going out there to get enough money to spoil you all rotten. But now they were far away in time and space, on the other side of that glass screen, beyond the cotton-wool wedges that muffled her brain. Eric kept changing the subject back to exchange rates and bonuses. The Korean pianist started on 'Some Enchanted Evening'.

' ... and if we stay on till I'm fifty-eight and two months I'll get a Saudi state pension as well.'

'That's a funny age.'

'They've their own calendar here, 'tisn't like ours.'

'Do you remember this? From *Carousel*, wasn't it?'

Turf and Surf consisted of a vast plate laden with steak, lobster, baked potatoes and broccoli cooked with almonds.

'Once you have found him, never let him go,' Mona hummed, and sighed at the sight of the food. 'I don't think I can eat all that. Very rich, isn't it?'

'It's smashing, is American food. Reckon I've eaten a steak a day since I arrived.'

Eric beamed and gleamed as if protein was a cleaning agent that had inwardly and outwardly polished him. He's different, Mona thought. She kept feeling an urge to touch him, to make sure he was really the same. But they had hardly touched at all since her arrival. They'd made love in that bed, as excessively big as the steak she was trying to eat, but hadn't cuddled. 'You may see a stranger, across a crowded room,' the Korean pianist insisted again with violent arpeggios. Well, he is a bit like a stranger, really.

'It does seem very American, the way of life out here. I thought it'd be all camels and sand and dates.'

'I'll tell you something, Mona.' Eric leaned forward so that their noses almost touched through the plastic flowers. 'I didn't think much of the Yanks when I saw them at the end of the war, but here they're bloody marvellous. Work hard, play hard, eat and drink like kings. We don't know how to live any more, back home.' And as if to demonstrate, he poured them more alcohol-free *sangría*, sat back, took a big cigar out of his top pocket and lit it up. He puffed clouds of evil-smelling smoke into her eyes.

'You look bigger,' she said suddenly. 'Not fatter, exactly.'

'I've bin doing a few body-building exercises with the fellas. We use a room near the swimming-pool, fitted up like a gym. When I first arrived I was that white and skinny, I was ashamed. Americans look healthier than us, too, have you noticed? The women are like film stars, even the ones your age. I dunno how they do it.'

'Make-up and face-lifts, I dare say. Well, I'm surprised to hear you talking like that. I thought you didn't like foreigners. In Marbella you went on and on about how dirty and ignorant they was.'

'That was the Spanish. Americans aren't like that – well, you'll see. They're having a barbecue Friday night, round the pool, so you'll get a chance to meet them all. And there are some nurses coming.'

'Whatever for? Is somebody ill?'

He laughed, louder than he used to laugh. 'Oh, Mona! Don't say things like that on Friday, will you?'

'But what d'you mean? What's all this about nurses?'

'Nurses are about the only single foreign women out here, right? So of course they have a ball. Men queuing up to take them out, parties every night – well, it's not surprising, is it? All these fellas stuck out here on their own.'

'I hope you haven't been queuing up,' she said sharply.

Mona baked some sausage rolls for the barbecue. Seiko didn't like her using the kitchen, but Mona insisted. She enjoyed cooking and, really, there wasn't much else to do. Sue-Ellen and Amber had dropped in for coffee that morning and stayed for a long chat, of which Mona understood about half. It was all very well Eric saying it was the same language, but it wasn't. They were all foreigners here and she had written as much in her first letter to Bev.

While she was sitting on the couch writing the letter, Mona had glanced at the photos of them all, on the coffee-table, and suddenly felt really homesick. Nearly cried in fact. Then she looked up and saw Seiko in the doorway, smiling. She sat beside Mona on the couch and showed her her own photos, of a wedding and a little boy in uniform. Mona thought she said that the girl getting married was her daughter and that the child in uniform was her son, who had disappeared. It's terrible, Mona thought, putting little kids in the army. But they aren't civilized in them African countries. She didn't like sitting too near Seiko, because close up her skin was so pitted and her tribal scars, or whatever they were, made Mona feel sick. Anyway she wasn't sure if it was right to talk to servants like this, though Seiko did call her madam.

The sausage rolls came out very nicely and Mona decided to make a trifle as well, since there was so much time. I've got all the ingredients, even the angelica. The shops here are wonderful. It was a very hot afternoon and they were all round the swimming-pool. Mona could see them out of the dining-room window, a dozen women and children and a couple of those huge, bulging men too. All very tanned and noisy. A lot of horseplay going on, splashes and screams and giggles as someone was thrown in the pool. Mona had brought her swimming-costume but she wasn't keen on swimming or sunbathing. I wouldn't feel comfortable, showing off me body in front of strangers like that. I did try on me costume and stood in front of that long mirror in the bedroom but, really, I won't do. All those white, crêpy, baggy patches, they'd only laugh at me. She had another shower and decided to knit some more mittens and bootees for her baby grandson.

Eric came home and stood by the dining-room window in a clean shirt, watching the preparations for the barbecue.

'Have you thought of getting your hair done while you're here?'

'Not particularly.' She patted it nervously. 'It's all right, isn't it?'

'There's a great social life out here, you know, once you start to meet people. Might as well look your best. Harmony does the girls' hair in her flat. She used to be a ladies' hairdresser. Why don't you go along? Oh, and here's some money, in case you need anything.'

Eric took out a new red leather wallet and handed her a thick wad of notes which Mona accepted, feeling guilty because she had done nothing for the money. She didn't even know how much it was worth. I don't want to go to the party, she thought. Eric was right about my hair, I look awful and I can't talk to these people. Mona was just about to tell him she had a headache when he jumped through the window, like a circus act. He landed on the Astroturf and bounded up to the group around the barbecue.

Mona went the long way round to the pool, through the gardens and white bungalows. It's very pretty, really, she thought, like a holiday village in a Club Méditerranée brochure. She introduced herself to everybody, including several people she had already met. These women, she thought, I know Eric thinks they're the bee's knees but to me they're all like Barbie dolls. And the men too, with those tiny heads balanced on enormous shoulders and chests, as if somebody started to inflate them and then ran out of breath. Not one of them under six foot. They make Eric look tiny. And all these funny hats. I've not seen so many men in hats since the war. Cowboy hats and baseball caps with RIDGID written all over them – what's that supposed to mean, I'd like to know? They all had deep, slow, nerveless voices and brown faces full of white teeth. None of them had heard of Nelson and she had never heard of Ah Cansaw, where most of them came from. They spoke so slowly that even familiar words were stretched beyond recognition. They kept saying they loved her accent, and after a while she realized this meant that they couldn't understand her, either. She edged closer to Eric, hoping he would act as an interpreter.

An oversized man approached them, his forefinger raised in the air, and drawled, 'Hi, Eric! How's ya hammer hangin'?'

'Does he want to borrow a hammer?' Mona whispered to Eric.

'Hi, Sam. This is my wife, Mona, who's just arrived.'

'Hi, Mona. How ya doin'?'

'Oh, hello. Very well, thank you,' she said hurriedly when the long, round syllables stopped rolling.

'What've you got there, Mona?' Eric asked reprovingly.

She looked down and saw she was clutching her dishes. The round trifle dish, balanced on top, had spilled red jelly and yellow custard all over the sausage rolls beneath and a greasy stain was spreading all over her dress. Horrified, Mona put the dishes on the nearest table and sat down heavily.

'Hi, I'm Bob.'

Bob was about ten years younger than she was, thin and quiet voiced, built on a far less superhuman scale than the other men. He was bareheaded, with a serious, anxious face, and he came from Dallas, which Mona had heard of. They sat at the small wrought-iron table, licking the jelly from the sausage rolls, and warmed to each other as misfits. Bob was divorced, had been in Riyadh for three months and had a lot of Saudi friends. He said this defiantly, and although Mona had been in Riyadh for only three days, she looked around nervously to make sure this eccentric remark had not been overheard. Bob didn't drink, either, and said he thought the Koran was a wonderful book which everyone living in Saudi Arabia ought to read. He was studying Arabic, and at weekends he often went into the desert on sheep-killing picnics with his Saudi friends. . . . Bob talked for hours, in a cautious torrent, as if he hadn't been listened to sympathetically for years. Mona understood most of what he said and was relieved to be involved in a conversation, albeit a one-sided one.

Nobody joined them at their table, with their abstemious bottle of mineral water and children's party food. Behind Bob's monotonous voice, Mona was aware that the barbecue was becoming wilder; vast quantities of big, bloody steaks and *sediki* were consumed. There were whoops and cackles of laughter as people jumped, or were thrown, into the pool. Mona heard a great crescendo of guffaws and, turning, saw that a girl she suspected of being a nurse had stripped and was about to jump in the pool. The watching crowd roared, stamped and clapped as the thin, white girl paused on the edge of the pool, her face for a moment terrified in the moonlight. Then she dived in.

'Pretty near time to go home,' Bob said without looking round, as if the girl's naked plunge was an alarm clock that went off at the end of each party. 'Reckon I'm too old for skinnydippin'.' He picked up his bottle of mineral water, nodded and walked away.

All around Mona couples reassembled like pairs of cards, gathered their belongings and went home to their respective bungalows.

'Why ever did you spend so much time with boring Bob?' Eric demanded as they made their cocoa.

'I don't think he's boring. He does seem lonely, though.'

'It's his own fault. In the refinery they say, "Ask Bob the time and he'll tell you where he bought his watch."'

'That girl's still in the pool, poor thing. All on her own. Do you think I should ask her in for some cocoa? She'll catch her death.'

'Stella? She's crazy. Comes from south Wales. Can't keep her clothes on for two minutes. These barbecues nearly always get out of hand,' he said with satisfaction.

Mona ran to the bathroom, got a towel and threw it out of the dining-room window. In the morning she found it on the window-sill, neatly folded.

3

Eric said she ought to have a coffee morning and invite all the women on the compound. But somehow Mona didn't and they no longer rang her bell. She spent days on end inside her bungalow, cooking, writing letters, knitting and reading the romantic novels she bought in the supermarkets. Once a week she and Eric visited these emporiums, monuments to consumer power, and after several trips Mona managed to fill up her freezer, which was big enough to store several bodies in, with ice-cream, fish fingers, peas, chips, meat and poultry. This gave her a sense of achievement: it was comforting to have enough food for months ahead, on a desert island. You had only to remember the war. Several times a day, Mona opened the lid of the giant coffin and stared at her supplies.

But Seiko's presence invaded her privacy. Mona moved from room to room, avoiding her, fearing Seiko's judgement on her inactivity. Eric started work at seven and came home in the late afternoon, exhausted, sweaty and usually furious about some incident at the refinery.

When Betty phoned, Mona greeted her like an old friend.

'Have you settled in?'

'Oh yes. We've a very nice bungalow. You must come and see it.'

'I thought you'd be all right on the IOP compound. How d'you get on with the other ladies?'

'Oh, they're very pleasant.'

'And have you got a driver?'

'Yes. Though I've not been out yet.'

'Mona! You should be ashamed. You've been here nearly a month.'

'I know. But time passes so fast here . . .'

'That's no excuse. It's very important not to let yourself get cut off. I'm going down the gold *souk* Wednesday with some of the girls. Why don't you come along? We'll pick you up. Is it the compound near the junction of Pepsi and Jareer, or the one near the Takhassukki Road?'

'I don't know,' Betty said guiltily, suddenly realizing that she had no idea where she lived. Behind a wall in a Club Méditerranée, a suburb of Ah Cansaw.

That night she had to ask Eric for a map. It had been drawn by hand and photocopied many times, and was full of strange references to the Coffee Pot Monument, the White Elephant and Camel Corner. The names conjured up places far more intriguing than anything Mona had glimpsed on their desultory drives to supermarkets. She posted the letter to Betty at her PO box number and began to look forward to her outing.

On Wednesday morning they rang the bell and surged into the bungalow, six women aged between thirty and fifty-five, wearing droopy black *abayas* over long cotton dresses. Betty seemed to be their leader. She stalked around, appraising and examining Mona's kitchen and bathroom, photographs, furniture and crockery. The others sat down in the sitting-room and waited for Seiko to bring them coffee.

'Very nice. And that's your pool – it's quite a small one, isn't it? I do like your picture window! Where's your maid from? Oh dear, that's where they're all fighting and dying of famine and that. D'you think she's all right? Did you let your husband find her? I'd never do that, I must say. After all, you're the one as has to live with her. Are these your clothes? Very unusual. Made them all yourself, did you? You should really get yourself an *abaya*, then you can wear what you like underneath. You'd better wear this one, love, to go to the *souk*. Not that one, it's a bit transparent. Who's that waving to you, Mona?'

'I think it's Amber. Oh no, it's Harmony.'

Firmly, Betty helped her into the appropriate kaftan, covered her head with a pink chiffon scarf and squirted her with perfume.

'Blue Grass? Me, I always use Chanel No. 5. Right, you'll do. How many coffee morning have you been to?'

'None.'

'Oh, Mona! And how many've you had?'

'I haven't yet ...'

'Mona! Honestly! Come on girls, we're off.'

They bundled Mona into a small bus driven by a thin, ferocious-looking Pakistani. He drove so fast that the women bounced, their jewellery rattling as they giggled to each other. Mona thought, it's like being on the school bus again. If only I could remember what made me popular then, it'd be all right here, I could make some friends. Betty issued peremptory orders to the driver, who looked increasingly angry. Mona wondered if that sarcastic, abrupt tone was the correct one to use with servants.

'Haven't you got any jewellery, Mona?' Janice asked pityingly.

Mona felt defensive. 'I've got a few pieces I wear when we go out.'

'You should get that husband of yours to buy you some,' said Betty, who had already cast Eric, unseen, as an avaricious, callous, domineering man whose wife needed help.

Looking around, Mona saw that all the other women were wearing at least two pieces of gold jewellery, the most spectacular of which was Betty's charm bracelet. 'Can I have a look at your charms, Betty?' she asked ingratiatingly.

'That's the Yeiffel Tower, and that's just an old boot my husband bought me years ago. This cricket bat's very unusual, it's got a real ivory handle. And this cat's got real emeralds in his eyes. He gave me that as an anniversary present. I lost me hand of Fatima playing golf last weekend. I'll see if I can find another one. What are you going to get, Janice?'

'I thought I'd get meself some more earrings. Mavis is going to get that chain we saw last week.'

'Are you, love? Good for you. It's all twenty-three carat here, you know, Mona. Purest gold in the world, and dirt cheap, compared to Europé – ouch! Are you all right, Rita? Honestly, Ahmed, why can't you drive properly?'

Mona looked at Ahmed, who was cursing to himself, and wondered if he understood English. She thought she had seen him look at them in the mirror with particular dislike when they were discussing jewellery. He probably didn't earn very much, being a Paki.

As they drove into the centre the buildings became older and more interesting. There were lots of arcades, buildings painted white or pink, shops lavishly stocked with jewellery, perfume and rolls of fabric. It was a far more feminine city than Mona had expected. They passed several gangs of foreign women like themselves, *abayas* flapping raggedly in the warm wind, and dozens of black-robed, black-veiled Saudi women.

'Don't they ever take those veils off?' Mona asked.

'Aren't they awful, poor things? My husband calls them the Guinness bottles. They're only allowed to show their faces to each other, their husbands, fathers and brothers. When they're not out shopping they spend most of their time in the harem. Never lift a finger.'

'Must be so boring for them,' Janice sighed. 'No wonder they go wild when they get to the Yookay. Night-clubs, shop-lifting, gigolos – we don't know how lucky we are, being free.'

'Ooh, talking of gigolos and that, guess what we're getting hold of soon.' Rita lowered her voice. 'The video of *Death of a Princess*. It's not a very good copy, apparently. Still, I've been dying to see it. Let's watch it after bridge next Tuesday, shall we, ladies? Are you coming, Mona?'

'I'd love to. I can't play though.'

'You'll soon learn. There's the Blackpool Tower, we're nearly there.'

Ahmed stopped in a vast square surrounded by public buildings. The women climbed out of the bus, reminding Ahmed not to be late like last time.

'You know where we are now, don't you, Mona?' Betty asked gleefully.

'No.'

'Chop Square, where they do the executions. And chop their hands off if they're caught stealing. Still, I'll say this for them, they're very honest. I left my handbag on the counter in Safeway's last week and nobody touched it. You wouldn't get that back home, not nowadays.'

'And over there, under the palm trees,' Janice said, taking Mona's arm, 'is the falcon market. A good trained falcon'll fetch about ten thousand quid. Ooh, look, there's a baby gazelle for sale today. Aaah, intit lovely!'

The women stood and stared at the dignified, ancient transactions being carried out on the small patch of balding grass. Several urban Saudis wearing *thobes* and *ghutras* were examining a falcon which was chained to a red velvet pedestal. The Bedu who had spent months in the desert, training the formidable bird, squatted beside it, describing its merits and haggling over its price. The gazelle, tied to a palm tree by a piece of string, shivered fastidiously.

'Fancy paying all that money, just for a bird.'

'It's like a racehorse back home.'

'Of course they don't look after their animals here. Look at that pooer little thing. It's just a baby.'

They clucked and cooed, stroking the gazelle, which looked terrified. The Bedu indicated that they were not to touch it, and several of the beaky, stern-faced men broke off their conversation to glare at the women, who backed away.

Arm in arm they set off for the gold *souk*, loudly discussing all that they saw. Again Mona had that sensation of being behind a screen, walking amongst waxworks in fancy clothes and flimsy cardboard buildings which might collapse if you pushed them. Her companions gave her the same sense of unreality, although she tried to like them, warm to them, belong with them. For weren't they just like herself? They turned into a labyrinth of concrete corridors lined with cells stacked high with rugs and carpets. Men with leathery faces, wearing long, white garments like night-shirts, stood around in groups, talking. They became silent as the bevy of Western women swept past. There was a heavy cloud of spices, incense, leather and an ancient smell of new rugs. Mona wanted to linger. She liked the sights and smells of the place, and smiled at a young boy in a pale-blue night-shirt who was trying to sell her a carpet woven in rich, dark colours. But Betty and the others dragged her off, as if she was a child in a toy department and they were her impatient parents.

'Now don't get lost here, whatever you do. We never come
down the *souk* on our own, do we, girls? They're not used to seeing
women, specially not blondes, you see, and they can't control
themselves.'

Mona smiled sadly at the idea that anybody would be driven
wild with uncontrollable lust at the sight of her or any of the others.
Only Betty could be described as a blonde, and her hair looked as
if it had fought a long, painful battle with peroxide and other
chemicals. None of them looked their best in the ankle-length
shapeless cotton dresses which, it was true, covered bulges, but
also suggested there might not be any curves to disguise. The
ungainly black *abayas*, which all the women wore knotted at the
throat, made them look like a gang of witches on the prowl. Mona
decided not to buy an *abaya*. I won't make a fuss about it, she
thought, but after all I'm old enough to know what I want. It's like
the coffee mornings, I just don't happen to fancy it.

The labyrinth opened out into a sandy space lined with cubicles.
More goods were spread out on the ground here: baskets, copper
bowls, coins, necklaces, bracelets and chests studded with nails.

'Ooh, I'm glad to be out of there,' Janice said, as if she had just
escaped pursuit by an army of rapists. 'This is the antique *souk*.
Quite interesting, really.'

'Are they antiques?' Mona asked, squatting to examine a
necklace of battered silver beads irregularly strung with turquoise
cubes.

'Some of them, probably. Of course they've not got much
history here.'

Mona decided to buy the necklace for Lorraine, who liked
ethnic jewellery, and also bought a tiny brass coffee set for her little
granddaughter. She paid the price the stallholder asked, stripping
off the notes from the wad Eric had given her.

Betty turned around in horror. 'Oh, Mona! You should never
give them the price they ask, they'll think you're daft.' And she
snatched the notes back from the elderly stallholder, who looked
furious. He coldly indicated that he wouldn't sell Mona anything,
and withdrew inside his cubicle. Mona was annoyed. He hadn't
asked very much, she had such a lot of money and nothing to
spend it on. She didn't like to offend people and this morning it
seemed to her they were offending everyone. They were in discord
with their surroundings, too loud, too aggressive, too rich.

Betty took her arm and propelled her down more corridors.

'You mustn't let them take advantage, love. You could've got it for half the price. We'll go to the ladies' *souk* now, get you an *abaya*.'

'I don't want one, thanks.'

The women looked alarmed.

'But all the foreign ladies wear them.'

'The Saudis prefer it. It shows respect for their culture.'

'Well, I don't want one. I think they look awful.' Mona's heart beat frantically.

'Oh, well. We'll just go straight to the gold *souk*, then.'

4

They marched back through the dark carpet *souk* in a different formation, Mona alone behind the others. On the street they blinked at the shock of sunlight and modernity. Soon they turned off the pavement again into another dark cave full of treasure. Brilliant yellow objects blazed, glared, sparkled. It was almost too bright.

'Is it real?' She asked incredulously.

'Twenty-three carat.'

Mona saw now that there were women everywhere, groups of Western women like themselves as well as Saudi women. They were all animated, eyeing, ogling, fingering and trying on the jewellery. Strange to think of all that gold under their mournful black, Mona thought. Strange to think of a woman like me let loose in Aladdin's cave. She stopped in front of a glass-fronted cabinet and gazed at the intricate display of gold, ranging from fine chains to elaborate sheets of chain-mail, like elfin armour.

'That's what the young girls wear on their wedding nights,' Betty confided loudly. 'Holes in all the right places, you see!' She chuckled.

Gold even hung from the low ceiling; you could reach up and pluck it like an apple. And no security, no metal grilles or keys. The only men were the smiling stallholders in their white night-shirts, who were far more dapper than the other merchants in the *souk*. They encouraged the drooling women to caress their wares. The cubicles were scrupulously clean and brilliantly lit, tiny theatres in which to set tableaux vivants of greed. Mona looked at a fine golden chain with a coral pendant on it. Cautiously, she reached out to touch it.

Betty was at her arm again. 'Go on. Try it on. Suits you. You ought to treat yourself. I'll lend you the money if you've not got enough.'

'But when would I wear it?'

'Whenever you want. That's what we're here for, after all. That's what's so gorgeous about gold, you can keep it on all the time, in the bath or in the pool. Will I get the price down for you, love?'

'All right, then.'

Betty's haggling was a formidable performance. Using her charm bracelet as an auctioneer's hammer she bludgeoned the price down by a third. The stallholder was at first amused, then indignant and finally sullen. Mona fumbled with the money Eric had given her, which was more than enough.

'There you are, love. No, don't wrap it up. Wear it. Let's show the girls.'

They crowded round Mona to admire the necklace and at last she felt she had done something acceptable. Then they were off again, swooping down the brilliant yellow corridors that branched off in all directions. The atmosphere between them was happier, warmer.

Rita was looking for a third gold necklace, Janice for earrings, Betty for a hand of Fatima, Mavis for a bracelet and Tina for rings. At stall after stall they jostled, giggled and haggled, thoroughly enjoying themselves. If one of them was left behind, the others searched for her in mock panic.

'Bottom-pinchers!' Betty explained as she dragged Mona forward. 'They're that sneaky, these Arabs. They'll walk beside you and you'll just feel a hand, like that, so you're not quite sure what they're up to.'

After an hour Mona was hot, thirsty and exhausted. She kept touching the necklace to make sure it was still there. In dozens of mirrors she caught sight of it and marvelled. Already the girls were egging her on to buy another.

'Oh, I feel so much better,' Rita said as they stood again at the entrance to the *souk*. 'Last Monday I was that depressed, I was talking about leaving again. Sometimes I miss the kids so much, and I'm not going to see my grandchildren grow up, am I, stuck out here? I mean it's very friendly on our compound but it's not the same, is it? So Jim said, I'll give you five hundred riyals, love. Go down the *souk* and buy yourself something nice. And he was right. I wouldn't really want to leave him on his own out here.'

'Asking for trouble,' Betty said darkly.

'Can we get a drink? I'm parched.' Mona felt the warm air was like an oven shrivelling her skin and throat. Yet this was only May.

Rita frowned. 'That's a bit of a problem. It'll be *Sallah* soon and we're not allowed in Kentucky Fried Chicken any more.'

'Why ever not?' Mona was still amazed by the number of things women were not allowed to do.

'Well, to begin with, a few years back when I arrived, half the expat wives in Riyadh used to go down there of a morning. They do lovely coffee and chips in there. We'd sit behind the screens and have a bit of a party. It was great. Then the word got round and there was so many women crowding in, there was no room behind the screens. There'd be thirty or forty of us squashed in there, and maybe one or two blokes sitting outside, in this enormous space. It was daft. So one morning somebody – was it you, Betty? – asked the blokes if they'd mind swapping. They were very obliging. They weren't Saudis, mind you, but Filipinos or Pakis or something like that. So for a few months we had the run of the place, and we sat in the windows bold as brass. It was just like being at home. Then the *mettahwahs* got to hear about it. Just before Ramadan they raided Kentucky Fried Chicken. Said they'd close them down if they let women behave immodestly and flaunt themselves in the window. Anyone would think we'd been soliciting. Well, it's enough to drive you to it, intit? Anyway, now it's a funeral parlour again and we're not even allowed in.'

'But can't we just get a can of Coke or something?' Mona asked desperately.

'Sssh!' Betty hissed. 'They don't allow Coca-Cola here. I think they invest in Israel or something. Let's see if we can find some Pepsi before prayer-time.'

As the skies crackled and buzzed with the first cries of nasal ecstasy, they furtively bought three tepid bottles of fizzy orange from a woman who sat cross-legged on the pavement with a basket of drinks and sweets.

'See that? Black as the ace of spades. They came over here as slaves and a lot of them stayed on. Is that Ahmed late again?'

'Look, there he is. Right round there on the other side of the clock tower.'

'Fast asleep at the wheel.'

'Oh, he's that lazy. I'm going to complain again.'

'That's right, love, you stick up for yourself.'

They piled into the minibus. Betty shook Ahmed, who sat up and yawned. Mona, sitting just behind him, thought he looked really ill.

'How many hours a day do you work, Ahmed?' She asked suddenly.

'Fourteen hours every day, madam.'

'No days off?'

'Sometimes Friday. I prefer working holidays because Riyadh holidays no good.'

'But don't you get any holidays? Don't you ever go home? Where are you from?'

'My country India, Bombay. In two years I have one holiday. One month. Next summer I am having holiday.'

'Oh dear.'

Betty nudged her. 'You really shouldn't talk to them like that, dear. He might get the wrong idea.'

Ahmed turned up his radio, so that all further conversation was drowned by Indian pop music.

'Are you coming to bridge Tuesday, Mona?' Betty asked doubtfully.

Mona thought, they don't like me. I want them to like me. 'Oh yes, I'd love to. And I have enjoyed myself this morning. It was ever so nice of you to ask me along.'

'That's all right, love. We all have to help each other here. I'll give you a map for your driver, then.'

It was only half-past twelve when Mona got home. Still at least four hours before Eric came home. She put away her necklace in her red leather, velvet-lined jewellery box and wondered when she would wear it again.

Seiko was sitting on a stool in the kitchen, reading a letter and weeping. When Mona came in she didn't hide her face or scurry away, as Mona would have done, but looked up at her with tragic eyes. For a moment Mona hesitated, remembering Betty's advice. Then she went awkwardly over to the woman and put her hand on her arm.

'What's the matter, Seiko?'

The letter was from army headquarters in Addis Ababa.

Seiko's fourteen-year-old son was reported missing.

'Go and lie down, love. I'll make you a cup of tea.' Mona put her arm around Seiko's shoulders and led her to her bedroom.

But later she wondered if she had done the right thing. Perhaps she shouldn't have been so weak. Betty and Eric had both warned her that they played you up and took advantage if you were too soft on them. Tomorrow I'll have to keep my distance again, she reminded herself.

Fretfully, Mona made frequent cups of coffee and waited for Eric. She tried to ignore the scene outside the dining-room window. Several of the men who worked night shifts were there, pushing each other into the pool again. Diving and showing off to the women. She was glad Eric didn't do night shifts. They were making such a din she couldn't concentrate on her knitting. Mona frowned at the offensive window and caught sight of two tiny children, naked and beautifully tanned, in a plastic padding-pool. They reminded her so painfully of her grandchildren that she could only go to the window and stare longingly. Then, for the first time since her arrival she opened the window.

'Would they like some ice-cream?' she asked the woman who seemed to be looking after them. She thought it was Sue-Ellen.

'Sure would,' said the woman laconically. She wore a white bikini and lay on a towel with a straw hat over her face.

Mona had bought a huge box of choc ices, out of habit and optimism, which were now stored in her giant coffin. She handed two of them through the window to the tiny children, a boy and a girl.

'More of your folk comin' soon,' Sue-Ellen remarked, her hat still over her face. 'Brits.'

'Really? Coming to live here?'

'Sam says they're recruitin' in England now.'

'Ah heard that too,' said Harmony, coming over to the other side of the window and looking inside Mona's bungalow curiously. 'The Refinery's not goin' to pay American salaries when they can git cheap labour from Egypt 'n England 'n places like that.'

'We were figurin' on leavin' in the summer,' Sue-Ellen said indifferently.

One of the night-shift workers strode into the pool enclosure with a cassette player booming country music, a yodelling, twangy male voice whingeing about balls of fire. Mona shut the window with distaste.

Eric also approved of the necklace. 'It's gorgeous. You'll have a collection by the time we leave. All the women do. You can wear it to the barbecue, Friday. It's a hill-billy theme this week.'

'You what?'

'Oh, cowboys, that sort of thing. Were you all right, down the *souk*?'

'What d'you mean?'

'Well, I've never bin but I have heard it's not safe down there. Tom, one of the blokes at work, went down there with his daughter last Christmas. She's only fifteen and well endowed, so I gather. Some old Haji comes up and offers him four hundred riyals for ten minutes with her round the back of the stall. "Top half only," he says to Tom.'

'I wonder he didn't take it. They're that interested in money, people around here.'

'Mona! It's only what we're all here for. Anyway, I don't think you should go down there too often.'

'I'm not fifteen and neither are the others. Oh, and Seiko's in a dreadful state. Her son's disappeared in the war, poor soul. Which country is it she's from?'

'I can't remember. One of them where they're always fighting and having famines and that.'

'Anyway, she's in her room. I hadn't the heart to make her work today. Not that there's anything for her to do. I don't really know why ever you thought I'd need a maid.'

'I want you to have a good rest, love.'

5

Mona thought, I'm looking forward to bridge too much. Like when I was a very young girl, waiting for parties. I was always disappointed when I got there. I used to warn the girls about doing that. In a middle-aged woman like me it's ridiculous. Pathetic really. And I'm dreaming far too much, always about home. Having the family around me again, children touching me, needing me. Then I wake up crying because nobody does and I can't get back to sleep until it's time to get up. Well, things were better then even if we had no money. Eric was never interested in money then in any case. He has changed, it's not just me, and maybe it's not just Riyadh either.

Sometimes she tried to talk to him about their past together, as if to check out his identity. On the night of the hill-billy barbecue, as they moved around the bedroom getting dressed, she said, 'D'you remember that suite we had in the old house?'

'Can't say as I do. Aren't you dressing up?'

'I'm too old to be a cowgirl. Old cow, more like. You must remember, it was orange. Then later when we gave it to our Lorraine. She had it redone in green.'

'Oh yes. We bought it at the Co-op.'

'No, it was Widdowson's,' she said sharply.

'Was it? I could've sworn it was the Co-op. Oh, well. That was a long time ago.'

He fails all me tests. Perhaps he really is an impostor. How he enjoys all that boozing and whooping and guffawing. He does it so naturally. Mind you, he's always been a sociable man – on the noisy side when he's tanked up.

Mona sat at her usual table, with Bob, stiff with embarrassment but smiling anyway. It is nice to see Eric enjoying himself and I am pleased, of course. I wish I'd gone home early, when they all got out their guitars and harmonicas and started wailing and yelping, but there'd be no point, seeing as how our bungalow's in the middle of the party, so to speak. Harmony, Sue-Ellen and the others are really unfriendly now. It's because I'm British. The words got round that the Brits're going to pinch some of the Yanks' jobs. And because I get on with Bob, they treat him like some kind of pariah, though he's a nice enough bloke even if he does talk too much. Makes a change from talking to meself all day. Still, it's hard not to take it personal, specially when Eric gets on so well with them all.

Even Eric's hangover, which lasted all the following day, confirmed his role among them. Mona started to think and talk a great deal about Betty and her friends. Although at first Betty had seemed to be a bit on the hard side, she'd turned out to be very kind. As she brought Eric his fourth cup of tea on Saturday morning, Mona remarked, 'It must be nice to be on a compound like Betty's, with plenty of other Brits around.'

'Give me the Yanks any day. I've lived with bloody Brits all me life and I can't see what's so flipping marvellous about them.'

'I don't know what you see in these Americans, to be perfectly frank. To me they're just a bunch of loud-mouthed, flashy show-offs.'

'I'll tell you why I like them – because they're fun, and they're generous, and full of enthusiasm. They're not moaning and whining all the time like most of the Brits you meet nowadays. Like you, Mona. Honestly, you haven't stopped since you got off that plane. You want to be careful, with a name like yours.'

'That's not fair, Eric.'

'If I'd've known you were going to be like this I'd've advised you to stay in Nelson.'

'I wish I had,' she said with all her heart.

'Well, go back then.'

But as he said it he looked so grey and tired and grim that she held out her arms to him, and he didn't push her away.

'I don't want to leave you here on your own, chuck. But it's so lonely for me here. Maybe it'll be better when there are a few more Brits on the compound, people I've something in common with. I'm going over to Betty's, Tuesday. She's really very nice. You'll have to meet her.'

'All right then. I hope you do settle in here, love.'

'I expect I will. Takes time, doesn't it?'

Mona kept picking up the map to Betty's compound, as if it was a love-letter. Grand Festival Palace, Fish and Chip Street, Al Akariah, baseball pitch in front of clinic. She wondered if the Sudanese driver would recognize all these curious landmarks. She made a potato salad and a sponge sandwich, Lorraine's favourite cake.

On Tuesday morning Mona put on her best mauve kaftan and her new gold necklace. She had wanted Harmony to do her hair, but hadn't managed to pluck up the courage to ask her. They were so glamorous, Harmony and her friends, so obviously initiated into mysterious processes and bottled magic of which Mona had no knowledge. She imagined them in and out of each other's bungalows all day, giving each other perms, facials, manicures and massages. Mona put on some pale-pink lipstick and waited for the driver to ring the bell.

On the way to Betty's she gripped her two bowls tightly. She was the only passenger on the minibus, which called each morning to take the women on the compound shopping or to visit friends. The Sudanese driver was, like Ahmed, cool and subtly hostile. With his back Seif managed to express anger, contempt and suffering.

Again, Mona felt compelled to talk to the driver and question him about his life. Seif worked a twelve-hour day six days a week, shared a villa where forty other drivers slept ten to a room and, after eighteen months, would be entitled to one month's holiday. His employer held his passport, and if Seif had an accident, which was only too likely in Riyadh's crazy traffic, he would either have to pay a heavy fine or go to prison. He had a wife and a baby he had never seen, in Khartoum. He explained to Mona that only foreign workers with a degree or equivalent qualification were allowed to bring their wives to Riyadh. It was on the tip of her tongue to say, Well, what's Eric got? He left school at fifteen like me. Then she remembered that Eric was white and had a British passport, which was a sort of qualification really.

'Like a slave,' Mona said, amazed, not knowing how to sympathize. She admitted to having her own apartment, maid and swimming-pool. Seif's tension was like a spring coiled tight. When the spring was released there would be violence. It made Mona nervous to think of all those lonely young men in the city, living in squalor and enforced celibacy, saving money and quietly performing their tasks. Hating.

Betty's compound was behind yet another high, white wall. There were six four-storey blocks of flats built around a swimming-pool, surrounded by lawns and flowers watered by a sprinkler system. Betty was wearing sunglasses, a straw hat, a T-shirt and shorts. They passed two women, chatting in their dressing-gowns and curlers.

'We're very relaxed round here. In and out of each other's flats all the time.'

'They're really very nice, the compounds here.'

'This is nothing compared with some,' Betty said resentfully. 'You should see the Oriental Bank compound – squash courts, playgrounds, a video-club and a clubhouse where they do aerobics. Gorgeous. Oh, well.'

Betty lived on the second floor, in a big, modern flat. The sitting-room was full of women. There were the five who had come to the gold *souk*, clad today in shorts and sun-dresses, and at least six more. They waved their coffee-cups at Mona in greeting, smiled, waggled their bare legs and looked playful. There was an atmosphere of youth and forced gaiety, as if Betty's Maxwell House had been a little strong for them.

'Move up, girls!' Betty said to three women sitting on a couch.

Mona squeezed in shyly and accepted the cup of coffee pressed on her.

'I mean, this is it, isn't it?' One of the women was saying. 'All take and no give. I think Arthur Scargill's a monster. And he's not going to suffer for his obstinacy, is he? It's the miners' wives I feel sorry for.'

Rita said, 'I'm glad Mrs Thatcher's taking the unions in hand.'

'They've too much power.'

'They should come to a country like this where there aren't any unions.'

'Or go to Russia.'

'They don't know the meaning of the word work, most of them.'

'Me dad was a miner,' Mona said suddenly, not knowing why it made her feel so sad.

Betty clapped her hands. 'All right then, ladies! That's enough gossip. Mona, you've not played before, have you love? You'd better stand behind Janice and watch, you'll learn a lot from her.'

With a great deal of giggling, nudging and coyness the women regrouped and sat at three tables. Three packs of cards were produced, shuffled, cut and dealt, and as they slid deftly down on to the table Mona saw the women's faces change. They became serious, intense and passionate.

'We playing for money today?' Betty asked hopefully.

'Oh no!' Rita giggled.

'Right,' said Janice. 'Five riyals a point.'

The game continued in fierce silence, punctuated by groans and nervous laughter. Mona tried to watch Janice's cards, but her attention wandered; she had never played games with any enthusiasm and cards bored her. She associated them with boozy masculine evenings and talk about football and racing. She was surprised to see these women grip their cardboard fans so murderously. Janice hissed at her partner, Tracy, who had committed some folly. Mona edged her chair round so that she could watch Janice's face. At the *souk* Mona had thought she was quite pleasant, less aggressive than Betty. Janice was about forty, with a son at a 'good' boarding-school in Yorkshire. Her large, florid face was anxious and her bloodshot blue eyes fixed desperately on the cards in the centre of the table. Although Mona hadn't been able to follow Betty's minimal explanation of the rules of the game, it was quite obvious that Janice was losing and blamed her partner, Tracy, who kept apologizing. This drama became so painful to watch that Mona wandered over to another table. Betty, whom Mona would have expected to be a ferociously competitive player, held her cards loosely. In between turns she sat back and made joky conversation. Mona's eyes strayed to the big table laden with the food they had all brought. She tiptoed over and helped herself to a piece of banana cake.

This game goes on for ever. It's like opera. Eric used to watch it on telly sometimes, but I never could make any sense of all them Italians taking half an hour to say good morning. Fancy grown women getting so worked up about a few bits of cardboard. I'd sooner have snap – at least it's got some life to it. Mona fidgeted, nibbled and yawned.

At last Betty remembered she was there. 'All right, love?'

'Oh yes.'

'Getting the hang of it?'

'I think so.'

'Come on, then. You can take over from Tracy. I think she's had enough.'

Tracy, almost in tears, got up and scuttled into the bathroom. Mona sat down in her chair, which was still warm from Tracy's bum, electric with the tension generated by the game.

Janice glared at her. 'Well, we're bound to lose now.'

Gwen and Hilda, Mona's opponents now, smiled at her as if to confirm Janice's opinion. Mona felt exactly as she used to do at school when she was the one nobody would pick for their side at netball. She wished she could get a note from her mother. She gripped the cards, relieved to have something to do with her hands. Janice leaned over to rearrange her cards into some mysterious order, hissing commands which Mona didn't understand. 'Yes, all right,' Mona kept saying, hoping Janice would go away. But instead she snatched one of Mona's cards and slapped it down on the table.

'I don't think we can allow that. You're not supposed to play both hands, Janice,' Gwen said coldly.

'Not when we're playing for money,' Hilda said.

'So we'll say this game doesn't count.'

Mona was relieved. She didn't mind playing a game that didn't count. Sitting back, she let Janice grab and bully. Although Mona did nothing to stop Janice, she decided she didn't like her and would never play bridge again. Janice glowed with triumph when she and her phantom partner won the game that didn't count.

Mona watched her big, coarse, greedy hand cut, shuffle and deal.
She looked round at all the other hands, encrusted with rings and
bracelets, and at the hard, staring eyes above them. Janice's hot
breath was on her again. Mona could smell her Nivea cream and
Miss Dior.

'Play the ten of diamonds!' Janice hissed.

But when her turn came Mona played another card. She
wouldn't look at Janice, though she could feel her angry presence
beside her. Why am I annoying her like this? Why can't I enjoy
the game, join in, team spirit, take things as they come? But there
was in this demonic game some force that brought out the violence
and aggression in all of them, made them be themselves. And their
selves were not cosy, not friendly or wifely or motherly or
grandmotherly or sisterly. Tracy came back into the room and
hovered over their table. Bitterly, she stared at Janice. Then she
winked at Mona, who put down the jack of diamonds because she
liked his face.

Gwen and Hilda pounced, gathered the cards together and
snorted with triumphant laughter. Mona looked at her watch and
saw it was lunch-time. Not since her last few years at school had
she felt such relief at the end of a session.

Janice hissed viciously. 'That's two hundred riyals we've lost,
thanks to you. And I'm not paying a penny of it. If you don't know
how to play, you shouldn't've come.'

'But I told you I didn't . . .'

'That's not fair, Janice,' Tracy said sharply. 'You accepted
Mona as your partner. We'll split the money three ways, seeing as
how I played for the first half of the game.'

Janice threw her cards on the floor and turned away petulantly,
quivering with anger. Mona had never seen such a large woman
throw a tantrum before.

'All right, girls!' Betty yelled. 'Time for lunch, or there'll be no
time to watch the film show before the yusbands get home!'

They crowded round the table, laughing again now, nudging
and joking. But Mona couldn't join in. She sat alone at the table
where Janice's hands had grabbed, pushed and snatched.

Betty came over to her. 'Come on, love. Try me garlic bread.
Don't worry about Janice. She always gets worked up about
cards.'

Over lunch they were all friends again. Tracy and Janice complimented each other on their cakes and exchanged knitting patterns. The cotton wool was in Mona's head again, the screen was between her and them, so that she could hardly talk to the other women although they kept talking to her and looking at her oddly.

After lunch they drew the curtains to shut out the dazzling afternoon sun and sat down to watch that other screen. This picture was dim too, Mona noticed; it wavered dimly and the sound-track crackled, whispered furtively then suddenly boomed. The film seemed to be about a young princess, who she had been and how she had died. But it seemed to Mona that the real subject was the dimness of this young girl's reality, the difficulty of living at all in Riyadh, let alone dying. Behind high walls this girl had danced, gossiped with other women, maybe fallen in love, maybe been caught. Inside the brand new buildings the women took off their veils and killed time together. Did they play bridge, have lunch-parties, coffee mornings? At least they're pretty, Mona thought, the child wives of Riyadh. They watch each other sing and dance with pleasure and perhaps their husbands and lovers visit them with passion. I hope so.

At the end of the film Betty said, 'Sad, intit. That poor young girl, never a moment's freedom.'

'Married off to some old man.'

'Not allowed to work. Mind you, I don't suppose they get much of an education, the girls here.'

'We should thank our lucky stars.'

'We don't know we're born.'

Mona said nothing. All around her in the dark she felt the warmth of other women's bodies, smelled their perfume, sweat, cigarettes and food, heard their breathing and their watches ticking.

'Now, there's just time for *The Muppets* before my husband comes home,' Betty announced.

'Oooh! Where'd you get it from?'

'Through that video club of Ron's.'

'But what's illegal about *The Muppets*?' Mona asked, bewildered.

'Miss Piggy, of course,' Janice snapped.

No ambiguity here. The copy of the film was in yucky

technicolour. The women ooohed and aaahed as Miss Piggy batted her eyelashes and Kermit the Frog sidled and wisecracked in a plague of cuteness. Mona was reminded of something: the big eyes and mouths, the loud voices and phoney graciousness of the females, the beefy, booming males – she had met the Muppets, in spirit at least, at the Friday night barbecues. She smiled to herself, pleased because she now had a private language in which to hate her neighbours. I won't tell the others, or Eric, but I'll write to Lorraine about it. Lorraine'll understand. Bev's got no sense of humour and Eric thinks they're the bee's knees. Following them around like a little kiddie, he's even bought a baseball rig-out now. He looks all skinny and shrivelled inside it.

'Did you say something, Mona?' asked Rita, who was sitting on the floor beside her.

The film ended. For a moment they sat on in silence in the dark and it was good, calm. They might have been anywhere.

Then Betty jumped up, drew the curtains and looked at her watch anxiously. 'Come on, girls. My husband'll be back any minute.'

'And mine too!' Rita squealed as she rewound the videotapes. The other women stampeded to the dining-table and collected their dishes.

Reluctantly, Mona stood up. For a moment she hoped that Seif would forget where she was. Eric wouldn't know and I don't even have my address or phone number in my bag. I could always stay on here, like a changeling. Learn bridge, put up with Betty's husband who can't be worse than Eric, just wait for Ramadan when I can go back home . . . then Mona realized the other women were making whispered arrangements for another bridge session, glancing at her uneasily. They don't want me, I've disgraced myself. Mona grabbed her food and was offended to see that her cake had only a small triangle missing and her mound of potato salad was hardly dented.

At the door Betty asked her, 'Are you coming to aerobics on Tuesday, love?'

'I don't know. I'll phone you. Bye.'

Choked with failure and rejection, Mona rushed down the white marble corridor, down the stairs and across the lawn. There were children playing in the swimming-pool and Mona turned to watch them longingly. If I had one of those I would know who I was. There was no shade between Betty's block of flats and the high wall. By the time she reached the gate Mona's skin was prickling and she could have drunk a gallon of water, though she had only just had a cup of coffee. I can't remember what time I told Seif to come for me. If he's not there, I've no way of getting home. They say it's not safe for women to get taxis on their own. Anyway, I can't remember where I live. I can't remember what colour Seif's car is. Or what he looks like. Black and thin – oh heck, there are four black drivers out there. I've lost the map Betty gave me, it's not in my bag, maybe I left it in the car. And the gate's shut now, locked, Betty's on the other side and I can't even remember the number of her flat. Or her surname. Her hands clasped under her chin, her face drooping with fear and confusion, Mona blinked helplessly at the cars. One of the drivers was honking and smiling. But what if he's one of them abductors Rita was talking about, he might drive off with me, no one would ever know. . . .

Wearily, Seif waved again at the gawky, frizzy-haired woman. They all looked alike to him, but he remembered her ugly, crumpled mauve dress. He wondered if they got drunk at these parties or went to meet their lovers. She was swaying oddly and her eyes were bloodshot. She didn't seem to see him, even when he drove right up to her and opened the door for her.

'Is it you, Seif?'

'Madam?'

'We are going to the IOP compound, aren't we?'

'Madam? You want shopping?'

Mona got into the car, recognizing his voice and the pale-blue seats. 'I want to go home, Seif.'

Mona was lying down when Eric came back that afternoon. He looked with distaste at her old pink quilted dressing-gown drooping over the side of the unmade bed, and at her shrivelled yellow feet sticking out like dead leaves.

'What's the matter? Been here all day, have you?'

'Of course I haven't. I told you, I went over to Betty's. I've just got a bit of a headache.'

'Another one? You want to watch it, Mona, or you'll be living up to your name. How was your party, then?'

'It was all right.'

'Going to become a bridge fiend like all the rest of them?'

'I don't think so, somehow. Yes, it was very pleasant really. We played cards and had lunch and watched some videos.'

'Watched videos? Were they dirty?'

'Certainly not.'

'You should've seen some of the videos they showed up at the clubhouse when I first arrived. Before you came out, of course. Disgusting, they were.' Eric chuckled. 'There was one of them called *Debbie Does Dallas*. Bloody amazing. Made me wonder where I'd been all me life.'

Impatiently, Eric drew the curtains, letting the cruel sunlight expose the dry pouches and crevices of Mona's face. Mona sat up, wounded by his tone and aware of her unbeauty as she clutched her dressing-gown and fled to the bathroom. An old bag. Empty, used, useless. She struggled into a bra, girdle, dress and make-up, into a more attractive form.

Eric sat in the dining-room with a glass of beer, riveted by the scene outside the window. The brown, energetic bodies laughing, chasing and lounging. Flat tummies and smooth terracotta skins, buns like apples. He can't take his eyes off them. That's why he always has his drink in here instead of in the sitting-room. Well, I hope they get cancer from all that sun.

She sat beside him, 'Eric?' He's tired too. The men here all go grey under their sun-tans. They age, wither, till only alcohol can lubricate them. 'Eric, I've bin thinking. I'm bored here. I know it's the life of Riley but I can't stand it. Honest. It doesn't suit me.'

'You don't do anything, Mona, that's why. You just lie around in the house all day. There's a pool right there outside the window and you never use it.'

'That's just lying around in a different place. I don't like swimming or sunbathing, I don't have to like them, do I? I want to work.'

'Don't be daft. I earn more than enough now. There's no question of your working.'

'Not for the money. Just to give me an interest. I enjoyed teaching. I never used to get headaches and funny moods when I was teaching. And there's plenty of opportunities here. I could set up dressmaking classes tomorrow if I wanted to. Advertise in the newsletter that Intercontinental Women's Group puts out. Women'll learn anything here, you know, they're that bored. We all are – Chinese cookery, Japanese gardening, batik . . .'

'What's batik, for Christ's sake?'

'I don't know. Something foreign that passes the time. I could get Bev to send me out a load of patterns, and clear out the sitting-room so there's plenty of space. I'd have to buy a machine – well,

I need a new one – and get the ladies to bring their own.'

'I'm not coming back to my own house every day to find a hen-party going on.'

'We'd do it in the mornings. Seiko would help me clear up afterwards, Eric?'

'No, I'm not having it. You've worked hard all your life, and I'm sorry you've had to. But I'm earning good money now and I want you to have a rest.'

'I don't want a flipping rest. It's driving me round the twist having a rest!'

'I'd never forgive myself if my wife had to work when I'm earning the kind of money I get here.'

'But I'm not talking about money.'

Mona stared at him, incredulous at his stupidity. His face looked as if it had been carved, clumsily, out of a rectangle of wood; frown lines all over his forehead, his mouth lugubrious, his eyes hard and glazed with complacency because he was taking a stand. This wasn't the first time. In the past he had taken stands about buying their own house, not having her father to live with them and not letting the girls stay out late. Lorraine said Mona was weak to put up with it. Emotional blackmail, she called it. But although she was disappointed, Mona was at the same time glad he still cared enough to interfere, to want to look after her. She saw in his mulish pride a kind of tenderness which she needed more than independence. Mona grabbed his rough, grey hand, which had veins bulging out like tree roots. He was like her, really. The sun hadn't touched him, he still belonged to the bleak, resilient Northern world. They were both aliens in this silly Muppet town. Mona stood up and hugged him, but he hardly responded. As if every nerve in his body was absent, taking a stand.

'They can see us through the window.'

'Who cares? We see enough of them. It's like a blooming striptease out there – like the Windmill, we never close.'

'I wish you'd try to make more friends on the compound, Mona.'

She dropped her arms. The cotton wool was in her head again and the screen, which was also the window on the pool, divided her from Eric.

7

Mona went into the sitting-room, where the picture window framed harmless grass, flowers and bushes. She sat with her head deliberately turned away from Eric, from Seiko preparing supper in the kitchen and from the Muppets disporting themselves beside the pool. Suddenly, to her annoyance, the neutral space was filled by Sam. Wearing a baseball cap and a tight T-shirt which displayed all his terrifying muscles, he pushed her sliding glass doors aside as if they were saloon doors in a Western.

'Hi.'

'Good evening.'

'Ya know what that sonofabitch Bob's gawn an' done?'

Mona said nothing, but Eric came in, sat them all down and poured out glasses of root beer and peach brandy. He was flattered by Sam's visit. They didn't get many visitors.

'Boring Bob, you mean? Bob Ponting? See, Mona, I told you he was a funny bloke.'

Sam had wavy grey hair and a heavy, rather noble-looking face. Grudgingly, Mona admitted he was handsome. He had an expression of immense disgust and drawled his words so slowly that she could hardly understand them. His vowels were dragged out like yodels.

'He's converted to Islam. Saw him jist now goin' to some mosque in his *thobe* and *ghutra*. Even gawn dyed his beard and mousse-tache, to be like them. Bin invitin' his Saudi friends in too. Nobody wants them creepin' round our compound. Next thing we know, they'll have the police over.'

'Oh my God!' Eric said.

'He did say he thought a lot of the Koran,' Mona said in a conciliatory voice.

Sam brought down his fist on the coffee-table, which bounced a foot in the air, and roared as if he was trying to outpreach Muhammad: 'Ya'll know what that hick's plannin' awn doin' next? Goin' on TV to tell the worreld how he's done gawn converted. How Ayrab values and Ayrab culture and Ayrab morals are the greatest. He just doesn't wanna know 'bout America. Says it's corrupt, decadent, doomed to blow itself sky-high. Well, I'll tell you something. I'm gonna have his balls for gravy. We're gonna git him awff of this compound. Ya'll wanna sign a petition, sayin' how all of us feel?'

'I'll certainly sign it,' said Eric, getting out his ball-point, clucking and looking solemn. Taking another stand.

Mona was uneasy, haunted by the image of Sam's huge fist slamming into Bob's pale face. At parties Bob looked like a frightened rabbit at a gathering of weasels. In this brutal world of macho 'oilies' Bob had only his droning voice with which to defend himself. Well, why shouldn't he dress up and change his religion? They all dress up here, anyway, with their daft hats. Sam's got a butterfly tattooed on his arm like a kid. The arm with the butterfly, its wings bulging and rippling indecently, held out the petition to her.

'No thanks. I don't think I'll sign.'

'The wife's a bit tired,' Eric apologized.

'No, I'm not. I'm not going to sign it because I like Bob. And who's this petition going to, anyway? They're all Saudis, aren't they, the directors at IOP? Well, what's a Saudi going to think if you all say you can't bear to live with a Muslim?'

Sam looked at her as if she had lost caste. His manner towards her changed, and he no longer spoke to her in the chivalrous, patronizing voice that had gained him a reputation for charm.

'Well, I don't happen to agree with that kinda liberal bullshit. Any man that's born an American, that man is born with one helluva privilege. Ah jist can't understand why any man would give up that privilege. To me, it's jist like a white guy choosin' to become a nigger. Well, we're goin' to have a meetin' 'bout Bob right now, in the clubhouse, and you're real welcome to come along, Eric.'

'Thank you. Yes. I will, I'll just have a bite to eat.'

Sam strode out, ignoring Mona. She sat hunched over her drink, surprised by how malevolent she felt; how frightened too. She wanted to warn Bob. She kept remembering some film she had seen years ago, set in an old-fashioned American town where they were persecuting witches. Shut up in a tiny, closed community, unable to escape. I feel like a witch meself, an ugly old outcast.

Eric was watching her. 'Honestly, Mona, you didn't have to be so rude. What's the matter with you?' He gobbled the sandwiches Seiko had made for him. 'Well, I'm off.'

After he left, Mona tried to read a novel about a Regency heiress who was constantly being bundled into carriages and things called phaetons by a masterful young buck called Beau Clarence. Seiko asked if she should serve the mound of rice and meat she had prepared.

'Come and eat with me, Seiko. Let's have it in here.'

Shyly, Seiko sat on the edge of an armchair opposite Mona. Whenever she was allowed to cook she produced this satisfying bulky food. Eric said she used too much garlic and spices, but Mona ate with enthusiasm and pleased Seiko by taking more. They smiled at each other over their food. Mona thought sadly, Seiko's the closest thing I've got to a friend out here. I didn't like it at first, having another woman in the house, but now I've got used to having her around. I don't want to be alone here any more. There's too much glass in the houses, it's too easy to look in. As if the architects thought there'd be monkeys living in the houses, wanting to show off all the time.

Seiko was showing Mona her photos again, of a pretty young woman and an old man in military uniform who looked very frail. Mona thought she said they were yet another daughter, who was getting married, and her husband who was sick. 'Going for dying,' Seiko said. Strange to think of Seiko, so alone and silent here, belonging to all those people. She was paying for her daughter's wedding, had to go back to Addis Ababa to arrange it, and her husband's funeral too. Or so Mona thought she said. She nodded gently, glad that Seiko, at least, had a real life to lead somewhere.

'You must come back soon,' Mona said, realizing how much she would miss her. She looked at Seiko, thought how her strength and power had been wasted here. How dreary this household must seem to her – no children, no relations, no friends. Mona's eyes filled with tears because it was so dreary. She couldn't stand it either. She ran into the bedroom and lay down.

Much later, Mona heard a baying, yelling, smashing, crashing, splintering commotion. It might have been the end of a more than usually wild party, or some kind of blood-letting. Soon after, Eric came back and she pretended to be asleep. She actually did sleep, but woke up at about three in the morning to find her brain twanging with fear and wakefulness. It felt like a glass cube revolving in her head, transparent, reflecting curious pictures. To her horror, Mona found she had peed in her sleep, wet the bed like one of her grandchildren. She worried about how to clean it up without Eric noticing. I can't change the sheets with him on them. She got up, tidied the sheets on her side of the bed and hoped that the desiccated air would dry the sheets.

In her pink fluffy slippers and dressing-gown, Mona drifted out through the picture window. The nocturnal compound was silent except for the pool licking the walls of its pit, dark except for the enormous stars, which were too big, too bright. Their beauty made Mona feel uncomfortable because they reminded her that Riyadh had a secret identity she would never begin to understand. Under the stars, the holiday village slept blandly, white cubes neatly planted on concrete steps. Flowers brushed her dressing-gown as she walked to Bob's bungalow on the far side of the swimming-pool. She couldn't remember whether, as a single man (that anomaly in Saudi law), he had to share it with another man. But she was sure nobody would share with Bob. His loneliness seeped out of him. It was impossible to imagine him gossiping with a friend over a can of Near Beer or asking a flatmate to throw him a towel. Perhaps that was why he turned to religion, because he found casual intimacy impossible. Yet he has been married. I wonder if he had any children. Yes, this is the direction he disappears in at the end of barbecues. Come to think of it, he didn't turn up last week. That's why I had nobody to talk to.

There were three bungalows in a row. Knowing that the plan of each bungalow was identical, Mona peered in at the bedroom windows. Curiously striped and dissected by blinds, two-headed monsters sprawled. The comfortable humps and multiple limbs of matrimony. In the third bungalow, both bedrooms were empty, the blinds pulled up to reveal bare, sad rooms, grubby sheets and piles of books. Mona crept round to the sitting-room window. She was suddenly aware that her errand of mercy might be interpreted more cynically by anyone who woke up and saw her.

She saw Bob through the picture window in his sitting-room. He was slumped in an armchair, under a reading-lamp which was still switched on. His face was squashed, swollen, blue and purple in the circle of light. He wasn't dead, though his eyes were closed. One of the sliding doors was cracked in a great star shape, as if it had been forced, and there were books ripped up all over the floor. Mona noticed how different it was from the other bungalows, although they were all given the same bungalows and furniture. Bob had barricaded himself in the middle of the room behind walls of armchairs, sofa, TV and bookcases. There were no pictures, knick-knacks, photographs or plants in the room.

Bob opened one swollen eye and looked at Mona. She stepped back, her heart thundered. She was terrified that he would speak to her, wake the others, compromise her. I've that first-aid kit in the bathroom. There's an ointment that will heal those bruises, and some pills to help the poor lad sleep. I could go in there now and look after him. That's what he needs. But I'll have to go back to the bungalow first to get the ointment and the pills. I might wake Eric by mistake. People will think.... Nervously, Mona smiled at Bob, trying to convey by her smile that she was glad he was alive and sorry he had been beaten up, though of course she couldn't let herself be dragged into such an unpleasant situation.

8

In the morning Mona woke up just after Eric had left for work. She dressed, washed, drank her coffee, gathered her medicines and briskly set off for Bob's bungalow. The harsh sunlight illuminated the dust on the flowers and the peeling plaster walls. She felt no guilt about visiting Bob's bungalow so openly, and waved to the first shift of sunbathers as she crossed their Astroturfed glade. They were preparing their towels and unguents to protect themselves against the sun, which would be hot by eight o'clock.

Mona knocked at Bob's front door, with that falsely cheerful rhythm her father always used, even when he knew he was dying of cancer – ra-ta-ta-ta-ta, tum-tum. There was no answer. Mona went round the back, where the sliding doors were still cracked and the sitting-room in chaos. She looked around to check that nobody was watching her and then remembered that it didn't matter if they were. She opened the glass doors a few inches and neatly piled the ointment, bandages and pills just inside the room. Then she withdrew quickly, glad that she didn't have to talk to Bob, or stare into his pitiful face. It was only as she scurried back inside her own bungalow that Mona realized he wouldn't know who had left the medicine.

That night Mona asked Eric, 'What did you lot do to Bob last night?'

'Didn't do anything, personally.' Eric smirked. 'But I heard Sam and the others go off.'

'Bloody disgrace. Like those Ku-Klux-Klan stories we used to hear about the South.'

'Why? Bob's not black.'

'He is far as they're concerned.'

'Rubbish, Mona. Anyway, he won't be back.'

'What d'you mean?'

'I heard at work. He's going to get a flat somewhere off the compound. Live with some of his Saudi pals. Well, he didn't fit in, did he?'

'That's no crime.'

But of course she knew it was. And she began to behave in an increasingly furtive, secretive way. That Friday night she refused to go to the barbecue.

'Oh, Mona!' Eric said, finding her in bed again when he came home. 'What is it now?'

'I've got a bit of a gippy tummy.'

'What about the food? Shall I take it?'

'I didn't make any food this week. Anyway, nobody ever eats it.'

'Oh, well,' he said with relief. 'I'll have to go along on my own, then.'

She listened for his dashing exit through the dining-room window. Then she crept out of her room, shut the window after him and got out the keys from the box in the cloakroom cupboard. Nobody uses them, Eric had explained when she first arrived, we're all in and out of each other's houses on this compound. Well, I'm not having anyone in and out of mine. When all the windows and doors were secure, Mona felt better. The yells, giggles and squeals from the barbecue sounded less menacing. Eric can just ring the bell like anyone else.

After Seiko went back to Addis Ababa, Mona thought of the bungalow as an island floating in an ocean where tempests, sharks, crocodiles and barracuda fish were commonplace. She thought of Eric as a marauding pirate who occasionally returned to her island, buried his treasure and went off again. She missed Seiko, although in many ways it was nice to be left alone. In letters to her daughters and friends Mona described every detail of 'my little bungalow', enclosing plans and photographs of all the rooms. Every day she spent hours cleaning, moving pictures, rugs and furniture. Sometimes she thought that Riyadh would be tolerable if it wasn't for Eric, who nearly always returned from work in a bad temper, exhausted and grey. Most evenings, Mona got up when he came in and let him lie down instead. He would sleep until supper, which they ate in silence. Eric gazed out of the dining-room window while she sat with her back to it.

'Why are you here?' he asked after one of these silent meals.

'I came to be with you, Eric. Seems stupid now, but I did.'

'How long is it now before you go back for Ramadan?'

'Thirty-five days.'

She struck them off on his IOP calendar, which she didn't look at too closely because it was really very suggestive. Worse than page three. June had a picture of a busty girl in a G-string caressing Self-Lubricating Tools with Maximum Thrust.

'You don't really want to come back here in the autumn, do you?'

'I want to be with you, Eric.' She wiped her eyes because it wasn't true, although she wanted it to be.

'Oh, for God's sake. Don't start the waterworks again, I can't stand it.' He disappeared into the bedroom.

Mona wasn't tired, or hungry, although the bread-and-butter pudding was in the oven. It was nearly sunset, the hour when Riyadh was briefly transformed. The desert reclaimed its own at dawn and dusk as the brutal modern contours of the city were mellowed, washed over with sandy orange and warm pink. Cautiously, Mona opened the front door. There was nobody out there; they were all inside their houses or around the pool. The crisp white steps led down to the wall, the gate, the street. I've only been out there to get into cars driven by men. I've never walked down my own street. How I used to walk up on the moors, donkeys years ago now. Inhale all that lovely cold, damp air, stride over the grass. Of course we always used to complain about the weather but at least it made you feel alive. That smell of damp grass and earth. Here it's tepid, you never feel really invigorated. Take a deep breath and all you get's a mouthful of air-conditioning.

She pressed the button that opened the heavy metal gate at the bottom of the steps, and turned right to go down the hill. The street was deserted, high white walls on either side of her, a ghost town. The muezzin sounded in adenoidal triumph. Now all the shops'll be shutting for prayer-time. I should've changed really. You're not allowed out in short sleeves like this. If one of them *mettahwahs* sees me wandering around at prayer-time in a short dress, I could be arrested. Betty told me how this woman rushed out of her house at one o'clock in the morning, after a row with her husband. Ended up in police custody for days while they checked up on her. Couldn't understand what she'd been up to. They don't think like us. A little hysterically Mona started to giggle,

because this walk from nowhere to nowhere was so pointless, so
ludicrous. If I shut me eyes I could be at home again, or on me way
to the airport. . . .

Eric was annoyed when the doorbell woke him up. 'What've
you been doing to yourself?'

'I walked into a palm tree.'

'There aren't any palm trees on this compound.'

'Not here. I went for a walk down the street.'

'Whatever for? I told you it wasn't safe to walk around on your
own.'

'Well, I know that now, don't I?'

She stumbled over to the couch and lay down on it, shielding her
right eye with her hand. From her forehead to her cheek a huge red
circle was turning wine red, purple and yellow.

'People'll think I've been having a go at you,' Eric said
affectionately as he applied ointment to her poor battered face.

'I won't go out for a few days. I don't have to.'

Mona smiled at him, enjoying his touch. This is the most
interesting thing that's happened to me for weeks.

They say down together to eat the bread-and-butter pudding,
which was burnt. In bed they put their arms around each other,
kissed and made love. Eric was very gentle, as if apologizing for
something he hadn't done.

9

In the morning, Eric woke her up before he left for work.

'You look dreadful, love. You'd best get Seif to take you along
to the clinic. Get your eye looked at.'

Mona calculated that her visit to the doctor would take up most
of the morning. When Eric comes back this afternoon I'll have
something to tell him about. As she cleaned her teeth, she stared in
amazement at her victim's face: a circle of livid bruises like an eye-
patch. She tried applying some make-up, but foundation only
turned the savage marks from dark purple to mauve. It's a pity me
face is the one part of me I'm allowed to show. Before going out,
she even tried to attach a red chiffon scarf to her straw hat as a
makeshift veil. But it merely drew attention to the top half of her
face and made it blaze all the more.

At nine, hatless, Mona walked down the steps to the waiting car.

Sue-Ellen and Harmony were already sitting in the back, on their way to the supermarket.

'Oh, my gracious heavens! Whatever have you done to youah face?'

'Walked into a pálm tree. Daft, intit?'

Sue-Ellen forgot all her hostility in avid curiosity. 'It looks just terrible. Have you seen the doctor?'

'I'm on me way over there now, if you wouldn't mind dropping me off at the clinic?'

'Why, of course we don't mind.' Harmony clutched Mona's arm and looked incredulously into her technicolour whorls and wheels. Then she turned to Sue-Ellen and remarked, as if continuing a conversation, 'Don't you think the men out hyeh drink too much?'

'Sure do.'

'Mike now. Back home he'd never have more'n a coupla cocktails or byehs. Over hyeh he's drinkin' with Sam or Chuck most every night, and they git through gallons of the stuff. Ah don't say it always makes them act mean, but pretty often it does. Well, you know it does.'

'Ah know,' Sue-Ellen said bitterly, and when Seif stopped outside the clinic she helped Mona out delicately.

'Thank you,' Mona said, smiling and waving at them as if they were old friends.

The clinic was an expensive private one, a perk of Eric's. There were marble floors, plants everywhere and copies of *The Lady* and *Country Life* piled on tables.

'What have you done to your face?' The Irish receptionist asked Mona briskly.

'I walked into a palm tree.'

The girl glanced at her with a brief, cynical smirk. 'They're awfully ferocious, the palm trees over here.'

'What do you mean?'

'Never mind. The doctor'll see you in a minute.'

Mona began to wish she had worn a veil. All the other patients were men in early middle age: a Saudi, an American and a Frenchman. One by one they stared at Mona and smiled knowingly, insultingly, as if her battered face was a secret they were proud of. She tried to look at the magazines, which represented an England she had never been a part of – nannies, horses, collections of porcelain. Viciously, Mona stared at the

photograph of a girl who had just become engaged. She was
wearing a pearl necklace and a cashmere sweater, and her face was
utterly bland and unmarked. Not pretty, just born in the right
place and stayed there. Mona's face was stinging now and she
could hardly open her right eye. As each new person stared at the
bruises around it she felt as if another bulb had been lit behind the
ugly marks, making them brighter and more obvious.

The doctor was a hearty ex-army man who roared with laughter
at her story. 'Looks as if he's been hitting you with the
frying-pan.'

'He hasn't,' Mona said desperately.

He applied some ointment and gave her a tube to take home.
'The swelling'll go down in a few days. Going back to the Yookay
for Ramadan?'

'Yes.'

'Don't walk into any oaks.'

Betty was sitting at reception. Mona instinctively raised her
hand to hide her eye.

'Oh my God! What's happened to you, love?'

'I, er, had an accident.' Mona sounded so embarrassed that it
wasn't surprising Betty stared at her with voracious sympathy.

'Whatever did you do?'

'I walked into a palm tree. I really did.'

'All right, love. Oh dear. You'd best wait here until I'm
finished, then you can come shopping with us.'

'What are you here for?' Mona asked defensively.

'Varicose veins. It's the heat. Feels as if they're going to burst.'

Mona envied Betty her respectable, middle-aged ailment.
'Perhaps I should just go home and lie down. I'm not keen on
going out at the moment.'

'Nonsense. Come out with us and have a bit of fun. Else we'll
not see you till September. We'll all be going off for the summer
soon.'

So Mona told Seif not to wait and turned towards Betty's
minibus. Rows of elderly schoolgirls thumped on the windows and
waved at her. They were wearing their war-paint of gold chains
and black *abayas*. With a pneumatic sigh, the doors opened for
Mona and she got on the bus.

'Hello, Mona! Been getting into more fights over bridge?'

'Put a raw steak on it, love. At least you can afford it over here.'

'Reminds me of when me and Bob had a fight, years ago. My

face came up like that. I couldn't go out for days.'

Mona was already wishing she'd gone home. But well-meaning hands, covered with rings and bracelets, pulled her to a seat and examined her.

The bus took them to a palatial white marble shopping precinct. Inside the automatic sliding doors was an air-conditioned lobby, in the centre of which was a fountain surrounded by troughs of immaculate flowers. There were the luxury shops which the city seemed to be able to support in indefinite numbers: flowers, perfumes, books, jewellery and toys. In the cool air, Mona's face felt less uncomfortable. The women spread out and prowled around, egging each other on to spend, as they had in the gold *souk*; toys for grandchildren, face cream that cost five times as much as in Boots, Swiss chocolate that had to be eaten before it melted. Cheered up by their consumer power, they linked arms and almost danced across the marble floors, which were being washed by squads of Korean cleaners.

They met up with another gang of black-robed women, bridge and golf cronies. Mona tried to hide, but she attracted the now familiar jokes. She had decided not to mention the palm tree again. Mona watched as Betty talked to Joan, a tall, big-boned Londoner, whose *abaya* fluttered round her shoulders like a cape. Betty knows everybody, Mona thought enviously, I wish I could be more like her. Oh, well. I'd best get meself some sunglasses.

When she came back, her eyes transformed into two shadowy, symmetrical circles, Joan had taken Betty aside and was whispering to her. Betty's face expressed horrified delight and her charm bracelet rattled as she clutched Joan's arm. Joan led her gang back to their bus and Betty turned back to her friends. She looks as if she's had a real shock, Mona noted with surprise.

But Betty couldn't bear to spoil her story by telling it in too much of a hurry. 'We'd best all stick together this morning.' She added enigmatically, 'And don't go to the toilet, whatever you do.'

'But I'm dying to go.' Janice hopped from one foot to another.

Betty looked so nervous that they were all silenced.

Mona, more confident now that her bruises were covered, went over to her. 'What's the matter, love?'

'Something Joan said. Something terrible's happened here, it's not safe any more. And Ahmed won't be back until midday prayers.'

They followed her gaze. With an expression of absolute terror she was watching the orange-overalled Korean cleaners swab out and disinfect the women's toilets.

'There's only an hour and a half before Ahmed fetches us,' Rita said cheerfully. 'Let's go upstairs to Mothercare. They've some gorgeous new baby clothes in. And some lovely cards in Hallmark, too.'

'I'm not waiting two hours to go to the flipping toilet,' Janice said, and strode off.

But Betty grabbed her arm. 'No, you mustn't. Or if you do, we'll all have to go in there together. Come on, girls.'

In convoy they marched to the lavatories.

'Leave the door open,' Betty ordered Janice, looking around in horror. The others were bewildered, but took their mood from Betty, who seemed suddenly older and smaller. She clutched their hands for comfort.

'Puts me off, having you all standing there.'

'Hurry up, Janice! Let's all get out of here. This place gives me the creeps.'

'What is it, Betty?'

'What happened here?'

'Something nasty?'

'I always thought it was too much of a good thing, them boasting about having such a low crime rate.'

'Some of the things you read about in the *Arab News*! Disgusting. What happened, Betty?'

'I'll tell you upstairs.'

Gliding up on the escalator, Mona had a pleasant sense of luxury. Like that hotel where Eric took me out to dinner. Marble floors, flowers, perfume, fountains. Makes me feel a bit like a film star, what with the dark glasses. Then she remembered that something nasty enough to shock Betty had happened here.

At the top of the escalator Betty turned round and counted them all. They went into a restaurant where they guiltily ordered ice-creams garnished with whipped cream, syrup and nuts. Then they all huddled together in the tiny Women's Section, behind screens.

Betty felt too ill to touch her Ice-Cream Dream. 'Do you know, today I don't think I mind it being just women in here. Makes me feel safer.'

'Tell us, Betty,' Janice said impatiently, wolfing her banana sundae.

'All right,' Betty whispered hoarsely. 'Joan told me there's been two foreign women murdered in the toilets downstairs. Where you went,' she glared at Janice. 'The first one happened last week. A young Dutch girl went in there, and her mum waited outside. Well, she thought the girl was taking a long time. Then she saw another lady go in there, a Saudi. This Saudi lady comes out, and her daughter's still in there, so finally the Dutch girl's mum goes in to see what's the matter. And she finds her daughter slashed – blood everywhere. Been raped and murdered. That Saudi lady was a man.'

'Oh my God!'

'The perfect disguise!'

'What about the other one?'

'You mean they didn't close the toilets after that?'

Betty was divided between titillation and genuine fear. 'Joan says they cleaned them out and then opened them again. Didn't warn the public or anything like that, because of course crime here doesn't exist till they catch the criminal and bump him off, chop him up or whatever. Joan only heard about it because she knows one of the girls on the compound round the corner, and the police've been round all the houses, asking questions. Then yesterday there was a second murder. An American lady, been shopping like us. She goes to the toilet and doesn't come out. Her driver comes to fetch her, hangs about in the car-park. She doesn't turn up, so he goes off home and the police're called. They find her in the toilet – her body, I mean. Same as the Dutch girl. They were still cleaning up the blood when we arrived this morning.'

None of them were able to eat their ice-creams. Mona felt sick, paralysed with fright. 'It's funny really. At home, you read about crimes like this all the time. But somehow you don't think of it happening to you. But here, I don't know, it's all so quiet and strict, but you feel helpless. As if there's a horrible violent current running underneath it all, waiting to strike you, and there's nothing you can do against it. Well, I'm going to stay at home in future.'

'I won't be back here in a hurry,' Rita agreed.

'I'll go to Safeway instead. At least it's always crowded there.'

'Safety in numbers, girls.'

'Coming to me coffee morning Wednesday, Mona?'

'No thanks, Hilda. I shan't go out any more.'

They smiled at her overreaction. But Mona meant it.

10

'There's plenty to do in the bungalow, what with cleaning and cooking, knitting and reading and writing letters to all of you.'

When Eric came home he noticed very little difference, in fact Mona seemed calmer than before. For the first two weeks her refusal to go out wasn't too much of a problem. She pleaded headaches and sickness to excuse herself from two barbecues and from their Friday shopping trips. Grumpily, Eric went off to Safeway to fill a trolley, not without a sense of triumph. He didn't like shopping, of course, it was a woman's job, but still he could remember rationing and knew what it meant to be able to help yourself to anything you fancied in a bloody great emporium.

Then one afternoon Eric came home to find a big piece of hardboard nailed over the dining-room window.

'What's happened to the window? Did the kids break it?'

'No.'

'Did Nabil do it?'

Nabil was the odd-job man.

'No. Did it myself.'

'But where'd you get it from?'

'I found it in the cupboard in the hall.'

'But what for, Mona?'

'I prefer it like this. I never did like the windows here. They're too big. Don't give you enough privacy.'

Eric rushed into the sitting-room. But the picture window there was still intact.

'I couldn't find a piece big enough for it. I'll ask Nabil in the morning.'

'But Mona, you can't do this. It's not even our bungalow.'

'Why can't I? I'm here all the time, so I reckon it's up to me how I arrange it.'

'But it blocks out all the light.'

'I don't like the light. It's too bright, hurts my eyes.'

Eric looked at her more closely. She was still wearing the dark glasses she had bought to cover her bruises, although her eye had healed. Around them her face was very thin and white. She had lost so much weight that her wedding-ring slid up and down on her finger.

'You're not well, Mona. It's a good thing you're going home soon. But you shouldn't have done that with the window. I'll have to go all round the houses now, when I want a swim.'

'Do you good. You're getting a beer belly on you again.'

Her manner with him had become cool and sour, as if he had done something she couldn't forgive. He went out with his towel, and soon she heard his voice, jovial now, joining in the laughter and ribald banter of the others. Disgusting the way they carry on out there. Perhaps the Saudis are right when they say men and women aren't allowed to go swimming together. It's not like back home where you just go in for a quick dip and then hurry off to get warm and dry. All this sun has a bad effect on people, makes them lazy. Vain. I'm glad I don't have to watch them any more. It feels more like my own house again. It wasn't so bad when they all ignored me, but since I had that accident with the palm tree they've been knocking at the window, ringing the bell, asking me out. I know what they all think, I've heard the children sniggering.

Mona went into the sitting-room to measure up the picture window. When Eric came back from his swim she double locked the front door behind him.

'But Sam's coming round for a drink, later on.'

'Then he can ring the bell like anyone else.'

'Oh, Mona! It's so embarrassing, living in a fortress. Nobody else does.'

Eric had no defence against her anger. Every day when he came home he found a new offshoot of her hostility: another window blocked, an invitation refused, the telephone unanswered. She decided to decorate the hardboard window screens with photographs of their children and grandchildren. In every room now there was a defiant collage of their past and present together: letters, birthday cards and other shrines to family life.

Mona was proud of her skill at avoiding excursions. She hadn't been out for three weeks and now it was only fourteen days before she got the plane home. She had already packed and was living out of suitcases, so that every time she cleaned her teeth or changed her clothes she was reminded of her departure. She had written to Lorraine, asking for more photographs of the interiors of all their houses. Now they wouldn't arrive before she left. She had explained to her favourite daughter that she and Eric had decided it was too dangerous for her to stay on here. In fact they had never really discussed it, but Mona had always presented decisions to her daughters as joint ones. They had been a 'we', a pronoun which had sustained Mona even though most decisions were made by Eric.

Now that she was quite alone, moving all day long in the curious rhythms inside her head, she saw that Eric's 'I' and her own were two separate balloons floating off in opposite directions. She knew he would be relieved when she didn't return in September. Mona imagined him coming back here on his own, holding parties to which nurses were invited. All the women looking at him, admiring him because they thought he had beaten up his wife. Given her her come-uppance. How pleased everyone on the compound would be when they heard she wasn't coming back. . . . Almost every day Mona imagined herself into a coma of misery. When Eric came home in the evening she was silent, pale and numb. She flinched at the sound of his key in the lock, as if he had no right to come in. It struck Eric that, since her accident with the palm tree, she had been looking at him as if she expected him to hit her. And he felt guilty towards her, as if he had.

As the time for her to leave drew nearer, Mona rehearsed. Last of all, I'll take down the pictures on the blind windows, change into a knee-length skirt and a short-sleeved blouse to celebrate, and put on my new necklace so the girls'll see it at the airport. I don't want them to think I couldn't cope here. I'll have duty-free bags for them, more presents on top of my suitcase – oh, it will be good to see them again. I'll have so much to tell them. I've told them most of the stories already in the letters but I'll tell them again.

In these rehearsals there was always a break, a gesture she couldn't make even in her imagination. Mona stood in the hall, which was dark now the windows were blocked. In the small mirror on her right she could see the shadowy reflection of her face, thin and dry as a camel. She slid back the bolts on the front door and then quickly locked it again. Leaning against the door, she pushed aside the small brass eyelid and peered out. Through the distorting circle she saw the fat concave steps she would have to descend. Slowly, and with dignity. I don't want anyone to think I'm running away. I might need Eric's arm, going down to the car. Perhaps I should start practising with him in the evenings.

A figure bulged up the steps. The bell rang and the face looked straight at her: a big nose, eyes couched in bags, hardly any chin and a dumpy body on foreshortened legs. She giggled, because it was such a good caricature of Eric. He rang again. Mona fingered the bolts but decided it would be too risky to open the door again so soon. The eyes were bloodshot, irritable, he didn't look pleased to see her. He put his key in the door but couldn't turn it because her own key was in the inside lock.

'Mona! What's the matter? Are you all right?'

When he shouted, his mouth was a landscape of decay. She stared down into dusty pink caverns, the slimy horizon red above disintegrating cliffs of brown and yellow. He continued to shout and ring the bell. She had to go into the bedroom to stifle her laughter. Once in there, she grew firmer: I'm not letting him in, he's disgusting, whoever he is. Mona lay down and waited for her privacy to be restored.